I0664422

Lunar Kingdom

The Richard Jackson Saga, Volume 15

Ed Nelson

Published by Eastern Shore Publishing, 2024.

Table of Contents

Other books by Ed Nelson

The Richard Jackson Saga
Book 1 The Beginning
Book 2 Schooldays
Book 3 Hollywood
Book 4 In the Movies
Book 5 Star to Deckhand
Book 6 Surfing Dude
Book 7 Third Time is a Charm
Book 8 Oxford University
Book 9 Cold War
Book 10 Taking Care of Business
Book 11 Interesting Times
Book 12 Escape from Siberia
Book 13 Regicide
Book 14 What's Under, Down Under?
Book 15 The Lunar Kingdom
Book 16 First Steps
In the Richard Jackson World
Mary, Mary
Stand-Alone Story
Ever and Always
Cast in Time Series
Book 1: Baron
Book 2: Baron of the Middle Counties
Book 3: Count
Book 4: Earl
Book 5: Earl of the Marches

Dedication

This book is dedicated to my wife Carol for her support and help as my first reader and editor.

Thanks to my editors, Old Rotorhead, Ernest Bywater, Lonely Dad, and Antti.

Edited by Janet E. Rupert

This fictional journey started with the Bellefontaine Ohio School class of 1962.

Quotation

That's the way it happened; give or take a lie or two.

James Garner as Wyatt Earp, describing the gunfight at the OK Corral in the movie *Sunset*.

ISBN 979-8-89434-019-7

Library of Congress Control Number: 2022911369

Chapter 1

On Monday, January 6th, 1964, I received notification that our moon station had successfully achieved lunar orbit. Our original launch calculations had been almost exact. It had only taken a few minor burns to put it in a polar orbit around the moon.

I had a congratulatory message sent to the crew on board. Both Empress Ping and Queen Elizabeth sent theirs. President Kennedy also sent one, but it was much shorter as we had once more upstaged NASA.

Television pictures of the moon's surface were sent back continuously. The landing was shown in classrooms all over the world. It was at the time the most viewed broadcast in history.

Besieged with interview requests, I finally decided that I had to give in. It wasn't going to be a Rick Jackson victory, though. It was going to be a team victory.

To emphasize that, I flew back to our launch site in China and gave my interview from there. Unlike the first interviews with the international press, they had representatives on-site. We were generating enough news that they now stationed people there.

The reporters were all young people who were in line for better positions. For some reason, the edge of the Mongolian desert was considered a hardship duty station.

The questions all rotated around, "When are you going to land on the moon?"

"The moon landers are in transit right now. Upon arrival, a thorough inspection will occur. If both of them are in good condition, then we will make a landing."

"Why two?"

"Safety. We don't want to send people down and have a vehicle fail. Can you imagine what the deathwatch would be like?"

From the looks on some of the reporters' faces, they imagined it and saw themselves as the center of a painful long-drawn-out process. The ratings would be sky-high!

At times I hate reporters.

While awaiting the arrival of the lunar lander module, Jerri Cobb and the crew were surveying the moon's surface for a landing spot.

Our criteria were different from NASA's, or I should say stricter. They wanted a flat, stable surface with no small craters filled deep with dust.

We looked for that but added that it also had to be a place to start tunneling down for a permanent base.

We hadn't scheduled the base to start on this mission. But we were trying to find an initial starting point. If we didn't find it the first time, we would keep trying until we had one. We were landing on the moon to stay, not to say we had done it and go home.

My sister Mary had asked if she could send some clothes to the moon and ship them back. She wanted to sell t-shirts that said, "The Space Ladies went to the moon, and all I got was this lousy t-shirt."

I told her, "No!" Then she went to Mum and her gang behind my back. The gang now consisted of Mum, Jerri Cobb, Queen Elizabeth, and Empress Ping. They overruled me.

They also decided to ship everything from t-shirts and sweatshirts up to fancy dress clothes. They would have different messages depending on the formality of the clothes. The lesser items were to be sold. The more expensive items were auctioned off at charity functions they supported.

When told by reporters that I had been saying that private enterprise and capitalism would be the ones to open up space rather than governments, I was surprised. Was I a hypocrite?

They don't play fair.

I think it was karma when one of the capsule loads of clothes had an engine failure and went sailing off toward Jupiter. It would take years to get there. If there had been people on board, we would have launched a rescue mission.

The value of the clothes wasn't enough to spend the time and effort to retrieve them. If there were Jovans, I wondered if they would appreciate Earth styles.

The space station in orbit around the moon was a large affair. It is one hundred feet on each side. That is one million cubic feet. That sounds like a lot until you realize what we had to cram into it.

The first consideration was radiation protection. Since this is a long-term station, the question wasn't if there would be a solar flare, but how big and how hard it would be. The solution was a series of containers, ten feet by ten feet by three feet. These were the outer hulls of the space station. Filled with water, they gave us radiation protection and our water supply.

The containers would hold thirty thousand cubic feet of water. It would take 225,564 gallons to fill the tanks. Each tank was a stand-alone so that if a small meteoroid punctured one, we would only lose that container.

There were automatic feeds from each tank, along with a set of manual controls as backups.

It took a minimum of one gallon of water per day for each person. We allowed two gallons. Ten people would take twenty gallons a day, so we had plenty of water.

The water was the most expensive part of the whole station. It weighed 1,872,180 pounds or about 849 metric tons. We could lift 50 metric tons a launch, so it took seventeen launches to place the water in orbit.

Each launch cost two hundred and fifty thousand dollars or over four million dollars total. Our goal was to cut the launch cost down to twenty-five thousand dollars per launch, but that was in the future.

As I told the launch team, "The only part of the explanation that I could do the math on was the cost. Everything else was beyond me."

The team's next concern was being able to breathe. The primary source of oxygen will be generated by water electrolysis, with O_2 in pressurized storage tanks.

Each molecule of water contains two hydrogen atoms and one oxygen atom. Running a current through water causes these atoms to separate and recombine as gaseous hydrogen (H_2) and oxygen (O_2). We vented the hydrogen as we had no current use for it, along with some other trace gases.

The major gas we had to remove was carbon dioxide, using a machine based on a new material called zeolite, which acts as a molecular sieve.

Along with the hydrogen and CO_2 which we needed to remove, we had to face that people also emit small amounts of other gases. These are called farts.

Methane and carbon dioxide produced in the intestines are what make farts. Sweat creates urea when it breaks down. People also emit acetone, methyl alcohol, and carbon monoxide. These are byproducts of metabolism in their urine and their breath.

Activated charcoal filters are the primary method for removing these chemicals from the air.

If you think I came up with any of that, you are kidding yourself.

The food supply was fairly easy if you like to eat out of a squeeze tube. We allowed one and a half pounds of food a day. For ten people, this was 1350 pounds for ninety days. One launch covered this.

I do understand eating.

The largest technical issue was the generation of energy. We could handle our food, water, and air supply using known technologies. We were using solar cells to convert sunlight to electricity directly for energy. Large numbers of cells are assembled in arrays to produce high power levels. This method of harnessing solar power is called photovoltaics.

A detailed mission profile was constructed and assessed to ensure that the power system design would support the station.

The station's electrical power system used twenty solar panels to convert sunlight to electricity. The twenty solar panels made an array 120 feet long by 50 feet wide.

Solar panels are not efficient by any definition. We were generating our energy by brute force or, in this case, by a very large array. We had several different development groups working on increased efficiencies.

We also placed a huge backup battery system to run the station for two days. This backup would give time for an orderly evacuation of the station if needed.

Each of the ten people permanently on board had their private room ten feet by ten feet by eight feet. The many arguments about such a "waste" of space came down to a mental health issue.

The threat made to the engineers who thought it a waste of space was to put them into isolation for a month, with no private space, which settled the issue.

Workshops and exercise areas rounded out the main areas of the station. There was a "lounge" area with entertainment and a separate dining area.

All in all, it was a spectacular construction.

Chapter 2

I needed to explain some things to the main space program team. They would find this all hard to believe, but it would have a major impact on the space program and, ultimately, all of the Earth.

It had to do with my baby sister Mary. She had always been precocious and seemed way beyond her age.

Only recently had the full extent of her intelligence come out. While being super brilliant, she was also still a nine-year-old girl.

She had developed cold fusion, which wasn't so cold. To start with, even though everyone called it "cold fusion," it was only "cold" compared to the temperatures of an H-bomb, which rivaled the center of the Sun. Its energy was produced as heat, but in controllable amounts and with no radioactivity.

She had always kept a diary of her days, so I will let that speak for her. When I explained the situation, she agreed to share several days of her life that explained what was going on. I pieced this together from her diary, conversations with our parents, and Jim and Sally, among others.

Being tested:

When our principal told me he would talk to my parents, I thought I was in trouble. I was but not the sort I thought it was going to be. Instead, he wanted me to be tested!

I didn't get it. I was tested in school and always got an A. Maybe he thought I had cheated on those. I had cheated a little; I always turned my paper so Patty could see my answers. She had trouble with some subjects, and I wanted to help her.

Once when I was really mad at her, I took two test papers and filled them all out. The one I showed her had all wrong answers, the one I turned in got one hundred percent. She got a zero.

Maybe that's why she spilled ink down my back later that day. She swore it was an accident. I looked out our classroom window while the teacher droned on about how important it was that we knew our times tables. I think I had memorized the Poisson Table of Probabilities but wanted to practice them to have them down pat. Maybe if I set the drapes on fire, she would shut up.

Nah, it was raining outside, not much, but I didn't want to stand in it and get soaked. Mrs. King had called on me five times today in class, so there was a less than three percent chance of her calling me again. It would probably be Connie next as she hadn't been called on yet, so it was in the ninety-nine percent category she would be next. She was.

While I looked out the window, Mum and Dad's limo pulled up. Not only had the principal called them, but he also had them come in for a meeting. James went home with his parents the last time that happened, and we never saw him again.

The word was that he was being held in Alcatraz. I thought Chino was a better bet but didn't know how to find out or place a bet on it. I could write a letter to him at both places, in the care of the warden. If he weren't there, they would probably mark it, "not at this address."

While I was thinking about this, the teacher called on Connie. She knew the answer like always and had been paying attention, so I didn't have to worry about her.

The next one up would be either Jimmy or Stevie. They were both paying attention, so I didn't have to pass a note or, in Stevie's case, kick him as he was next to me.

As Patty had said, if I didn't have the whole class to keep on track, I would have been bored out of my gourd. I'm sure it made Mrs. King's day easier when all her students were alert and had the right answers.

I had the right answers when I paid attention. I got my numbers mixed up when she asked me what seven times six was when I was trying to work a trigonometry problem in my head. I always got my secant and cosine tables mixed up when I memorized them.

When I missed hearing what she asked, I always said 42, my answer for everything.

I was finally pulled out of class to go to the office. My parents had been there for a long time. Mrs. King looked puzzled as I hadn't done anything today.

Everyone looked serious when I got to the office, but my parents didn't seem upset, so I didn't know what to think. Every time they had to show up in the past, I got my butt spanked when I got home.

Today didn't look like a spanking day. I had put the extra handkerchiefs in my undies for nothing.

The principle started with, "Mary, do you find your classes to be boring?"

If I say no, I'm lying. If I say yes, then I might get Mrs. King in trouble. It wasn't her fault she had to teach boring stuff. It was like that book in our library, *Catch 22*, by Joseph Heller. I couldn't win, so better not to lie. I knew how those ended on my rear end.

"Yes, they are boring, but Mrs. King is a good teacher. The other kids don't know the stuff she is teaching, so she needs to do it, but I already know that stuff."

"Who taught you that 'stuff'?"

"Mum did when I was little like before I started school, then I did most of it on my own using books in our library."

"Most of it on your own? Did someone else help you?"

"Ben, who takes care of our horses and is studying to be a veterinarian, helped with the medical books. Then Mrs. Hernadez would help with the hard books in Spanish like *Don Quixote*.

"What about math?"

"That is easy. I just read the books. I would work out problems on the blackboard in the library. Then I would have to erase them when they filled up. That was a pain because sometimes I needed the information for other problems.

I finally realized that I could take a picture of the blackboard and have Denny develop it for me. I read that in *Time Magazine* when they did a story about Professor Einstein. Now that guy is impressive. I wrote him a letter and told him that quantum effects weren't spooky.

I understand how they work, but he never answered me back. I shouldn't have told him I was eight. He probably only writes back to teenagers.

"You will have to explain what quantum effects are later. What books have you read?"

I named off a bunch of them, mostly classics from the library. I think *Plato's Republic* was my favorite. I didn't mention *The Catcher in the Rye* or anything by Reverend Fielding. Those might give Mum and Dad fits.

"What about history?"

"I've read everything on Western Civilization, now I'm working on the Asians, after that North and South America."

"Since the Aborigines in Australia only use verbal traditions, I'm hoping to go there and walk in Dreamtime with them."

I hastily added, "When I'm old enough to do their drugs."

Dad cleared his throat, "Mary, we would like you to take some tests to see what grade you should be in. It seems you are more advanced than we ever thought."

"I'm not in trouble?"

Mum asked me, "Why did you think that?"

"Every time you have come to school in the middle of the day, I have ended up getting a spanking."

Mum grabbed me in a hug.

"You poor dear, you have gotten into so much trouble, and it's because we didn't know how bored you were."

Now I knew the answer when I got caught. I would tell the teachers I was bored. Today was turning out to be a good day after all. I wouldn't need those handkerchiefs.

I was told that I would be tested at Stanford University on Saturday. I wasn't to worry about the tests or study because they would be about many different things.

"Will they have Latin on them?"

The principal told me, "They might."

"Ouch, my medical Latin is pretty good, but I haven't had a chance to speak with anyone who uses it for daily conversation."

"That's why they call it a dead language. Not very many people in the world use it daily. Maybe the Pope."

"Mummy, can I call this pope guy and see if he will talk to me in Latin?"

"Don't worry about it, dear. I'll see about getting you an audience later."

"I thought audiences were those people who went to see Rick in his movies."

"You would be a small audience of one."

"Oh cool, like a private screening."

"Exactly."

"What does one wear to see the pope? I have a set of those new capri pants I can't wait to wear."

"Later, dear, it takes a while to get a private audience with the pope. Fashions might change."

"Yeah, like those stupid Nehru jackets all the boys wore last year. I noticed Ricky didn't wear any. He is lucky he has Harold as his valet."

"If he didn't, he would be wearing his cowboy hat everywhere."

"Yeah, it would look silly when he is in his morning suit."

The principal cleared his throat and asked if we were done here. Dad told him we were. Mum and I could continue our important conversation at home. Men didn't understand what counted.

Chapter 3

Jim and Sally took me to Stanford on Saturday, to take their tests. They seemed easy to me. I think the hardest was on comparative religions. They wanted a long essay, and I found that to be boring.

I wrote that religions were man's attempt to find their place in the universe, and as man learned more about the universe, religion had to evolve.

The only problem was that different nations, races, and areas' knowledge didn't grow at the same rate, so it became awkward when the difference became too great, like *auto da fe* great.

I had to wait a week for the test results. At least the school did, and they shared it with my parents. I don't know what the problem was, but they had several conferences at school. I knew they had been to the office, but I was never called in.

Mummy and Daddy seemed distracted at home, as though they had a serious problem. One evening after dinner, they had me meet them in the library. I didn't even get a chance to collect any handkerchiefs.

"Mary, starting next week, you will be going to a different school."

"Which one?"

"Stanford University. You will major in mathematics as a senior. You may be tested again in other subjects and, if you do well, be made a senior."

"What about my friends?"

"You will have lunch three times a week at your old school to catch up with them."

"Will being in class with all those old people be scary?"

"Jim and Sally will be with you at all times."

"Okay then, if anyone gets mean, Jim can show them his handgun, or Sally can pull out that dagger she hides under her skirt on her garter belt.

"Or I even could pull mine out."

I showed Mummy the garter belt I was now wearing to hide my Fairburn-Sykes Commando knife that Ricky had got me for my birthday. My dresses below the knee hid it well.

"You will do well in school, my dear."

First Day at Stanford.

I was excited to start my first day at my new school. It was a long way from my house, so Daddy had bought me an apartment. He called it a condo. That was a short form of a very long word that I couldn't pronounce.

Sally, Jim, and I would stay there three nights a week. I thought that would be so neat. Mummy wouldn't be there. I could stay up as late as I wanted.

Mummy and Sally had spent two days at my new pad, as Denny called it. They bought furniture and had it all set up, sheets, blankets, and all sorts of kitchen stuff. They even went grocery shopping.

It looked like a lot of work. I asked Mummy why I just didn't stay at a hotel. She told me it was a matter of security. I thought about that. Suppose Sally or Jim had to shoot someone? There was less chance of hitting an innocent bystander. Hotels are full of people.

The place had four bedrooms, so we each had our own, and the extra one was my office! My very own first office. It had a phone line, a copy machine, a typewriter, and other stuff like staplers.

I would have to learn how to type. In the meantime, I would write out all my assignments.

Sally took me to a bookstore on my first day to buy textbooks. They cost a lot of money. I had to pay five dollars for my math book. English was cheap at four dollars.

I took English 101, Arts 101, Physics 401, and Calculus 401. The 101 courses were required for a degree. I hope they won't be boring.

The next morning, I had my first class. Jim drove Sally and me to the right building and dropped us off. He had to get a parking permit for the school.

The class started late, like nine in the morning. I couldn't understand why all the other students looked like they weren't awake. I had been ready to leave since seven in the morning. They looked like they had just gotten out of bed.

Sally walked me to class. She would be sitting in the last row of the classroom for each of my classes. That was embarrassing. She would see me passing notes.

I sat up front where I could see the teacher. The desks were so big I couldn't see over the people in front of me. I was the only person in the front row.

When we first came into the room, some guy told Sally she couldn't bring her kid to class. I looked around and didn't see any kids with Sally. She ignored him.

People kept coming into the room until all the seats were filled. Everyone looked at me funny as though I had cooties. I sneaked a look in the small mirror in my handbag, but my face was clean.

When our teacher came into the room, he stopped when he saw me. Sally had been waiting for him and handed him some papers. He read them and smiled.

"Welcome to Calculus 401, Mary."

"Thank you, professor."

I had practiced how to talk to my new teachers on the drive-up with Sally. Jim told me to call them dude, but he couldn't fool me. Some of them might be ladies. Should I call them dudettes? I decided to go with professor as Sally recommended.

She told me that I couldn't go wrong with that, even if the teacher were only a teaching assistant. I wondered about that. Mrs. King didn't have any teaching assistants.

Maybe that was what she meant when she said she needed a referee some days.

Just as the teacher was about to get started, some guy asked. "What's the kid doing here?"

I still didn't see a kid. The professor told him that Mary Jackson had tested into the class. They were talking about me! I crossed my arms and glared at him. If it had been Patty, she would have known trouble was about to start.

One of the older girls, who were all older, asked me a question. "Are you the Mary Jackson with the clothing line?"

"Yes, I am."

"I thought I recognized you from your TV ads."

"Thank you. I thought the ads made me look fat."

This statement got all the girls in class talking about my clothes. The boys were asking what clothing line and what TV ads?

The teacher finally slammed a book down on his desk to get their attention. That allowed me to shoot a spitball.

I shot it at the guy who called me a little kid. It hit him on the end of his nose. He went cross-eyed looking at it. When he realized what I had done, he whispered, "Nice one."

Maybe he wasn't a jerk. I wouldn't spill any ink on him after all.

Ricky had been visiting at home just before I came up here. He explained how important it was to read the book and work on the problems before class at the end of each chapter. That way, I would know what I didn't understand and ask to explain it in class.

I had done that and was glad I did. It took me a little while to figure out, but there was a typographical error in the book, or the author was dumb. I was betting on the typo.

I thought I had better help the teacher by letting him know about the error so he wouldn't look stupid in front of the class.

I held up my hand as soon as everyone was quiet. The professor called on me, and I explained an error in the textbook. A plus sign at the end of chapter three, problem number four, should be a minus.

I had taken what Ricky had told me to heart, as Mummy would say, and read five chapters ahead.

The teacher told me I was probably wrong, but he would look at it tonight. He did ask me, "Why do you think it is wrong?"

"With a plus sign, there is no way you can get a smooth curve, or any curve for that matter. Using a minus works out nicely. I think it must be a typo, or the person who wrote the book is stupid."

A quiet burst of laughter in the room died away at once.

"Mary, I agree. If it is wrong, it is a typo that didn't get caught."

Sally later explained that the teacher had written the textbook we were using.

After class, several girls wanted to talk to me about my clothes and the different princesses I used as models. Were they nice?

The guys all left immediately. I was getting ready to leave when the teacher called me.

"Mary, if you spot any other errors, will you please tell me in private."

"I can do that. What is it worth to you?"

When someone asks you for something, the negotiations start. For some reason, Sally interrupted me.

"Excuse Mary, please. This is a game they play at her house."

The teacher looked a little red-faced. I don't know if he was embarrassed or angry. I took Sally's hint and told him that, of course, I would bring it up in private in the future.

On the way home, I asked her why she didn't give me a chance to negotiate good grades. All I would have done was work out all the problems in the book to get an A. She gave a huge sigh.

Chapter 4

Math was a morning class on Mondays and Wednesdays. I had art appreciation in the afternoon of those days, followed by English literature. I don't know why we had to take the literature class; I already could read.

The first day in art class, the teacher was snotty with me. He said children couldn't appreciate the nuances of fine art. I couldn't resist it. I held up my hand.

"Yes, Mary."

"What's a nuance? Is it like a nuisance?"

"Exactly, just like you."

"Thank you for your explanation. I will be certain to tell the chancellor how helpful you have been when Mum and I have tea at his house this weekend."

"Perhaps I was misspoken. Nuance is the subtle details of what makes a painting, for example, great rather than a more mundane copy."

"Oh, you mean like Henri Matisse compared to fellow Fauves, Barquet, and Dufy. They were good but not up to his standard."

"Err, exactly. How do you know about those painters?"

"My brother Ricky told me I should read ahead in all my classes so I could ask intelligent questions about what I didn't understand. He loaned me his books and notes from Oxford."

The teacher turned to the class and told them, "Out of the mouths of children. I recommend you take that advice to heart."

He then went on to show us pictures of and tell us about great paintings. When he got to Van Gogh and *Starry Night*, he stopped.

"Mary, you are turning up your nose. Don't you like this?"

"I think it is okay. I'm not sure about Van Gogh's choice of colors."

"What's wrong with his colors?"

"They clash with the drapes in Mummy's hobby room."

"Your Mother has a copy of *Starry Night*?"

"I don't think so unless they sell copies at Sotheby's. Daddy bought it there for her birthday."

"It's hard to believe that your family owns that. It would cost millions of dollars."

"It wasn't that many million, only two or three. I could afford that if my parents let me have my money."

"Your parents take your money?"

"Yeah, they put it in a trust fund. I don't know how you decide to trust the fund, but they do. They wouldn't even let me have the money to buy a new limo this year. They said I had to keep the one I had for two years."

All the other students were laughing at the professor and me for some reason.

The professor finally asked them what was so funny. One of them told him, "The Jacksons are one of the wealthiest families in the world. If they wanted, they could buy the Musée Jacqueline et Pablo Picasso."

"Daddy tried. He hates Picasso. He met him in the war and didn't like him at all. The US State Department wouldn't let him do it. They said it might cause a war with France."

"Why a war with France?"

"Daddy was going to burn the paintings."

"Why?"

"Daddy was a military policeman, and he had to interview women when Picasso was charged with physical and mental abuse. He didn't think he deserved to be considered great."

"That brings us to a good point. Class, your next assignment is to write about how a great artist can be a bad person. One thousand words and give examples."

I held up my hand. The professor didn't want to see my hand for some reason, but I kept waving it. He finally recognized me.

"Can we use examples of great villains who were very bad and were terrible artists?"

"Like whom?"

"Adolph Hitler, for one."

"I suppose your dad knew him also."

He sounded snide to me. I think that was the word. I would have to check it out.

"No, that was Grandad Newman. He met him right after World War I at a beer garden in Munich."

"I suppose he hated him on sight because he saw the evil in him."

"I don't think so. According to Grandmum, Grandad thought he should take a bath. He smelled."

A bell rang about that time, and we all got up to leave. I heard the professor mutter, "Thank god we're going by the quarter and not the semester."

I didn't understand that at all. I enjoyed today's class.

Sally walked with me to my next class, English Literature. Two other girls were headed that way, so we made a small group. They wanted to talk about the latest fashions.

One of them wanted to know about the drapes clashing with the painting. That gave me an idea for an extra credit problem. I could bring the painting and drapes to class and show them how they didn't match.

All I had to do was talk Mummy into loaning me the drapes. She liked them. I don't think she would have a problem with the painting.

English literature was boring. The teacher gave us the reading list for the quarter. I held up my hand.

"What if we have already read all of these?"

"That's unlikely young lady, but if you have, you can take the final and test out of the course."

"When can I sign up to take it?"

"You mean to tell me you have read *Pride and Prejudice, Vanity Fair, Frankenstein, David Copperfield, Wuthering Heights, Bleak House, Jane Eyre, Great Expectations, Middlemarch,* and even *Mrs. Dalloway* and *To the Lighthouse* by Virginia Woolf. I don't think your parents would allow that."

"I didn't ask. They were all on our library shelf, so I picked the ones that sounded good."

"You are too young to read anything by Virginia Woolf. She is too mature for you."

"She's tame. Now *The Decameron* is risqué."

"You've read that!"

"It was just sitting there on the shelf. It was hard to read, I had to use my Italian dictionary, and even it didn't have all the words."

"You read it in the original Italian?"

"I got most of the way through. It is like Spanish, you know, but I gave up, especially when I found out that we had an English translation. My brother Denny had it hidden in his room. He had to pay me fifty dollars so I wouldn't tell Mum that he had hidden it. She hates it when we leave books around the house."

"See me after class. We will discuss this further."

"Yes, ma'am."

The teacher told the class Mary had brought up an issue that we face in literature. When is it literature, and when is it pornography? I want a thousand-word essay on the differences between the two on Wednesday.

The class all groaned at that. One guy said he wished the brat wasn't in this class. She caused nothing but trouble.

Since he was looking at me, I knew he meant me. I glared back at him and crossed my arms. I would have to start carrying a bottle of ink with me, or maybe a jar of fire ants.

I had another thought and held up my hand. Once more, the teacher didn't want to recognize me but finally had to.

"Yes, Mary." She sounded a little tired.

"Can we bring in examples?"

"Like what"

"I also found Denny's collection of *Playboy* and *Hustler* magazines. I think they are examples of each."

"I supposed you blackmailed him for fifty dollars not to tell."

"Oh no, I got a hundred for that. I think blackmail is too crude of a term. I prefer to think of it as Denny paying me tribute for my silence on his crimes against Mum."

"Crimes against Mum; why not Dad?"

"Dad is the one who gave them to him. I still haven't figured out how to approach Dad to gather tribute for not telling on him."

"I suggest great caution."

"Of course. I just can't figure out how much to ask for."

For some reason, Sally was having whooping fits in the back of the room.

After class, I talked to the teacher. Sally was there and assured the teacher that she had seen me reading the books in the back of the limo. She didn't know how well I understood them, but I had read them.

She asked me about water imagery, and if I understood that. I told her it usually referred to birth and rebirth or even purification. I gave the example of Horace's figuration of Lucilius as a river churning with mud and the transformation of that image at Juvenal, where the Orontes flows into the Tiber.

"I suppose you read that in the original Latin."

I was embarrassed but confessed, "We have it in English at home."

"I'm a little disappointed, but you can take the exam tomorrow morning if you want."

"I would like to do that; I don't want to get in trouble in your class."

I told her about the guy who called me a brat and what I planned on doing. She told me to be here at 9 a.m. sharp to take the exam.

That's how Mary got into college and came up with the formulas that proved cold fusion was possible. JE Research took it from the theoretical stage to proof of concept, then built the first working models.

Chapter 5

Continuing on my mission to divest most of my business, I had a long session deciding which should be disposed of and how. After deciding what JE businesses to dispose of, I went to Mum and Dad. As software people called it, they were my alpha testers.

Wanting a sanity check on my ideas, I asked for their time in the library after dinner that evening. I thought it would take about half an hour of their time.

I would tell them what I wanted to do, and they would tell me my ideas were great, go for it, now let's watch some TV.

Dad's first question was, "Have you checked out if the markets will bear all these businesses selling at once?"

"No, I haven't. That sounds like it would be a good idea."

Mum came up with, "How much are you asking for each company?"

"I haven't settled on a price yet."

"How much are your companies worth? That should give you an idea of what you should be asking for them."

"I have no idea, and I think some multiple of sales would be a starting point."

"True, but some of your businesses like the shipping and freight company have capital equipment, while others such as software are intellectual property," from Dad.

"It sounds like I have a lot of homework before I can put them on the market."

"There are companies that will evaluate their worth. Banks and Wall Street trading companies that specialize in IPOs. They can handle the evaluation of the share costs."

"So, I have to find the right people to handle the sales and IPO, but then they will do all the rest of it?"

"All but pay the taxes."

Dad and his taxes.

What I thought would be half an hour turned into two hours and three cups of coffee, along with attendant bathroom breaks.

Dad brought up, "Rick, you will have to manage the news of these sales carefully. You don't want people to think you are having a fire sale. Plus, you have employees who will panic at the news of you selling out."

"I intend to make it a part of every deal that all employee's jobs are protected for one year unless the discharge is for cause."

"Even so, unions will be knocking on the door trying to convince your people that they now need the union's protection. If the unions get in, the value of the company will drop."

"This gives me a lot to think about. Thanks for your input, Mum and Dad."

I lay awake a long time that night, running scenarios through my head.

My next step was to talk to Jim about selling most of my businesses. I had no idea of how he would take it.

Fortunately, he took it very well.

"Jim, I need to talk about divesting most of the business units.

"Thank God!"

"That was enthusiastic."

"I have been hoping this day would come. Things have been growing faster than the rest of the team or I can manage. There will be champagne toasts when the news gets out. You realize that you have made us all millionaires at the top three levels of the company. Some of us have been scared that we might lose it all because of loss of control or the government stepping in and calling us a monopoly."

"I thought we had taken steps to avoid the Sherman Antitrust Act and all the rest."

"We have, but the government can change the laws when it wants."

"Yeah, I almost had that happen in Australia. I had to bring the queen of England and the empress of China in as part-owners to stop that move."

"Okay, Rick. How do you see this playing out?"

First, I described how I would like to divest each business unit. Then, I described what needed to be done before selling the companies or having an IPO with a straight face.

"We are going to have to look at each market that we deal in to see if it is even appropriate to try to sell or have a stock offering.

"After that, we have to identify possible purchasers."

These thoughts resulted from my midnight tossing and turning while playing through scenarios.

"All the divisions and operations need some evaluation as to their worth to give us an idea of what we should be asking. I suspect we will have multiple companies in different countries doing the evaluations. For the IPO, we will have to decide on which commercial bank or trading house will manage the offering.

"Then there is the news factor. We don't want to panic the markets or our employees. We will have to be careful about unions seeing this as an opportunity. I know I would if I were them."

"Rick, you have given this a lot of thought."

"That, and some good advice from my parents."

"That's a given."

We agreed that a team of upper-level management had to be put in place to handle the sales and IPOs. I let Jim know that I was now going to talk with the queen and the empress to make certain I wouldn't cause problems with them.

When all was ready to go, I would talk to JFK. He was last because, at that point, the news would spread fast. The White House leaked like a sieve. Everyone there would want to get rich off of insider knowledge. That wouldn't happen in England or China, but they were monarchs and could keep a lid on things.

After a brief discussion with Mum and Dad about my conversation with Jim, I headed to England.

As usual, I didn't get in to talk directly to the queen until after explaining all to Mr. Norman. He was another one not surprised by my desire to sell. While not as vocal as Jim, he agreed that it was getting too much for me to control.

He asked for several days to investigate how all this would affect England, to which I agreed.

That night, I stayed at my suite in the Plaza and went for a morning run on Rotten Row in Hyde Park. I wasn't surprised when a young lady came barreling towards me on horseback, giving me the finger.

What surprised me was after she passed me, I heard a commotion. A lady pushed a pram right in front of the young lady. She managed to turn the horse enough to miss the pram but got thrown in the process.

I rushed to her aid. My only thought was to help, not to find out who had been rude to me so many times. Well, maybe it did cross my mind.

When she was thrown, she twisted her right ankle when she landed. I bent down to help her trying to ignore the unladylike language. She was as bad as my Mum when she got upset. Both of them would put my Uncle Popeye to shame.

For the first time, I got a good look at her. She had always been flying by. If beauty is in the eye of the beholder, then my eyes were beholding beauty.

She was a brunette with brown eyes. No feature stood out, but they all came together. A modest trim figure completed the package. After I helped her stand, she asked if I could help her round up her horse.

She had settled down, and it was now only her blankety-blank horse. I looked around and saw her horse calmly eating grass a dozen yards away. I helped her limp over to capture the blankety horse.

As she calmed down, her speech was nicer. She and Mum would get along.

I took a chance and asked her, "We have passed half a dozen times, and you always make a rude gesture. Why is that? I don't believe we know each other."

"Oh, we don't. I had a bad experience with a man who looks a lot like you. Every time I see a look-alike, I give them the finger. That way, I won't miss sharing my feelings if it is him."

That was an interesting take on life. According to that, I should be shooting every Russian, North Korean, and East German that I ran into. Now that North Korea and East Germany weren't separate countries, it could get messy.

We exchanged names, hers being Sandra Wilson. I gave her a plain Rick Jackson in my American accent. I had to think about doing it. I had used the English one so much that it had become second nature.

I helped her get on her horse to get back to her stable. She was a nice handful. I thought about asking her for her contact information but thought better of it. I had so much going on that I didn't need any more complications. Besides, I reminded her of a bad boyfriend. That couldn't end well.

I went to Treacher's for fish and chips. I wondered if I could talk him into opening franchises in America.

Chapter 6

The next morning, I met with the queen. Her advisors had reviewed my plan and found nothing that would hurt the United Kingdom.

"Richard, there is nothing in your plan to divest yourself of your companies that will hurt the United Kingdom. Since you are keeping the Space Division intact and under your wing, our countries will continue to prosper.

The queen continued, "I do have a personal request. Three families lost their fortunes in the last war while aiding Great Britain. Since their senior members died in that war, they have never recovered. If you could see your way to allow them to participate in one of the IPOs, I would appreciate it.

"If you provide their names, I will have them invited, Your Majesty."

"Mr. Norman will provide the particulars."

I was excused and backed out of the small room. Mr. Norman was waiting for me with the list of three names. They were Smyth, Wilson, and McTavish.

"Rick, these families have given their all for queen and country, and we have never been able to repay them. While not living in poverty, they have fallen greatly."

"I will have them invited to the IPO for the container company. To ensure that all goes well for them, I will invest one million pounds in stock for each family. That way, if things don't go well, they won't be out anything more."

"You are a fine young man, and I'm certain that you will be well rewarded for your actions in the future."

"I have been very fortunate. I'm glad to be of help."

"Yes, but this is a large sum you are gifting them."

"You do realize that the goldfields alone will provide me with over fourteen billion US dollars next year?"

"One forgets your circumstances. Would you be interested in repaying the kingdom's war debt?"

"No."

With a cheeky grin, he told me, "I had to ask."

Later that day, I boarded my 707 to fly to China. There was a new one on order, but it would be another six months before I saw it. The flight via India was without excitement. The best kind.

I was getting better at gin rummy. I won seven dollars on this trip.

I was whipped by the time we got to Beijing. I spent the next two days recovering.

I couldn't have held an intelligent conversation the first day if my life depended on it. The next was better, but I still wasn't up to par.

I had an appointment with the empress's chief of staff the morning of the third day and dinner scheduled with the empress that evening.

The meeting went well with the chief of staff. He almost wet his pants when I told him that I wanted to sell the Noble House bank. You could see the dollar signs turning in his head.

He wasn't as enthused when I told him it would be an IPO on the Chinese stock market rather than a private sale, but there would still be opportunities to make money.

China is China.

He couldn't come up with any objections against China's best interests, so he told me to proceed. Unlike the UK, where advisors reviewed things, he made the decisions.

At dinner that evening, I broached the subject with the empress. She assured me that she had been kept up to date on events and that the disposal of the Noble House had been reviewed before I arrived.

She thought a public offering would be good for the Chinese people and that she would hold the chief of staff and his cronies in check. They would get a share but not the lion's share.

If the chief didn't agree to this, she could always replace the late chief.

Her spy system was very good, and she was ruthless.

I worked up the nerve and asked her why May-ling blew hot and cold about our relationship.

"Rick, I think she likes you a lot. You have never been told, but she had a childhood disease that left her unable to ever have children. Being infertile will lead to problems when she ascends the throne. A second cousin would replace her, but frankly, we don't consider him or his heirs able to do the job. She doesn't want to involve you in a mess and also deny you the pleasure of children.

"She is also afraid that if she is killed or dies of natural causes on the throne, the people will want you to take her place. There will be others who will try to kill you. They would install the second cousin who would be their puppet."

Wow, that gave me a lot to think about.

It was a sober flight back to the US. Not that I drank a lot, it was a sober reflection about May-ling and where we could go, if anywhere. I had never given having children much thought, but after thinking about it, I realized that I always assumed I would have them someday.

As far as taking the throne, I didn't see that happening. Many had tried to kill me and look where the attempts had gotten. It wasn't a pleasant flight.

Returning to Mum and Dad, I updated them on the business portion of my trip. I wasn't ready to talk about May-ling.

They saw nothing wrong with helping the families as the queen had requested. Since the empress agreed with our plan, there was no problem there.

They were a little relieved when I told them that Jim agreed it was time, and the matter had been discussed previously in the upper management levels.

It was a good sign that Jim wanted to put together a team to ensure the timing of each event and to take care of all levels of current employees while forestalling unionization.

They thought I had a plan in place, and it was time to start the process.

So, it was now back to Jim. I shared Queen Elizabeth's minor requests, and he had no problem with them, especially since I would be funding them.

The Chinese position agreed with ours, so it was now full speed ahead. While I was gone, he had selected a team of managers who would lead each divestiture. They would each head up a team handling the separate projects.

At all team levels, they were long-term employees who had done very well financially from the company and should continue to do so if they chose to stay on. There should be no internal issues.

I explained to the team why I was doing what I was doing. Ultimately, I protected us all from the company. It could become an unmanageable monster that would collapse under its weight. From the nods around the table, they agreed.

I explained what I wanted to be done with each company division. We would be a holding or licensing company when all was said and done. After additional thought, even the Space Division was spun off into a separate company.

The *estancia* and stations were my holdings, so they weren't involved in this. I agreed that when all the sub-teams were formed, I would explain the why and how of what was to be done.

The execution of the explanations needed to go smoothly. One hiccup could affect it all.

My next step was to arrange a meeting with JFK. The changes I wanted to make were normal business flow in the US, but they were also of a magnitude that could affect the national economy.

When I called for an appointment, they practically demanded that I come in immediately. Since I had to fly from California to Washington, DC, it would be the next day.

Upon arrival at the White House, I didn't have to wait at all. The president and his economic team were waiting for me.

It seems that the US also has a good spy system.

President Kennedy didn't mess around, "Rick, what's going on? We have heard a hundred rumors in the last two days. Is your health okay?"

"Nothing like that, Mr. President, the long and the short of it is that I have decided to divest most of my companies."

"Why?"

"They have become too large for me to handle. I don't want a failure because I didn't do the job. I'm either selling to the current management, putting the companies on the open market, or having an IPO."

One of his advisors pumped his fist in a victory sign. He had guessed right. From the scowls around the table, they had disagreed with him in public or, worse yet, lost a bet.

"What are your plans for the container business? That one will have the most impact."

"I'm selling off Howell, Narrow Freight, and the Scottish Lines. The main container business will have an IPO."

"Who is handling the IPO?"

"That hasn't been decided yet. We need to select partners for each divestiture and then evaluate the worth of each company."

"Who is your leader on this?"

"Jim Williamson is the leader of the project. Under him, a team leader has a team that will handle each project. These are in place and starting the process. Each team will select the financial institution they will work with."

"Do you mind if we make suggestions about which financial institutions they work with?"

"Not at all. If you work under the same conditions as the queen and empress have agreed to."

"What are those?"

"Elizabeth will have those who don't work in our best interest beheaded. The empress will have them strangled."

So, I made it up. It was still worth it to see the looks on their faces. What were looks of greed now became fear. After a weak grin, the president asked, "What's your next step?"

"The one I hate the most, a press conference."

Chapter 7

That evening, I flew back to California to have the press conference at my offices. The new office campus had a room set up for that. If things went badly, I could go home and hide in my room.

I got home late Tuesday night, so Jim had a press conference scheduled for Friday. Friday was the traditional day to drop bombs on the news cycle. You hoped that by the time Monday rolled around, other events would overtake your story.

It didn't happen that way for me. Nothing happened over the weekend, so on Monday, my story was the lead story.

The conference went as predicted. I announced that I would be doing a major restructuring of the company, including selling off some operations and taking others public.

"Why are you doing this?"

"The company has gotten too large for me to control, and I want what is best for the employees and the company."

"Do you have health issues?"

"No. Next."

"Are you in financial trouble due to your space venture? It appears you are ahead of NASA, and they are a federal agency."

"Have you read the news out of Australia? No, I'm not having any financial issues.

"To restate it, the company is now larger than my span of control. I could turn it over to a high-powered individual who could handle it, or I could downsize. I choose to downsize."

"Which companies are going public, and which are being sold?"

"That decision hasn't been finalized yet. I have several management committees analyzing each business unit.

"How much do you expect to make?"

"Until each division is valued, I have no idea."

"When will you know?"

"When my management committees recommend how to dispose of each division, and then select a financial partner to work with."

"What about your employees? How many will lose their jobs?"

"One of the criteria I have set is that we will not be selling a division to a company that is a direct competitor, so they have a lot of cross functions. The only cross-functions will be high-level accounting and purchasing. We plan to keep them onboard at the downsized Jackson Enterprises. We have always operated in a lean fashion at that level.

"I would also like to add to potential investors: we will not make ourselves an attractive target for unionization. The unions must take a run at us as this is an opportunity for them. We intend to take care of our employees in all selling contracts, so they do not have to fear layoffs or cuts in pay."

A reporter spoke up, "That's for the first year; we've seen this happen before."

"This will be spelled out to last for at least five years. If a buying company finds itself in financial trouble, I will buy back that division at its selling price to keep my people employed."

"That's hard to believe."

"Frankly, Mr. Reporter, I don't give a damn if you believe. This conference is over."

I loved that finishing touch. It got better later when I learned the reporter's last name was Butler.

Then there were the follow-up interviews. Every major newspaper and television network wanted an interview. An exclusive would be preferred.

Since I had met Walter Cronkite when he went into space, I agreed to talk to him. That was TV; for a newspaper, I chose one of Dad's. I'm not completely dense.

Mr. Cronkite had a nice interviewing manner. He let me tell my story without interruptions. After hearing me through, he asked if he could summarize what was going on.

I agreed.

"Rick, it appears your company has grown so large that you feel it is going beyond your control. Rather than let it fail, you are breaking it up."

"That is correct."

"While breaking it up, you are trying to protect all the workers who helped you build the company. Once that is done, you intend to focus on your space program rather than be a playboy."

"Thank you for listening to me. You understand what is driving these decisions."

"One last question?"

"Okay."

"What about May-ling, the crown princess of China? You have been seen in her company many times. Is there anything between you two?"

"If you find the answer to that, please let me know."

He ended with, "And that's the way it is."

Dad's reporter was also correct in his conclusions. He just wasn't as personable, but then he wasn't in front of a camera.

Other requests kept coming in, but I turned them down. The press conferences didn't stop the speculation. More importantly, it didn't seem to impact the financial world yet.

One night-show host gave his opinion that this could be a disaster. I kept getting myself into trouble while running my company. What could I get into without them to take up my time?

He didn't get many laughs.

The Russians didn't help when they tried to extradite me. They kept going to different courts worldwide, but none accepted jurisdiction. The US said see the UK; the UK said see China; Australia said go to hell.

I was in a meeting with Jim, and I remembered to ask him if he had set it up that no matter what, Smyth, Wilson, and McTavish would be included in the IPO for the container operation and that I would be funding their share.

He assured me that it was all set up. He had a file with the particulars. He handed it to me for review. One name jumped out at me, Sandra Wilson. It seems she was the last of the Wilsons.

According to the report, she was living off of the last of her family's trust and would be dead broke by the end of the year. Talk about a surprise. She is the young lady giving me the finger because I looked like an old boyfriend.

Now I had to take care of her. Just when I thought I understood life. I told Jim to find a way to push some funds her way. We knew the IPO wouldn't be completed by the end of the year.

He wanted to know why I was doing this, as I didn't seem to care about the Smyths or McTavishes. I told him the story, which he thought was a hoot.

I had second thoughts about the Smyths and McTavishes and told Jim to make certain they were taken care of also. He would arrange an advance based upon a recommendation of the Crown. Let the queen handle this one.

We let the board of directors of Narrow Freight and Scottish Lines know that we intended to let them make the first offer to purchase their respective operations and provide financing if needed.

All we needed was a price evaluation for those operations, and they would be the easiest ones to move.

Both boards sent back enthusiastic responses. I loved the Scottish Line board. They even offered to hire me as a deckhand if I needed work.

Don Pearson was just as easy when we talked to him about the Personal Products Division. He only asked that he would be allowed to continue to use, "By Appointment to the Duke of Hong Kong."

I told him he could, but he had better keep the quality up. I think he was a little offended that I thought he might let it go down. I assured him I was trying to be funny, but the joke didn't work.

He told me not to worry. He had a better name lined up. Mary Jackson was making it her official hairdryer. Ouch, paybacks are tough. He got me. As far as my bratty sister, she knew how to wind me up.

I flew to Detroit to talk to Mark and Sharon Dawson about what I wanted to do with my share of Detroit Faucet. I had been a silent partner for some years now. I was willing to let it go, and I didn't need to wait for an evaluation of the company's worth.

I sold them my share for one dollar. We had been through a lot together, and I thought of them as family. Now, if it had been Mary, she would have had to pay millions.

Sharon cried while she hugged me. Mark had a goofy grin. When they calmed down, they told me that Sharon was expecting again, and if it was a boy this time, they had already decided to name him Richard Jackson Downing.

It was my turn to tear up.

We had a wonderful dinner at the same restaurant where we had our original meeting. During dinner, they told me that Anna Romanov and her line of specialty items were doing better than ever. Sales would go up every time she was in a movie.

I called Colonel Frade about Howell, and as I expected, he told me he wanted to buy me out. As soon as we could get the company appraised, we would complete the sale. I did ask him how his family was doing.

He told me they were fine. His only regret was that he had chased me out of Argentina. He should have had a shotgun wedding.

Sometimes you get lucky, and you don't even know it.

Chapter 8

Since it was still several weeks before the moon landing and I had done what I could in the divestiture project, I decided to head to Australia to check up on the two stations.

I planned to be in China at the launch center for the landing. Early arrival would give me a chance to adapt to the time change. No matter how many times I had done it, it never seemed to get easier.

My first two days were spent in Sydney checking up on my household. Jeeves had it all under control. It seemed strange to wake up in the morning, go to the bathroom, and come out to coffee and toast waiting for me in my sitting area.

After taking a shower and using my Jackson brand hairdryer, I dressed in the clothes that Harold had laid out, then went down to a full breakfast buffet.

There would be the daily papers waiting for me at the table. I noticed these hadn't been ironed. I thought about tweaking Jeeves about it but decided I might live to regret it.

Once breakfast was finished, I would adjourn to my office, where my day's first appointment was waiting. I could get used to this life.

Waiting for me were the engineers who had drilled the water wells. They had additional information for me about the water source.

We had been working with the assumption that the water was from a huge groundwater pocket that had been accumulating for thousands of years, if not longer.

Once the wells had been drilled, the pockets of gas created by the layer of oil were forcing the water up. Now that they had more information, they had formed a different opinion.

After exchanging information with the oil exploration people, it became apparent that the oil was not situated to produce the amount of pressure we were seeing. There was a lot of oil, just not in the right place.

Their new theory was an underground river flowing south from the Darwin region. If this was true, we had an almost inexhaustible source of water that could open up the entire Australian interior.

I asked how this could be proved. Silly me, it would only take money. The water people wanted to drill wells to establish the river path. I permitted them to drill wells to the north on my property.

The first wells would be in an arc north of the main body of water. Hopefully, the arc would narrow down to a straight line north if they were correct.

If an underground river course were identified, I would start buying land to the north like crazy. I asked them to keep this quiet but didn't go so far as to demand NDAs be signed.

I wanted the land and water if it was there, but when it became public, which it would, I didn't want to come across as greedy and grasping. Well, maybe a little bit greedy.

Next up on my agenda was oil. The test wells had been finished, and it was confirmed as the largest find in Australia, rivaling the Texas oilfield. They didn't think it would surpass Saudia Arabia, but it might approach it.

They informed me that several wildcatters were working on the fringes of my property. I told them not to interfere. Something about those risk-takers made them feel akin to me. I wished them well. It turned out I wasn't that greedy.

Now that the oilfield had been mapped out, it was time to start drilling seriously. Once more, all it would take was money. Fortunately, I seemed to have a lot of it.

They presented a drilling plan for the placement of wells. They had plans for storage and transportation in place. They even asked if I had considered building a refinery.

I told them of course I had, and that it was part of the long-term plan. Once the wells were producing, crude oil would be piped to the coast. Then we would start on that project.

I didn't tell them I had never given any thought to a refinery until they mentioned it. My consideration period was when they stopped talking until I opened my mouth.

Now that I had a moment to think, I added, "Here in the Outback away from housing is the best place to put such an operation. While large enough to create a bother near cities, it won't be a blip here. Not even the Aboriginals will be disturbed by it."

I made a mental note to confirm my thoughts with the local Aboriginals.

They did have a concern about the pipeline. There had been no progress on laying one out between different federal and state departments and environmental groups.

I replied, "I will look into it, but I'm afraid we will have to let nature take its course."

They weren't thrilled to hear that as it would delay getting the product to market, but they couldn't do much else.

I didn't tell them that Dad and I had discussed this very issue while in America. The only way we could see around this was by sending oil by rail.

To this end, I had commissioned my land company to start surveying an extension of the railway from our station to Alice Springs. From there, it would be a narrow-gauge track to Tarcoola to join the trans-Australian.

I made certain this information would leak to the press. Let the politicians stick that in their pipe and smoke it. The pipeline would be best, but it seemed prudent to develop an alternate route.

This meeting took me up to lunchtime. My lunch was served on the veranda on this pleasant Australian summer day.

After lunch, gold was on the agenda. Sheila Armstrong had come to update me. She was in town for other reasons, and her next stop would be back at the goldfield.

The security fencing was now in place, with guards patrolling the perimeter. The guards were all part of the Aboriginal workforce so that no one would get by them in the desert.

All the mining equipment was in place, and water had been trucked in from the first wells. It had taken hundreds of truckloads to fill the retention pond.

These truckloads of water would run through the wash plant. Ore had been sent through the crusher and was waiting to feed into the trommel. The trommel and wash plant both were due to be started tomorrow.

Housing was being put in place for the on-site workforce. Most gold operations were temporary, using travel trailers or even tents. This site was to be a permanent operation, or at least for the next one hundred years or so.

One thing that hadn't been established with the goldfield was how deep it ran. We knew its length, width, and height above ground but not how far down it went. If it were as deep as it was high, it would last for two centuries. I didn't even try to calculate its possible worth.

The smelter was constructed, and a vault to store the finished gold bars. We hadn't decided how to ship them to Canberra for storage. The Australian Royal Mint was almost finished being constructed, and that is where the government wanted us to ship their share of the gold and our taxes on our share, which we had agreed to pay in kind.

We didn't have a plan for what to do with our share of the gold. I was all for selling it to all comers freight on board, to be picked up here.

That is, they would be responsible for its transportation, and they owned it the moment it was loaded onto their vehicles, whether it was a truck, train, or plane. Or even a ship, but that one was hard to fathom. Pun intended.

All payments were to be in hard currencies. We would be using the Royal Bank of Australia as our clearinghouse. I had briefly thought of opening a bank to handle the transactions.

Mum and Dad both discouraged that. Their thinking was that I was having an enormous effect on the Australian economy. I should leave something on the table for the Australians.

That made sense. I didn't want to become a national boogieman. Besides, I was trying to divest companies, not create more.

What I thought was neat was that the smelter would stamp each bar with my coat of arms.

Sheila and I spent the entire afternoon on the gold operation. I invited her to dinner, but she had a prior engagement.

The time zone changes caught up with me, and I called it an early evening and was in bed by eight o'clock. That meant I was wide awake at 4 a.m.

I went for a long run in the dark. I don't know why I was surprised when the police pulled me over. The police must have thought I was a thief on the run.

I had picked up one good habit along the way. I always had a passport with me. They cautioned me of the dangers of running alone in this area in the dark and let me go.

I wonder if I can get Jeeves to run with me.

Chapter 9

Updates in an office are one thing. Walking the ground another. I had planned to make a trip to Lasseter Station before coming to Australia.

The next morning, I hogged the left seat of the DC3, so I could remain current in that aircraft and flew out to Lasseter. By this time, I had a choice of two landing strips, the one at the water drilling site or the goldfield.

Since I planned to check out the water situation first, I landed there. The site managers even had the control tower manned. It seemed like reporters or other nosey parkers were flying in every day.

It was a typical January day in the Outback. One hundred and four degrees with ten percent humidity. It hadn't rained here in at least thirty years.

There was a field office set up, so I checked in there. They had a map of the entire station with all the current well sites.

They were also surveying the land to see what was arable. Most of the station wasn't useable for crops or grazing. Even with water, it couldn't be used. This land was bare rock covered with sand or dunes that would drift back in if removed.

Still, I was told that tens of thousands of acres could be plowed and planted if water was made available. They recommended that a circular irrigation system be put in like those used in the western United States. Even for the land used for grazing.

The heat was so bad that the livestock wouldn't survive without being cooled. I tried to picture the irrigation system circling the field and the cattle following it around to keep the cool spray on them. That would be a sight to behold.

One concern that would have to be addressed was wild dog packs. These would have to be eradicated. We wouldn't have to fence the fields as the cattle would stay with the grass and water.

Our initial plan was to start with fifty of these circular fields and see how they worked. We even decided to put in CCTV. A field office would monitor the cameras swiveling to survey the whole field.

Each field would have a pole barn shelter for the cattle. Thinking of sand storms, we placed a closed side to the prevailing winds and half of the adjacent sides. There would be water troughs in the pole barn and around the fields.

The field office would also house a veterinarian's office. We would need three vets on staff to handle the first herd of five thousand cattle. That would be one hundred heads per each of the fifty fields.

In the future, it was estimated we could have five hundred fields. This station would rival those of Argentina.

There would also be random patrols for security.

A separate group of stockmen, jackaroos, and jillaroos would watch the herds. This station was going to be a major operation. It would rate separate slaughter and butchering facilities. We would ship the meat out by railway in refrigerated cars.

This ranch would end up larger than Jackson Station in Queensland. I would have to get Ron Ferguson's input on this station. His station would be our model.

There would be a thousand miles of sixteen-inch pipe to distribute the water around the ranch. The US Steel plant in Lorain, Ohio, would be providing seamless pipe for the station. It could be used for water or oil.

They shipped piping worldwide and maintained stock in Australia to get what we needed immediately. I even thought about opening a pipe plant here but shut that thought down. I was divesting, not investing.

I moved on from the water field to the oil field. There wasn't as much to see there. Drilling rigs were all over the place. Several even had permanent pumps with storage tanks.

There was a tank farm being put in place. The tanks were the floating top atmospheric type. They had to explain what they were. I had seen floating roof tanks from the air, but now I understood it was to keep gases coming off the crude oil contained.

These tanks were huge. They were eighty-eight meters in diameter and twenty meters tall. They were made from carbon steel for strength. Each tank could hold thirty-two million gallons. We were starting with ten of them!

I could see that we would keep US Steel in business for some time to come as they made the miles of pipe needed.

I also began to see the urgency in getting Canberra off its butt. We would be sitting on a sea of oil.

Our oil had been classified as sweet, with low sulfur content, the same as West Texas Intermediate (WTI). This grade is desirable and easy to distill into gasoline and allied products.

There would be a headquarters building here for the administrative staff. There would have to be housing as people couldn't fly back and forth every day. Since what I thought of as the water field was only ten miles away, they would host the amenities, and this would be a bedroom community.

Since there would be quite a few roughnecks who would come and go, we had to have barracks for them. Facing reality, they had to have a recreation center that included a bar. I was resistant to having a brothel on the station, but I knew that one would appear as an open secret.

It was too early for the conversation, but when the time came, I intended to tell security if the brothel caused no problems to let it be. The one thing I wouldn't tolerate was the drug trade. That was to be rooted out and destroyed.

If it took a few deep graves in the great Outback, so be it.

Each of the sites, cattle, water, oil, and gold would have an infirmary. Anything serious would be airlifted out, but there would be broken bones along with various illnesses.

I saw a pattern developing. Each time I visited an area, I saw a need for another infrastructure facility. I suspected that it would take several trips around the stations to identify the needs. Or maybe I should find a town planner?

Here on this station, I needed a town and three satellite villages. The cattle operation would be so spread out that it could be combined with the water field. I didn't want it in the goldfield because of security or the oil patch because of overall safety.

Heh, who needs a town planner? As I continued to add to my list of needs, I once more realized that I needed a town planner. I didn't want this operation to grow like the disorganized mess of an old west mining camp.

I moved on to what Tony called the goldfield. Driving me around, he was my first taxi driver and mayor of the Aboriginal contingent, or the blackfellas.

He could do that because he was one of them. I felt uncomfortable using the term, although I had done it frequently. He told me once more that it was okay, just don't call him an Abo.

When we drove into the main gold camp, there was a disturbance. A man was shouting orders to two security guards, and they were looking at him as though they had no idea what to do with him.

I had Tony pull over. The guy recognized me, as he came over to me right away.

"Good. Tell these nitwits that I need a large tent put up with chairs for my revival."

"Revival?"

"Yes, I'm a man of God, and I'm here to save these heathens!"

I turned to one of the guards, "How did he get here?"

"He hitched a ride on a supply truck and was inside the gate before we knew he was an intruder. He has been ranting and raving at us to do things for him. We were about to send him away when you showed up."

"Take him to the gate and shove him out."

"Into the desert?"

"No, I guess we can't do that. Put the preacher on a truck to the water field, and then the next flight out. Do you have handcuffs?"

"Yes, the boys need to be controlled some nights until they sleep it off."

That answered booze being available.

"Cuff him and get him out of here."

He began shouting, "You can't do that. I'm a man of God."

They hauled him away, him shouting until he was out of sight. Here I thought the priest on the *estancia* was pushy.

For some reason, I was mentally exhausted even though it wasn't that late in the day. I had them land the DC3 at this landing strip, as it was making a run back to Sydney, and went home to bed.

Chapter 10

Feeling better the next morning, I flew back to the station. I hadn't had a chance yesterday to check on what we were providing the blackfellas.

I had made some promises, and I intended to keep them. Tony was waiting for me as we landed. He must have a good network because I hadn't told him when I would return.

We went to see the elders. They didn't look unhappy, which I took as a good sign.

"Honored Elders, has everything been done that I promised?"

"They have. We are pleased with the housing that has been provided."

These weren't the permanent housing we provided at the Gold Reef. The elders had requested that a small camp be put up about five miles from the main site. That was for those wanting to maintain a more traditional lifestyle.

We were in the process of running a small water pipeline out to the camp. In the meantime, water was trucked out to them.

The houses were basic with no running water. That had to be obtained from the water tank in the housing center.

Sanitation was provided by a large community outhouse, similar to those found in rest areas in the US. They also had showers. A honey dipper would empty the sewage collection tank weekly.

A school bus would collect any children who wanted to go to school. It was a little hard for me to swallow, but their lifestyle didn't have compulsory schooling. It had to be honored, but there must be some way for them to see the advantages.

They had no problem using the medical facilities, so that was one worry handled.

On-the-job training was given to anyone who wanted to work. We had over-hired so that the blackfellas could go walkabout if it hit their fancy.

I heard a commotion coming out of one of the elder's houses. It seems his wives were disagreeing.

The elder, who wasn't thrilled about schooling, spoke up.

"Rick, do you plan on adult classes, and if so, how many hours a day? I might be interested."

The other elders all laughed at him. His wives were notorious for not getting along. Why would anyone have more than one wife?

Satisfied that my promises were being fulfilled, I moved on to the cattle portion of the station.

These operations were headquartered in the water field where most of the construction was. This area was Waterton and would be the main town on the station.

There would be a small village at the Gold Reef, known as Gold. The oil field would be known as Oil. Not very imaginative, but it worked.

The cattle would graze on irrigated land. The circular watering system would prevent overgrazing in any particular area, so it was a good thing. I hoped paths wouldn't be created, killing the grass.

That would take care of raising the animal. We had vets on-site to keep the animals healthy. You always lost a few, but usually, they were pretty hardy. Being raised in a grass pasture is better than a cramped feedlot.

After the cow is mature and ready for slaughter, we would try to do it as easily for them as possible. We chose to use carbon dioxide to stun, so the cattle would gradually fall asleep from lack of oxygen.

We did this rather than with an electric current or a captive bolt pistol. We wanted the animal to remain calm throughout the process, not just for ethical reasons: Adrenaline means that stressed animals make for tougher meat, and bruised meat can't be sold.

Before you can start butchering, you need to remove the cow's hide. Workers cut the hide from the cows. Once the cattle's hide has been removed, it's time to dress the carcass, removing the innards. The hides would be sold to a tanning facility.

Workers must carefully avoid rupturing the innards or getting any contaminants on the carcass for food safety reasons.

The meat would have to be graded. Meat is given a grade depending on the animal's size, muscle mass, and fat deposits. The USDA certifies certain beef cuts as Prime, Select, or Choice, based on the marbling and tenderness.

Here in Australia, it is a whole system where the MSA grades by two, three, or four stars.

We would be shipping out the whole sides of meat rather than cutting to the size seen in the grocery store. These would be shipped out in refrigerated trucks and rail cars. In the case of extremely well-marbled Wagyu, it might even be shipped by air.

We were going to grow crops. They would be wheat, barley, oats, and corn. There would also be soybeans, peanuts, chickpeas, sugarcane, cotton, fruits, grapes, and vegetables.

I wanted to prove that this could be made into a complete farming area if water was provided. The one crop that I wouldn't let the station grow was tobacco.

There would be another fifty fields dedicated to raising crops. These additions would cause an increase in the buildings and equipment needed. Now it was tractors and attachments, trucks, wagons, and a host of other machines.

Then there was the maintenance and spare parts issue. More people would be required, which in turn required more infrastructure support.

We needed schools, stores, public buildings, banks, and a library.

The public buildings would house things such as a county courthouse like in the US, plus offices to obtain a driver's license, a fire department, and a police station, in other words, the support for a small city.

There would even be a roads department. Since it was all private property, the station would have to fund it, but all the equipment and manpower would be in place.

There would be a bowling alley, movie theater, football pitch, stables, roller skating, tennis courts, basketball courts, and a field for baseball and softball.

I almost forgot cricket and rugby pitches, but the town planner whom my engineering group hired caught that almost fatal error, fatal in Australia anyway.

I insisted on a golf course. Nine holes to start. I intended to expand it as the station grew. I would love to host an international tournament.

Then there was housing. It would all be station-owned and rented out or be included as part of the pay packet. There would be individual dwellings of two, three, or four bedrooms and apartments with one, two, or three bedrooms.

We discussed a barracks, but we decided to go with a residential hotel setup. Having separate rooms would stave off the problems of having many young people living on top of each other, and we hoped the better living conditions would reduce employee turnover.

Another decision I made was that there was no separation by race or sex. There would be no all-black or white neighborhoods. There wouldn't be separate men's and women's hotels. There would also be a lot of CCTV cameras in the hotel hallways and lobbies.

I was told that it was like Big Brother was watching. That was fine with me, rather than having some poor girl raped.

When all was said and done, it was estimated there would be over fifty thousand people living at the station. That would make us one of the larger, if not the largest, cities in the state.

Darn, that meant I had to let the politicians in when they were campaigning. That also meant we needed a meeting hall or even a convention-sized building. I wondered if I could make them work out of a barn, preferably one that hadn't been shoveled out. They would be right at home.

I had no idea what I was getting into when I found the goldfield. This operation would be as all-consuming as my businesses were. I could let them elect a mayor and town council. That would shift a lot of the headaches.

It would also create a lot more. I had to think about that for a while. Tony and I talked about all of this while he drove me around. I started to ask him if he wanted the job, but he cut me off with a sharp, "No way!"

Things were in motion, and I was worried about problems down the road. I decided not to borrow tomorrow's troubles today.

It was almost time for the moon landing, so I headed back to Sydney and let the aircrew know that we would be flying to China in two days.

After a good night's sleep, I was feeling more balanced. The wonderful morning breakfast service was easy to wake up to. After my exercises and cleaning up, I made an appointment with the prime minister.

I paid taxes to Australia and sorted out how my stations should interface with the state and nation. I'm sure it would be more bureaucratic than I liked, but it probably would go that way no matter what I wanted, unless I chose to live there and run it all. That wasn't about to happen.

Chapter 11

The trip back to China was the best sort, uneventful. The Chinese Air Force wasn't as paranoid as it had been in the past. Two jets did a fly-by to make certain we were who we said we were, and that was it.

No threatening passes or attempts to make us put our wheels down. They may be getting ready to allow international traffic without scaring them to death.

We went directly to the launch site. I would stop in Beijing on the way back if needed. The empress would be on hand for the landing, so I would see her anyway.

There was a message waiting for me when I landed. It was from the director of NASA. He wanted me to call him.

I had no idea what this could be about, but I returned his call as a professional courtesy.

"Richard, thank you for calling me back. We are willing to help you on your upcoming moon landing."

"What are you offering?"

"We know you have only women on the flight who are not even combat-trained. We have a man available to lead the mission and provide the direction and support that can only come from a man."

I replied, "We have a strong team in place. I think they are up to the job. They have many hours working in space. What could your guy bring to the party?"

"Colonel Glenn is the first person to orbit the Earth. He has five hours in space."

"Most of my crew have a thousand hours or more on many missions."

"But they are women."

"What's that got to do with anything?"

"Well, everyone knows that men are the natural leaders."

"I don't."

"If you don't buy that argument, the first person to land on the moon should be an American."

"Jerri Cobb is an American."

"You are sending her? You know she didn't make it as an astronaut."

"Because of politics led by Glenn if I remember."

"That was the correct thing to do. Cobb has no combat experience."

"Our craft won't be armed, so that isn't an issue."

"Combat experience means he knows how to react in an emergency. Cobb doesn't have that experience."

"If I remember right, she has had to face three in-flight emergencies in the seventy-plus missions she has flown. How many inflight emergencies has your man faced in his five hours in space?"

"I can see you won't help the country of your birth. I will have to call the president."

"I was born in England, and yes, call the president."

The nerve of that man, thinking they could waltz in and take over our accomplishment. Being the fine calm person I am, I only kicked the trash can in the office I was using. I thought about punching the wall but valued my knuckles.

We had intended to make the landing a soft historical event. We would land and get right to work. Now I wanted to rub it in that a civilian program was doing what the mighty governments couldn't.

Governments were involved passively. It was my money, paying people who, in some cases, were seconded by their governments to assist with the program. There weren't any direct government programs involved.

I got together with the launch team and told them we would make a bigger deal of the moon landing. They had to come up with a sentence that Jerri would say as she stepped on the moon. The landing was to be broadcast far and wide.

The group teased Jerri about her becoming famous. They wanted to know who would play her in the movie. She told us that Anna Romanov would be perfect for the part. Anna is older than Jerri, but not that much older.

I told her I might have some pull in that direction and would see what I could do. I don't think any of them believed me.

That night I called the US to speak to Mum. I invited her and Dad to view the landing at the launch center. She told me that she was hoping I would call. She wanted to bring the whole family if it was okay with me. Of course, it was.

I asked her to invite Anna Romanov. I explained that when I had a movie made of the event, Anna would be offered the role of Jerri Cobb. She told me that Anna would be there even if she had to kidnap her.

With anyone but Mum, I would have taken that as hyperbole.

Their new 707 was in service so they could provide their own transportation. This event would be the first time our two jets would be on the ground together. It would be a sight.

I did get a threatening call from the White House. It wasn't from the president. Some flunky tried to come across strong but only made himself sound weak.

He told me that I would have serious tax issues if I didn't comply with their request to have a NASA person command the landing. I replied, fine, I will start moving all my businesses out of the US.

He started to stutter and try to retract his statement, but I hung up. There was no way to take my businesses out of the country. It would cost too much, but that jerk didn't have to know that.

I then placed a call back to the White House, and after the usual wait for an international call, I was put through to the president.

"Rick, how are you, and what do we owe the honor of this call?"

"Are you aware that NASA wants a man to lead our moon landing, and now they are having someone in the White House making threats?"

"I know nothing about this."

I believed him. Either he was innocent or had plausible deniability.

"I'm not going to cave, but it is irritating, to say the least."

"I will look into it."

"Thank you, Mr. President. While I have you on the line, I would like to extend an invitation to you and Jackie to view the landing from the launch site."

"We would love that. I will see if my schedule can be cleared."

"The landing will be in five days, so you will have to move quickly."

After I hung up, I realized that I had opened a can of worms. I had invited the president on an impulse. The empress was going to be there. Now I had better invite the queen.

I immediately placed a call to London and went to dinner as these calls took time to go through. Naturally, I only got halfway through when I was summoned to the phone.

As usual, I spoke to Mr. Norman. When I informed him of the invitation and that the empress and president would be there, he told me he would get right back.

While waiting for the return call, I had time to think. It ended up being five hours when I was awakened in the middle of the night for the call. The queen and her husband would be delighted to attend. Who should their security people be talking to?

"I will have them call you."

"Please make it soon. You know these events can get complicated."

What have I done? Maybe I should notify the launch facility security people and the invited hospitality group.

That brought up another issue. To keep international peace, I should invite the leaders of Germany, Hong Kong, and Australia. I had significant interests in each area and didn't want to slight them.

I thought about other major powers such as France and Spain but drew the line. It was drawing a line or inviting the entire United Nations.

Since it was the middle of the night, I sent the security night desk a message about the high-level invitations and asked them to arrange a meeting and hospitality after breakfast.

I realized I was flirting with an assassination attempt, but in for a penny in for a pound. I would also need to place calls to Germany, Hong Kong, and Australia.

Thinking of the time differences, I placed the German call right away. I dozed back off for an hour before the call went through. I didn't get through to the president but was able to talk to the chief of staff. He told me they would get back to me, but they probably would attend.

His use of the word, they, alarmed me. I thought it would be just the president and his spouse. I slapped myself up the side of my head when I realized that heads of state never went anywhere alone.

I didn't go back to sleep. At the earliest time possible, I placed a call to the empress. I managed to get through right away. I soon found out why.

The empress was not a happy camper.

Chapter 12

"Rick, I understand you are making the landing an international event."

"I didn't think it through and started things moving before I realized how complicated this could get."

"I thought as much. We received a call from the security team a few hours ago. They are in a panic."

"What can I do?"

"Not what you can do. You have caused as much commotion as we can stand. All your guests will stay at the Forbidden City and be ferried in for the launch. We are set up to handle this. There will be a state dinner."

"Thank you, thank you, thank you."

"Is there anyone else besides the US, UK, and Germany?"

"I intended to invite Hong Kong and Australia."

"That would be fine. Why not the whole UN?"

"Wouldn't that be a bit much?"

"Yes, it would. I just wanted to know how dense you are this morning."

'I'm sorry."

"You should be. Do you realize that you have upset the schedules and plans of the most powerful nations in the world on a whim?"

"I got carried away, I was talking to the president about NASA trying to horn in on the landings, and almost an afterthought, I invited him and Jackie to the launch site. After that, it snowballed as I realized I needed to invite all the involved heads of state."

She replied, "We intend to make the best of this mess by calling it an international space summit. Having Germany, Australia, and Hong Kong is a bit of a stretch, but we can say they support you. I understand everyone but the Germans."

"They are one of my largest business partners in the container business, though they don't do anything in space."

"I suggest you get them and the two others involved to save face."

"I will, and I apologize for this mess."

"The ones to whom you owe an apology are the launch center personnel."

"I will make certain that they know I recognize my error and give my humble apologies."

She added, "A bonus might go a long way."

"You are correct, and I will make it happen."

No matter what I did, my name would be mud with them even if they didn't know the story of Dr. Mudd.

The moon landers had reached the moon station.

The American project, as currently planned, would have a single unit encompassing the launch vehicle, cabin to the moon, lander to the moon, vehicle to return to travel cabin, and Earth lander.

Ours was in stages, the first a launch vehicle to orbit, then two separate vehicles to travel to our lunar space station. Then two landers and return vehicles for the trip to the surface of the moon. Redundancy was the key thought in our planning.

This attitude paid off when the moon landers arrived at the lunar station. They both were taken on board for a thorough going-over before the main event.

This inspection was possible because the station was large enough that the landers could be inspected in a shirt-sleeve environment.

Lander One had a failure on a connection in the return engine firing mechanism. Tearing it down, they found a connection had come apart. This separation was not considered possible as this was a dagger connection.

When male and female parts were joined, they would click into place and permanently join. This connection would be tested by a pull by the person who joined them, an inspector who followed behind, and an electrical test to ensure it was in place and working.

They measured the two ends on the station and found that the male end was at the maximum diameter and the female end at the minimum diameter.

This loose fit made it possible for the parts to be mated without going all the way past the dagger connection point. They would pass the pull and electrical tests with enough interference fit between the two.

Once in the cold of space, the metal would contract. The male end had less mass than the female to contract faster. Vibration would then cause the parts to separate.

Lander Two was examined, and the connection was as it should be. Manufacturers' records on Earth showed both parts in the center of the allowed specification, which fit correctly.

It was an easy fix but would have doomed the crew if it hadn't been found and with only one vehicle available.

We released all the information to the public but didn't compare it to the NASA plan. The facts would speak for themselves.

The events occurred on the third and fourth days before the scheduled landing, so nothing was held up. That was good as my big mouth had world leaders flying in.

I was surprised by the attitude of the launch center staff. I thought they would be upset by my overreach. Instead, they continued with business as usual.

They either thought this was a non-event as the visitors wouldn't be straining their resources or were so used to Ricky Jackson screwups it was just another day.

One can hope.

One of the more difficult things to prepare for was Jerri Cobb's first words as she stepped on the moon.

Proposals went from the slapstick, "Hey, it really is green cheese," to more serious thoughts. Serious won out, but the comedy helped relieve the tension. They even printed t-shirts to that effect.

I took the high ground and didn't wear one of the shirts. I bought one for later.

The world leaders gathered in Beijing. I attended the opening ceremonies and the first meeting, which brought everyone up to date on the event schedule.

There was a luncheon after the first meeting in which I had a chance to mingle with the various leaders. The German delegation sought me out. Politicians travel in flocks.

They wanted to know why they were invited as they weren't directly involved like the US, UK, and China. Since they were diplomats and politicians, they couldn't let themselves ask me the question directly.

They danced around the subject until I got a little bored and suggested that since they were the world's leader in heavy mining equipment, they might be able to help with building infrastructure on the moon.

I had thought this through beforehand. While speculation was that we would build a permanent base, this was the first direct statement to that effect.

To say they were electrified was an understatement. I told the two heads of state they would be contacted after the landing to bring them into the process. It made their day, that is for certain. They could now hold their heads up as part of the inside group.

I had a similar conversation with the Australians. This time it was about the need for an alternate launch site and a future landing strip. We were still working on reusable space planes to go to Earth orbit.

Hong Kong was simple, "I'm your duke. I couldn't leave you out."

I did have a wild thought but bit my tongue. We would need an Earth-based clearinghouse for the Lunar Bank. Did I mention that we would have a fully functioning city on the moon?

I spoke briefly with JFK and Jackie. Anna Romanov and my Mum joined us to say hello. This conversation was cordial, but I noticed Jackie get a strained look when talking to Anna. Anna was her usual calm self. I didn't dare look at JFK.

Anna, Mum, and I drifted away from the president as others came up to speak to him. Jerri Cobb joined us and was most interested in speaking to Anna.

No one had mentioned that Jerri wanted Anna to play her in the movie. We all assumed there would be a movie.

When the idea was broached to Anna, she was receptive. She only had one question. Who would be the love interest?

That stopped us cold. It was an all-female crew.

"Does there have to be a love interest?" I asked.

"Most successful movies have them."

I thought for a moment.

"Jerri does have one burning love interest that has consumed her life so far."

Even Jerri looked puzzled at that.

"What is that?"

"Being in space."

Anna got a thoughtful look.

"Yes, that would work. Jerri's passion for space could show why there are no men in her life. We could have flashbacks of her turning men down so she could follow her dream."

So, one of the highest-grossing movies of all time was born.

I had a chance to talk to Mum and Dad alone. They complimented me on how this had come together. I explained the truth of the matter and how I, a twenty-year-old kid, had upset the plans of the most powerful leaders in the world.

I thought Dad would chew me out.

"Rick, where does this place you in the scheme of things?"

Mum added, "You are now a person who must be listened to."

Chapter 13

My parent's comments took me aback. It was hard for me to picture myself as important. Then I realized I wasn't important for being Rick Jackson. I was important by being the rich Rick Jackson, who had the phone numbers of the most powerful people in the world.

As long as I had my money and their phone numbers, I would be powerful. Lose either, and I was just another kid. Yes, I had accomplished many things, but this is the world of, "What have you done for me lately?"

My money was my power base. I didn't have the power of a nation behind me. If I lost my money, my power to do things would be gone. Maybe I should found a nation? All the land was gone, well, except for Antarctica, but who would want to live there?

I decided not to worry about what I couldn't control and get back to what I could, the moon landing. Even that had been set in motion, and there was little left for me to do.

A special room had been set up for all the visiting dignitaries at the launch center. It had TVs set to view the control room, the action on the lunar satellite, and inside the moon landers. There were fixed cameras to see the outside where our astronauts would be setting foot when they landed.

The room had several seating areas. Some set up to view the screens, others in a conversational setting. Nothing as crass as folding chairs. This furniture was like out of a reception room at the Forbidden Palace.

I later found out that the furniture had been brought from the palace for this event. There wasn't time to get it anywhere else.

From how people talked and mixed, you could tell many an international deal was being set up. This gathering was a rare opportunity for world leaders to get together with no announced plan creating pressure.

The inner circle of the event was centered on the US president, Chinese empress, and British queen. They were chatting away as best of friends. This group was sending a message to the whole world that it was okay to deal with each other.

There were no reporters in this room. They were being held in another room to view all the proceedings on TV. The staff called this the dog pound. The reporters demanded to be in the main room but were told that wouldn't happen.

They could ask for interviews later from any leader who consented.

While all this silly stuff was occurring on Earth, the real action was in orbit around the moon. I left the dignitaries and went to the control room. There I could hear the transmissions from the satellite to control. All was going well.

Everything was in that dry humorless voice heard in every control tower. All business, just the facts, ma'am, nothing but the facts.

Six people were going down to the moon. Four would be staying at the station. Each of the two landers would have three crew members. Our eggs were not all in one basket.

As the countdown proceeded, I found myself tensing up. Everything dangerous in my life had occurred so quickly I didn't have time to worry. This time was different. Other people were working under my direction, and time was slowly moving.

The two-hour descent seemed to take forever, and all of a sudden, the surface of the moon was rushing toward the cameras. The landers had taken off with a five-minute separation.

Jerri Cobb was piloting the first lander. She realized at the last minute that the crater picked for the landing was boulder-strewn.

She flared out into a clear area and landed successfully. There was more than enough fuel onboard to perform the maneuver safely.

The second lander followed her actions and landed about fifty feet from her. There now followed a period of double-checking the status of both crafts.

The famous moment arrived. Jerri Cobb exited her spacecraft and, as she stepped onto the moon, uttered the famous words, "One small step for a woman, one giant leap for mankind."

Later it was claimed that you could hear her mutter, "It's not green cheese." Close examination of the tapes revealed that wasn't said, but it sold a lot of t-shirts. I had nothing to do with it.

I had my suspicions from the smug look on a little girl's face but couldn't prove it.

One Space Lady of the three remained in their vehicle. They would switch places with one another in a while. We wanted the craft to be manned or womaned—well, crewed, at all times.

Upon exit, the first item was to walk around each craft to ensure they were okay. Then the crew erected a flag pole from each of the three nations, US, UK, and China and one with my coat of arms.

The flags were printed on sheet metal to stand straight as a real flag wouldn't display well. We had made certain that a lady from each nation was on the first landing.

I would have been there if I could, but too many powerful people said no, and they said it most emphatically.

They lined up and saluted the flags for the cameras. Their next chore was to pick up rocks and dust samples to take back to Earth. It was arranged that the chosen representative of her nation would choose and hand-deliver a rock to their nation's leader.

We had a wonderful publicity team. The team didn't miss a trick, except the green cheese bit.

After that, we scheduled what was called "Playtime." They were to bounce around in the moon's low gravity to prove they were on the moon. We knew there would always be some deniers, but most would believe their eyes.

One lady had brought a golf club and teed up a ball. She whacked it. Some claim she hit it into orbit, but the math said it wasn't possible.

The Guinness Book of Records wouldn't accept it as they had no official witness present but did put it as a footnote as the longest drive in the solar system.

We made no mention of the main reason for the landing. That was to identify a spot to start drilling into the moon's surface for an underground lunar station. Pictures were taken of all three hundred and sixty degrees around the landing spot. These were cameras with long-distance telephoto lenses.

Our people on the ground were viewing the TV cameras to see if places merited closer examination. There were several extra pictures taken. All of this was conducted on a different encoded radio channel.

There was no doubt that other nations would copy the messages and break the codes. It would take time. Since Mary's computer had developed the code, and it was the most powerful in the world, they would have a difficult job in front of them.

After two hours on the ground, when everyone had a chance to do their job and ensure they got in front of the TV cameras, they all reentered the vehicles. After a rest period, they launched off the moon to return to the satellite.

The next step was for the six women who had been on the moon to return to Earth and be replaced by others. The four who hadn't landed would remain on station and be in the next group to land.

We would do this until all of our astronauts had a chance to walk on the moon. Their astronaut wings with stars would have a moon placed on them to indicate they were moonwalkers.

Yes, I was jealous.

The pictures taken for a possible permanent station had several promising sites. One in particular looked good. It was estimated to be less than a mile from the landing site.

It was a ridge that was high enough to be drilled into. The drills would slope down, but a solid starting point had to be in place. There was a huge flat plain outside, which was large enough for both landings and the establishment of a huge solar farm.

Our next landing had a small vehicle to get around. It was based on an electric golf cart. The seats were much bigger to accommodate a person in a spacesuit. I guess it was more like an electric truck as it had a truck bed in the back for equipment.

This event was to occur in the next two weeks without any fanfare or external TV. It would be kept in-house. We wanted to present a fait accompli to the world. Not even the US president was read in as he had a conflict of interest.

The queen kept it at a royal level as all the British investments were from her funds. I think the empress shared it with May-ling but didn't know it for certain.

I did know that there would be an international furor raised when our plans became known.

There would be claims that the UN owned it. All I could say was they would have to enforce their claim. Once we were dug in, not even nuclear bombs could touch the colony.

Chapter 14

It turned out that even landing on the moon had the international community upset. The central theme was how you could do this without our permission and letting us share the glory?

France was the most bent out of shape. There were no Frenchmen or women on the flight, and we didn't plant their flag. We had asked them for support, but they wouldn't provide any. Neither financial nor personnel. According to them, their refusal should have had nothing to do with it.

When asked at one of the press conferences I attended why France had turned us down, I gave a reply that wasn't the best.

"I'm not sure, but if I remember correctly, it was because we would only allow the wine to be served in the squeeze balls. They considered it sacrilege."

The funny part is that the French people agreed that it would be sacrilege to serve wine that way. I don't think the French people understood the gravity of the situation.

On a more serious note, the UN wanted to include observers in our space flights to ensure that we weren't damaging the pristine environment or trying to weaponize it.

I sent a message to the president of the General Assembly of the United Nations that we weren't ready to take paying passengers on our flights but would let him know as soon as we had the capacity.

This payment request upset the UN even more; they thought we owed them free passage. I could see that things would get much worse before they got better. This relationship would take a lot of thought and planning.

So far, the votes in the UN Security Council have been on my side. I could understand the Russians wanting to take everything away from me, but I didn't understand the British government's attitude instead of the monarch's attitude. The US kept dancing around the issue. That was due to NASA's influence.

With the US elections coming up later this year, you could already see JFK turning to his base and promising social programs. This shift would reduce the military's and NASA's budgets.

That, in turn, would help me in the UN. What a strange turn of events.

The Australians were lobbying hard for a space facility to be put in the Outback. It would do wonders for their economy. They were offering all sorts of incentives. I liked best an extension of the trans-Australian railway to Darwin.

The Germans were eager to sell mining equipment. We were eager to buy, so that was proceeding well.

While all that was going on, I decided it was long past time for me to become certified to fly the 707. I could get type-qualified, and that would be it. I was multi-engine certified. I would have to get an endorsement on jet engines, then once more on the 707 types.

There was only one problem. All 707 pilots were commercial pilots. The only privately held 707s in the world had a professional crew. That even included my aircraft.

There were no private pilots rated on the 707. The FAA didn't even have any forms that covered that eventuality. Without getting into a long-drawn-out legal battle, I had to get a commercial license, and then the 707 types added to my license.

Fortunately, by this point, I already had enough hours and endorsements to qualify for an Air Transport Pilot rating, and it was not unusual for experienced non-airline pilots to pick up such certifications.

By the time this was done, between parachuting and flying, I would have so many wings on my uniform that I might be able to fly without a plane.

These requirements would include pre-flight preparation. My pilot qualifications were completely covered, so missing a basic requirement would be no hard stop. I had passed a level two medical physical, so that wouldn't be an issue. To be a little bit of a showoff, I even attached my astronaut medical form, which far surpassed the commercial pilots.

Then there was knowledge of airworthiness, weather, cross-country flight planning, airspace, aircraft performance and limitations, and human factors.

I had to demonstrate an understanding of primary and secondary flight controls, powerplant, landing gear, electrical system, avionics, etc.

My inspector would watch me perform pre-flight procedures during the actual check ride. I had to show knowledge of airport operations, including no fender benders on the ground.

There would be takeoffs, landings, and go-arounds, along with performance maneuvers.

Then they would want to see if I understood navigation. Getting lost was a no-no.

If I could do all that, there would be slow flights and stalls, high-altitude operations, and emergency operations.

Finally, there would be postflight procedures.

I passed the knowledge portion of the practical test easily as I had been studying that for several years.

On my side, there are no trick or surprise questions on FAA check rides. Everything asked on the check ride must be listed in the ACS endorsements. I far exceeded the hourly or flight distance requirements for cross-country flights.

The check ride itself was anticlimactic. I used my aircraft and had my chief pilot as my co-pilot. There wasn't anything asked of me that I hadn't done many times before. Well, not that many stalls, but I had done them correctly.

The FAA check-ride pilot had one last request to turn into the final landing pattern.

"Rick, why don't you do a strafing run?"

That got my attention. When the FAA guy roared with laughter, I knew I had been had. It seems he knew Bill McGarry.

After I landed and had signed off on all of the paperwork, he wanted to discuss my emergency landing in a 707. He told me that was still used in training as to what a person can do with basic flight knowledge and good ground support. He added it also helped to have nerves of steel.

I could now fly a 707 as Pilot in Command and had a fallback position if I lost all my money.

At least this was a one-and-done event, not like everything else I had going on in my life.

I had to spend some time with Jim Williamson and the divestiture staff to see what they recommended.

Jackson Personal Products: Don Pearson had jumped at the idea of taking over the hairdryer and curler business. He needed a deferred loan to do the buyout, but it wasn't unreasonably large, and he was on a five-year schedule to pay it back.

Jackson Home Products: I sold Detroit Faucets to Mark and Sharon Downing for one dollar. This sale got me completely out of business. I had made more than my original investment, so I wasn't losing anything. The tax accountants loved the write-off.

The licensing of beer and soda can pull tabs would continue. The auditing group was sold to our outside auditing company.

Jackson Transportation was going smoother than I thought it would.

The board of Narrow Freight bought it out. As I thought, it was a long-term buyout. This sale was another help to my tax position.

Colonel Frade bought Howell Argentine holdings for cash.

The Scottish Lines went the same way as Narrow Freight and a long-term buyout by the board of directors. They promised to let me know if any more two-for-one ship sales came about; this was our inside joke.

I didn't change my decision to hold onto Freight Forwarding. It was such a money-maker and self-sustaining that it would be foolish to let it go. It needed very little input from Jackson Enterprises and nothing but my name and coat of arms for advertising.

The Initial Public Offering, IPO, on container manufacturing was in progress. It would take one or even two years to make this happen.

The Noble House would be sold off with Empress Ping in China making certain the country would benefit from the sale, rather than a few cronies.

I still was keeping the Spanish *estancia* and Australian stations. I wanted to see if a culture change would occur as the Spanish *estancia* became profitable.

The Australian stations gave me a power base beyond Hong Kong. There was no way to put a price on all the gold. I guess I could take the company public, but it could upset the world economy if turned loose.

IPOs have been started on computer manufacturing, software applications, and operating systems. It would take several years to sort out.

R&D would be kept intact, concentrating on better computers; the goal would be a personal portable computer. A major effort would be to develop better batteries.

My little sister Mary had proven to be a math genius. She had come up with a formula that indicated cold fusion was feasible. My R&D group made her prototypes. They were now starting work to design the first practical commercial models. If successful, they would have a key role in the space program.

I kept ownership of my FreightEx company to see how far it could expand. It didn't take any of my time, and eventually, I would let the people building the company for me buy me out.

I decided not to sell off the Jackson Entertainment Division. Between my promise to Denny about a beach movie and the Jerri Cobb story, it was worth keeping, at least for now.

Keeping it would also be another way to work if all this fell through.

Chapter 15

Our lunar satellite was now fully functional and staffed with ten astronauts at all times. A solar array was in place to provide energy to power the systems. The containers making up the outside wall of the satellite were full of water for life support and radiation shielding.

Using electrolysis, we made the oxygen. Nitrogen and trace elements were shipped up in pressurized tanks.

Two more lunar landers had been sent up for a total of four. We were ready to go to work on the moon.

The international community was upset because we stepped on the moon as a small group of nations and a private company. They resented being left out.

Building permanent structures would send them ballistic. There was no doubt they would find out. We could try to confuse them as to the mission and the timing.

I did not doubt that every intelligence agency on Earth had tried and, in most cases, penetrated the launch center. This spying could be reported from a janitor to a person in a critical position.

We started multiple rumors: we were having difficulties with the landers, the station itself, astronauts were ill. These rumors were laid out through separate groups, so we would know where to look for spies if the rumor became public.

The biggest secret was that the work near the original landing site was a diversion. We had announced we would be building an experimental station at the landing site.

We didn't say that we would be putting a permanent colony on the far side of the moon.

This colony was close-held information. We didn't let the US or British governments in on it. The queen was told, but not the president.

Empress Ping had to be told as everything would be launched from China. All the equipment orders were kept compartmentalized so that no one could put a picture together of what was going on.

They would know something was going on because of the number of launches. There would be more than could be accounted for by our light side actions. NORAD was good at tracking rockets.

They didn't have the rockets to follow us to the moon, so they could only guess what was going on. It wouldn't take too many guesses to figure it out.

Knowing your guess must be correct is not the same as having proof, so we had time before it went public.

The extra landers had been sent to support both projects.

Our first step in prepping the far-side building sites was to confirm a landing site. This situation was a bit of chicken and egg because we had to land near where we would place the colony, and we couldn't decide on that until we landed. It took three separate landings before we found a site that appeared satisfactory.

To explore the area around the landing site, we used oversized golf carts. These were the same as those used at resorts to carry groups of guests around. The spacesuits were bulky, so we needed oversized vehicles.

The tires had been replaced with much larger ones that were steel belted to handle the rocky surface. The batteries were in a pressurized enclosure, but we would be doing good to get six hours from a set.

We had to discharge the heat buildup caused by being in a vacuum. The buildup release was done by lowering the batteries to the ground when not in use. There was also a shiny foil above the batteries to prevent heat buildup from the sun.

Recharging the batteries required a small building set up as a recharging station. Then we had to have a solar array to charge the batteries. We had to go through this three times until we found a spot.

We were looking for a cliff face that we could drill directly into. The idea was to create an adit, dig back, and create a cavern. From there, we would drill down.

The cavern would be large enough to contain all the equipment being used, maintenance sheds, and housing. The only thing visible from orbit would be the markers for the landing site.

Those markers would be lit but would be almost invisible when turned off. Even if you knew the operation was going on, it would be almost impossible to find it.

Once the cavern had been created, we would supplement the solar array with a heat pump system, which would be more efficient than the solar cells, which were still infant technology. The temperature difference between the sunlit surface and the cavern's depths would provide an energy flow we could use to generate power.

Of course, all this would only work when the sun was up for two weeks at a time, replaced by darkness for two weeks, and so on.

The heat pump system would utilize a heat reservoir in the cavern to provide for continued storage and generation of energy during the period of darkness.

Finding us was unlikely as no one else had manned capability. It would be a very fortunate satellite to identify the site, and the US doesn't have the capability yet to put one in orbit around the moon.

I'm certain there will be a launch by the US Air Force from Vandenberg in short order.

At our third exploratory landing site, we hit the jackpot. There was a clear flat area to land on and a high ridge with a vertical face. Best yet, the vertical face was in the shadow of the ridge.

The temporary housing structures with airlocks were the first items brought down. We had thought a modified bulldozer would be first to clear the area, but it was fine.

One thing that had to be done was to have the astronauts go over the area with long steel rods. They were checking for potholes filled with dust. We had already found some that looked like level ground but were six feet deep.

Somebody had the bright idea to take the temporary structures, which were heavy-duty inflatable tents, and heap excess dust from the potholes on the "tents" while using a specially adapted sprayer to apply an epoxy-type fixative to it. We quickly got hard shells on the temporary structures this way, and the dust even provided some protection from cosmic rays.

The plan for the potholes was to fill them with rocks with dust on top. We thought that the dust could be tamped down. I keep saying "We," but several working groups were doing the heavy thinking on Earth.

The landing site was marked out with landing lights. Some clown put up a windsock. The bulldozer was finally brought down and used to make a road from the landing and housing area to the face of the ridge.

Again, it was lined with lights, so there was a clear road from one area to the other. Going off-road on the moon could take things to a whole different level.

The German mining machines were landed. The landing was the most dangerous part of the operation. Those things weighed many tons, and if they got out of control, the mass would destroy anything in its way.

The Space Ladies handled it like the pros they were.

The drilling machines had been broken down into major subassemblies. The Germans normally had a crew sent out to the worksite to assemble it. That wasn't possible this time.

After signing the NDA, the lead German engineer supervised the assembly from the Earth by using a TV camera to direct the work. I was there at the launch site looking at the same picture he was.

I was in another room. I can imagine what it would feel like if an audience were looking over my shoulder. As it was, you could tell the engineer was stressed to the max.

I asked him how it went when he was finished.

"This working by remote will never catch on. You have to be on site."

I didn't comment, but the fact is that it was done successfully.

While the equipment was being put in place, there were ongoing rocket launches from Earth to orbit, then from Earth orbit to the moon. They were ferrying supplies to support the new colony.

Somehow in my mind, it had gone from being a station on the moon to being a colony on the moon. I didn't use that in conversation, but I was now thinking about it.

A miracle occurred. The ladies who seemed to control my life agreed that it was now safe for me to go to the moon! I found out by a message from Jerri Cobb asking me if I was ready to visit.

"Oh yeah!"

It took two weeks in transit before I got to the moon. I learned to hate food from a tube and let's not even talk about space toilets.

When I landed on the moon, I thought I acted with decorum while touring the facilities. Later, when I was shown the tapes of my trip around the site, I was bouncing around like a little kid.

They had already made progress with the drilling. The Space Ladies had drilled a hundred yards back into the ridge and now were hollowing out a cavern. The next step would be to start drilling a ramp sloping downwards.

After my trip to the far or what we called on Earth the dark side, I had to land on the light side. This landing was sent live to the world to keep up our subterfuge. I don't think any of the intelligence agencies bought it.

I got the moon added to my astronaut wings. I'm hot stuff! I can claim that I was the first and only man to walk on the moon so far.

I mentioned that in the dining hall at the launch center. I was hit by about twenty dinner rolls from Space Ladies who had been there before me.

Aside from my swollen ego, things were going better than I thought they would. The UN was still bad-mouthing me about landing on the moon without their permission.

I did get a call from President Kennedy. He wanted to know when I would announce my real plans to the world. It was a good thing I had acting lessons because I had to keep him in the dark as long as possible.

He did tell me that Congress was reducing both military and space funding. The money would be diverted to social programs. The upcoming elections were close, and they wanted to get their base enthused.

It was good for me to help keep the space program secret. I wasn't sure further dependence on social programs would be good for the American people. It certainly hadn't helped the British in their economy.

Chapter 16

I reached a decision this morning. I'm having difficulty standing by and watching the development of facilities in Earth orbit and on the moon without being physically involved.

I informed the launch center that I would be put in the next astronaut training class. I needed to learn how to work in space. I wasn't asking anyone. I was telling.

I did get a phone call from Mum. I guess she had been elected to make the call. She asked me if this was the wisest thing I could do. As nicely as I could, I told her that I needed to be involved and that I could risk as much as everyone else was.

She didn't argue, just told me to be careful.

The astronaut training had changed dramatically. Before people were launched into orbit and working there, it was a bit of a guessing game as to what abilities and training were needed.

Now the requirements were known. Once a person was deemed physically fit and trained in on-the-ground knowledge of what they would be doing, the rest of the training occurred in orbit.

Most people who failed couldn't work in weightlessness without losing their sense of balance. No one would have to fail them out. They would self-select. No one wanted to be in space so badly that they would work with a helmet full of vomit.

I was lucky in that it didn't bother me at all. I could maneuver around and work with no proper sense of up and down with no problems.

I quickly learned about counter-spin when trying to tighten a bolt. R&D had developed wrenches that had built-in counterbalances so you could tighten a bolt without counterrotation.

We all had to try it without one of those wrenches to see how it would feel. After that, I never forgot to attach my wrench to my tool belt. I couldn't imagine being able to do the job without it. We also had a similar screwdriver though I didn't have to use it.

Things that used screws were usually in tight spaces. The Space Ladies handled those. I got to move a lot of big stuff. I could handle the mass. Any one of us could handle the weight in zero gravity; it was the mass that was the killer.

Being in a sleeping habitat with nine ladies quickly made me lose my body modesty. There was nothing sexy about any of it. Using a toilet with a flimsy curtain around it was horrendous, and the complaints about the smells were loud. I didn't think I was that bad.

How quickly the mighty can fall. I went from Duke Richard to Stinky Rick in one day.

I also had a lot of ground simulator time. I was training to be a pilot in command of a launch. It was the most intense training I had in any flying machine.

The flying was easy if everything went right. All I had to do was lay back and let someone else light the candle. It was when things went wrong, and I had to react.

I spent eight hours every day for two weeks with different failure modes thrown at me. I worked the module until I could react to each failure type without thinking.

I thought I had done well. I was informed that I had, so I was ready to take the advanced course! That was another grueling two weeks.

When I completed those two weeks, I was told that I had done exceptionally well. My scores were as good as the best, and the normal course took eight weeks. They didn't find out until later that I had bribed the night people to let me practice for another four hours every night. Whatever I had scored low on that day would be repeated time and again in the evening until I got it right.

After passing flight training, it was back into orbit to learn to maneuver donkey engines. This small craft was used to move bulky objects around for assemblies.

I was finally given the go-ahead to be the PIC on a ground launch. I had been up several times now, but there was no feeling like being the one who had to take action if something went wrong.

Nothing could go wrong with a vehicle that would generate 160,000,000 horsepower at liftoff, could it? Fortunately for me, these launches had become routine, and no alarms or red lights came on.

Next, I had to return to the ground and learn how to drive a rocket from Earth orbit to moon orbit. This training took another month. Most people learning the Earth to moon trip took two months. I had got the bribing down to an art and was able to put in fourteen-hour days.

Much later, I learned that the decision was made that since I had been self-taught most of my educational career, I would be allowed to push myself as fast as I wanted. It was used to create a baseline for how long training should take.

My bribes of food baskets and alcohol were shared with all of the staff. They thought it was a hoot. I was paying them to train me.

What hurt the most was that Empress Ping insisted she be sent a piece of fruit from every basket.

I was allowed to fly the trip to the moon at long last. I was now considered a full-fledged astronaut.

During the training, events were proceeding on the moon. The German open-face mining machines had dug out a huge cavern under the ridge. It was five hundred feet by five hundred feet. Pillars were left in place to support the roof.

All the equipment could now be stored out of sight of prying Earth eyes, of which there were none yet. The housing was also moved inside the cavern.

The entrance went a quarter-mile from the adit face back into the cavern. There was now a large airlock. There was no atmosphere inside the cavern at this time. It was planned for the near future, but supplies had to be stockpiled first.

The mining machines had drilled out past the cavern in a straight line. This went on for another quarter mile. A wide space was carved out then the machines backed up and started drilling down near the exit from the back of the cavern.

The idea was that if anyone ever got the idea of nuking us, the pressure would follow the straight line and dissipate. This idea was taken from the planning that went into Cheyenne Mountain.

A major problem was what to do with the spoil that was dug out each day. It had to be hauled and dumped outside of our tunnel structure. We had modified trucks to haul it to a deep and shadowed crater.

A road had been plowed and marked. All day long, drivers would be hauling loads of rock and dumping it. Guess what job I had. I wasn't about to complain. I was working on the moon.

I did learn the difference between driving in moon gravity and Earth gravity. I had to learn it the hard way.

What was rather forcibly explained to me later was that there would be less weight on the tires with lower gravity, making it harder for the vehicle to accelerate.

The incident that got me in trouble was caused by my getting bored driving so slowly. I tried to speed up, but the acceleration was like a grandmum's walker.

I did manage to increase the truck's speed. What I forgot is the thing called mass. The road had a bump, much bigger than the speed bumps found in shopping malls.

I usually slowed down to lessen the jolt to my spine. This time I couldn't slow it down enough. When I hit the bump, I prepared myself for a hit.

I got the hit. Instead of a sharp jolt like on Earth, it launched up into the air when the truck hit the bump, flipped over, and rolled a hundred yards. I had a seat belt on.

The seat belt saved my life. The truck was a write-off.

I went back to slow driving.

We did leave a series of structures outside. There were 42 satellite dishes arranged in an array. These dishes were six feet in diameter and, when linked together with our computers, made the largest radio receiver and radio telescope ever built.

There would be no interference as there would be on Earth. It was a wonderful research instrument, even though we used it to cover our project. We made certain the bill of materials was accidentally released on the Earth carefully so that an intelligence agency could find it.

We called the project SETI; this was short for Search for Extraterrestrial Intelligence. We thought it would take the CIA or MI6 or their Chinese counterparts at least a year to get to this point. It took them three months.

We couldn't safely work any faster, so it was now a race. The only thing we had going for us was that all the evidence agencies would have would be circumstantial rather than factual. They had no vehicles to send a satellite around the moon to take pictures.

The US Air Force proved us wrong with an unmanned launch from Vandenberg. We could have taken their rocket out on its journey to the moon. That was even suggested, but I shot that idea down as soon as I heard it.

There would be enough Cain raised when the truth came out. Taking physical action would put us beyond the pale.

Instead, we would let their mission proceed. The only things we would do would be to shut off the landing lights on the dark side and remove the lights from the road to the crater where we dumped the rocks. The road would have rocks added so that you couldn't tell a road was there.

These steps would create extra work for us, but they would also gain us time as we dug in. We wanted to present the UN with a fait accompli.

Chapter 17

While things were progressing on the moon, future problems came to life on Earth. The big one was cold fusion. My sister Mary had come up with an equation that made it look possible.

The engineers were able to develop a prototype device that worked. Now they were looking at commercial development.

Mum, Dad, and I had concerns about what effects this might have on the world economy and people in general.

We quietly commissioned a study out of London University to make projections. They were not pretty. It would destroy the coal mining industry worldwide.

Ending mining would positively affect the damage being done to the environment. It would also ruin the livelihood of those depending on the industry. It was easy to say retrain the miners. Retrain them to what?

Sad to say, most miners weren't suited for many jobs. The only path that looked promising was to let the current workforce age out and retire. This path included providing educational and training opportunities in the schools of affected areas.

In other words, we couldn't change the current workforce in developed countries like the US and the UK, but we could create a different future for their youth.

China and India were problems beyond description. Mass starvation was the most likely result. For some reason, this wasn't something that Mum, Dad, and I wanted to cause.

If the Chinese adopted fusion as their power source, they could always send their excess labor to farms in Mongolia or Siberia. It wouldn't take much retraining.

India was currently without an answer.

There would be a greatly reduced need for oil. The ones hurt most by this would be the Arabs. Since they were trending towards being religious militants, I didn't have much of a problem with not giving them the money to buy advanced weapons.

It would also lessen their ability to export their eighth-century brand of thinking.

Off-Earth fusion would be the power of choice.

Our bottom line on the whole fusion subject was not pushing it hard and fast. It would be best to let it develop over some time. We would educate the next generation before letting the genie out of the bottle.

Mary wouldn't become a trillionaire until she was at least twenty-five. That was probably for the best.

I worked on the moon and had radio conferences on the fusion situation with my parents. They handled it on Mary's behalf; they brought me into the picture for my world perspective.

Besides going slow, I recommended that they make it seem like the fusion project was not working as easily as planned; it would take more time, like years more.

This information was to be closely held among the three of us.

Mary didn't show any interest in the project after validating her equations. She was now looking into the possibility of breaking the speed of light; that or how to beat Patty at jacks.

While I was still on the moon, we had an unforeseen bit of good luck. While drilling down, they had run into the ancient remains of an ice comet. It had hit the moon millions of years ago and was buried deep.

We didn't have an estimate yet, but it looked like there would be a huge water supply.

This find required a change in plans. First, we had to get a rough estimate of how big the comet was. Then we had to come up with a method of melting the ice and storing the water until needed.

Just like that, we had a way to use the excess heat from our operations and environmental support. We also put in place preparations to capture and focus a large amount of sunlight and direct it through our tunnels using pipes and mirrors so we could focus an intense beam of sunlight on the ice.

This network was complicated by the need to fold and conceal the surface reflectors if surveillance satellites were orbited around the moon by the US or other Earth powers.

If there were a significant amount of water, the launch schedules could be revised downward, as water was the single largest component of mass sent to the moon.

Our costs would be reduced considerably. While I had more than enough money, I was beginning to realize there was no such thing as too much money. The more you have, the more you can accomplish. It was an endless circle.

It took a week of exploratory drilling around the edge of the ice comet to determine that there was a lot of water there, as in Great Lakes amount of water.

Once the amount of water was established, another cavern was drilled out to store the water after the ice was melted. It was sealed with a spray-on epoxy liner.

To melt the ice, we brought up the first production model of the fusion equipment. Deuterium, tritium, and He-3 were all present on the moon. Extraction machinery would have to be brought up, but it was known technology.

We would now have air to breathe, water to drink, and energy to spare. It would still take some months to put in place, but our major physical problems were under control.

I ignored the fine details like piping to bring water to all base areas. Housing, farming, and other such fiddly bits. All important, but it would just take time and effort.

I wondered if there was a way to create artificial gravity. Some simple inquiries at the R&D center received a negative response. The way the response was given made me think that it was suspected I was on something.

There was another change going on in the space program. We had run out of women. Not that women weren't applying for the program. There weren't enough of them.

The solution was simple. We started hiring men. We had enough pilots that we didn't need men for that. It was for the moving and lifting stuff that men were needed for.

These guys were our roughnecks in space. Not that they all fit the profile of an oil patch roughneck. We didn't want a bunch of drunk cowboys in orbit.

That would be a disaster in the making. The men selected were all physically and mentally fit. They were flown into orbit to work around the Earth or up to the moon.

We set up separate housing on the moon for the men. Short-term in Earth orbit, it seemed okay to share facilities between the sexes, but it was best to separate them for long-term living.

It was also recognized that men and women would get together no matter what, so we put communal areas where they could congregate. While there was a no-alcohol rule in place, we hoped to keep it down to a dull roar.

Keeping it down to a dull roar meant that we turned a blind eye to a small still built correctly. Any others were quickly found and destroyed. The people involved were shipped back to Earth.

A small unofficial police force was in place on my habitat advisor's recommendation. We called them the emergency response team, and they had uniforms, etc.

One of their official duties was inspecting all areas for safety violations. It was strange how they never came across that small still. It seemed when an inspection was scheduled for that area, a note would appear on the bulletin board listing the next day's inspection areas.

I was given a sample of the product being made. One taste was enough to put me off it for life. Bad as it was, if they could bottle it and sell it back on Earth, they would make a fortune.

Somehow the few bottles people tried to smuggle back to Earth were always broken in transit. Funny that.

Besides alcohol, some people even managed to get into fights without being drunk. We shipped these people back to Earth when they started trouble. I assumed it would be men, but the first person shipped back was a woman.

Our workers were split into teams. Teams had leaders. We used civilian Earth titles, like supervisor, director, foreman, etc. That was for the ones doing the drilling and assembly work.

The women who flew our space vehicles were given military ranks. These ranks were done with an eye to the future. We would eventually interface with programs like NASA and wanted our people to be even.

The highest rank, Brigadier General, was held by Jerri Cobb. She hated it. It cut down on her flying time as she now had administrative duties. The only bright spot for her was that there might be a chance in the future to work with Colonel John Glenn.

That was never to be as he resigned from NASA and the military to run for political office in Ohio. He lost as an unknown and faded into obscurity. One exception was his picture did appear regularly on a dartboard Earthside in the Space Ladies' recreation area.

With the addition of males to the workforce, we could move ahead faster on the moon. Upper body strength does count on certain tasks.

As a pilot in the space program, I was given a flying rank. I was made a full colonel when flying. When not flying, I was called Boss.

Weird, but it worked. I tried not to get involved with the day-to-day operations. If I did, the next thing you know, Jerri would have me doing her paperwork.

Chapter 18

No project of this magnitude goes without some problems. We had mechanical breakdowns that were a nuisance. One incident almost cost a man his life.

The roughneck was working at the drilling face. His job was to keep stray debris from jamming up equipment. He was nowhere near the actual large drilling device.

There are many takeaway tubes from the drilling face. The roughneck's job entailed not getting debris caught between the steel armor tubes and wearing the steel belting.

Of all things, I was involved in a safety tour of the worksite at the time.

The guy's suit arm got pinched between two of the tubes. He was lucky that it only got the suit's fabric and not his arm.

The tubes moved after pinching his suit material. In doing so, they wore a hole in the arm of his suit. He had been well trained. As soon as his suit alarm went off, indicating a leak, he immediately exhaled as much as he could.

If he hadn't exhaled, the sudden vacuum would have caused his lungs to swell and even explode. This action is counterintuitive and took a lot of practice.

The suits all have built-in sensors. The person wearing it is alerted by the alarm, and a radio signal is sent to the control room where all workers are monitored.

When the tubes moved, they loosened the suit's arm so that the worker could slap a patch on it. Later investigation revealed that the patch had a wrinkle and hadn't sealed one hundred percent.

Normally, if a person loses all their air to a vacuum leak, they become unconscious in fifteen seconds. He remained conscious for thirty-two seconds since he had a partial seal.

During that time, the workers closest to him and I were alerted, and I put another patch on his arm to seal the leak. He had just passed out when this was done.

All areas have plenty of spare oxygen bottles, so one was hooked up to his suit within the magic one minute. Any longer, and he would have died. As it was, it only took another forty seconds to get new oxygen to him.

My action was fast enough that permanent brain damage was prevented.

While his life was saved, the drilling equipment went into an emergency shutdown mode. In doing so, it practically destroyed the machine.

While a setback, it was better than killing a person.

The worker was taken to the base infirmary and quickly regained consciousness. He was fine. He wanted to go back to work as soon as he was fitted for a new suit, but it wasn't allowed.

He had to go on a forty-eight-hour stand down to make certain he was not only physically but mentally okay.

The events were broadcast on the working channel, so everyone knew the problem.

I went to the infirmary along with Jerri Cobb. She immediately started an accident review. Plans had been put in place for such events. No one knew when or what would happen. It was a statistical certainty that it would be something.

Along with the on-site engineers from the German drill manufacturer, I examined the drill remains. The Germans had finally left the ground and come on site.

It wasn't good news about our drill. It had eaten itself up while shutting down. The machine would have to be replaced completely. Strangely enough, the only parts that hadn't been damaged were the two tubes that had pinched the guy's suit.

It took a couple of days to figure out all the damage to the machine. The day after the accident, I stopped to speak to the worker who had the accident.

He was a mess. It had taken a while to sink in, but he now realized how close he had come to dying. He couldn't say enough good things about his trainers. He also thanked me profusely for putting the second patch on.

I told him it was my training kicking in, just like his.

Like all young men, he had thought he was immortal. He now knew different. As we talked, I noticed he had developed a fine shake in his hands.

I asked him what he wanted to do after things settled down. He told me he needed a job, so he would have to stay here no matter how scary it was.

I offered him a job ground side, and he jumped at it. He was done in space. It also was the beginning of a new policy for our group. If anyone realized that they were having a problem working off of Earth, we would provide a job ground side, no questions asked.

We had a lot of job openings on Earth. The space workers were well-trained people who had demonstrated an aptitude for our type of work so that they would make good employees.

The other side of the equation was that we didn't want anybody working on the high side of the company who might cause an accident.

The term high side had come into play somewhere along the line. Off Earth was the high side. On Earth, workers were groundhogs.

Each group made bad jokes about the other but did know they were on the same team.

It would cost two hundred million dollars to pull out the old machine, buy a new one, lift it into orbit, and install it.

While extremely costly, it wouldn't cause budget problems. I would have the gold miners work a few extra shifts if needed.

Our keeping the colony project a secret came to a screaming halt. When the new machine was ordered from the German company, errors occurred.

Several upper management people were on holiday. In advertising, a lower-level employee came across the order for a new machine to be modified to work on the moon.

The ad guy rushed a news release about how their company was the provider of mining machines for use on the moon.

Of course, no one picked up on this. Ha! Every intelligence agency and their governments knew about it in hours.

The Russians couldn't wait to get to the UN and accuse us of trying to weaponize the moon. Our kindest critics wanted to know when a moon hotel would be opened for space tourists.

We tried to downplay it, but the circumstantial evidence had piled up. Now there was something real to hang it all on.

The number of supplies we had put into orbit and then sent to the moon didn't add up. We had to be doing something major.

Everything we had stated about the project before had been true. We just hadn't told the whole story. Now the decision was mine to make. Would we stonewall and say nothing, tell lies, or come out with the truth?

My support team was mixed in their recommendations. I decided to go with the truth. It had served me well in the past. That is everywhere but in the Soviet Union's kangaroo court.

When it came out that we were drilling on the moon with the object of creating a permanent station, the outcry was enormous.

My entire team told me that I would have to allow UN observers to see that we were not trying to create a military base but rather a housing facility.

I didn't think it was any of their business but realized the pressure on China and the Crown had to be relieved.

I requested that I be allowed to address the UN's general assembly. The Russians fought it as they wanted me grilled in private, so they could say anything they wanted later on.

The votes were on my side, so I ended up in front of the General Assembly. I wore a suit and tie, along with miniatures of my honors. I needed that to remind them I was a person who had accomplished things.

I knew the truth that I was wearing them to remind myself that I was a person to be taken seriously.

I was given a standing ovation when I took the podium, so I guess my audience wouldn't lynch me on the spot.

I explained my goal was to establish a permanent manned scientific base on the moon. The design plans will be presented to all countries immediately after this meeting.

I also invited a team of observers to come to the moon at my expense to view what was being done.

I stressed the at my expense bit to remind them this was a privately funded project. The UN had no real hold over me. Countries could disrupt a lot of my supply chain, but we could keep going as long as China allowed me to launch.

The Chinese ambassador to the UN made it clear that China supported my efforts.

I had no say on the makeup of the observation team but wasn't surprised when a Russian was on it.

Worldwide, the general public received the news very well and supported the idea. We arranged for the colony efforts to be filmed and made available to all news outlets and any school requesting them.

Chapter 19

Have you ever been on the moon and received a call from the queen of England? Well, neither have I. I did get a call from one of her aides, Mr. Norman.

It was time for me to rob some dogs for the queen. Dog robber is an old slang term used for aides. Supposedly, we would do anything for our commander, including robbing dogs.

I was carried as a colonel in the Coldstream Guards as an aide-de-camp. She took me on to avoid the embarrassment of being rejected by the RAF after I was seconded to them by the Queen's Messengers. It was a complicated story.

The only reason I was a Messenger in the first place was to be able to fly people since I was underage everywhere but the military.

That was long past, and I had to wonder if I even needed to be an aide to the queen any longer. I was trying to simplify my overly complicated life. Maybe it was time to turn in my resignation.

Though I must say, I did like the Coldstream Guards dress uniforms.

Mr. Norman's call was at a good time. We now had enough manpower working on the moon base that I wasn't needed. Making certain that my shifts as a truck driver would be covered, I booked myself back to Earth.

We had enough capsules going back and forth that there were empty seats on the return trip, so no one had to be bumped.

I exercised while on the moon, so I hoped that I hadn't lost much muscle mass in low gravity. The return trip required working with rubber bands. While helping, they didn't cover all muscle groups.

Upon landing on Earth, I found that it wasn't as bad as I thought it would be or as good as I hoped. To say I tired easily was an understatement.

When I talked to Mr. Norman from the moon, he realized it would be a full month before I could be in London.

After returning for a week, I was up to England from China. I had talked to my parents in the meantime, catching up on the family and my business interests. The most exciting news was that scientists worldwide could validate Mary's cold fusion equations.

No one could build a device beyond the lab without information that we weren't releasing. We didn't want to throw the world into turmoil and cause people to starve by an early introduction of technology.

Mum and Dad had already donated funds to start technology training in the US, UK, and European coal mining areas in Mary's name. The money was being funneled in from my gold mine in Australia.

China would be self-correcting as they opened up Siberia to their people. I had let the empress know that coal mines would be a thing of the past in not too many years. Even with her, I didn't go into the complete details.

She and the rest of the world knew about the fusion projects, so she could connect some dots without me saying so. Deniability can be wonderful.

India was still a puzzle for which we didn't have an answer.

Upon arrival in England, I spent a day getting acclimated to the time changes. After that, I kept my appointment with Mr. Norman.

"Rick, I'm glad to see you. It has been a while."

"It has, sir. How have you been?"

"Just fine, my lad. By any chance, have you performed any new songs with Mr. Sinatra?"

"To coin a phrase, I think that tune has been played."

"Pity, I enjoy his work."

Notice it was Sinatra's work that he admired.

"Anyway, the queen needs some help with a delicate situation."

"Which lady do I have to escort to what ball?"

"My, you are getting cynical for one so young."

I raised a single eyebrow in his direction.

"It is a coming-out where debutantes are presented to the queen. There is a young lady who needs a high-ranking escort, but they can't be British."

"Why not?"

"Because the tensions between Great Britain and Argentina over the Falklands are at a high level. They may be going to war with us soon."

"Then why is she even being presented to the queen?"

"Her British aunt, who is a countess in her own right, has requested it. The girl's father, an Argentine general, is allowing it. I think you may know the family. The Frades."

Why me, Lord, why me?

"We think it may be the last gesture trying to keep the peace, but the general doesn't have enough influence in the Argentine army to change things."

"I do know the family and have done business with a Colonel Frade."

Mr. Norman told me, "He is a brother-in-law of the general."

"Could I call the colonel and ask him if it would be appropriate to escort the young lady?"

"That is a good idea."

I wasn't looking forward to that phone call due to my history with the colonel's daughter. At least he had seemed to have softened his attitude towards me the last time we talked.

I was given a small office to place my call to Argentina. The call went through in fifteen minutes, which must have been a record.

"Colonel Frade, this is Richard Jackson. Sir, do you have time for a short talk?"

"I do. I hope this isn't any delay in the sale of the Howell property. I want to get that back into the family."

"Not at all, sir. That is going smoothly from my understanding. There is another issue."

"What is that?"

"I have been asked to escort General Viola's daughter to a debutant presentation to Her Majesty Queen Elizabeth. Do you think it would be appropriate and productive? I have been given to understand tensions are high between Great Britain and the Argentine right now over the Falklands and don't want to do anything to make them worse."

"I don't think anything that you do will have any effect on the situation. I think your advisor is off on a flight of fancy. That said, there is no reason for you not to escort her. She is attractive and pleasant, so it will not be an ordeal."

"Thank you. I will do it."

"If you take a liking to the girl, you and your fortune would be welcome in the family."

That was one thing about the colonel. You always knew where you stood. After hanging up, I reported back to Mr. Norman.

"Colonel Frade sees no problems with me escorting the young lady but doesn't think it will affect the present situation."

"Very good. This brings up an awkward situation. You can't go as a member of the Coldstream Guards."

"Not in uniform or not in the guard?"

"Not in the guard, I'm afraid. This seems harsh after your service to the Crown, but your position has been the cause of some questions in Parliament."

"Heaven forbid that I cause questions to be raised in the House of Commons."

"I'm afraid it is both houses. Your wealth and power being so close to the queen make both houses feel their power is being threatened. You are giving her undue influence on policy. Parliament's only hold on the Crown is the exchequer. If you decided to fund the budget, they would lose all power.

"Do you mind if I sit and think for a moment?"

"By all means. Take as long as you need."

I felt like my brain was stuttering. Here I am, a twenty-year-old kid from Bellefontaine, Ohio, being told I was upsetting the balance of power in the United Kingdom.

I wanted out of the guard as my life was too complicated as it was, but this was mind-blowing. I could tell them I had no intention of funding England, but as long as I had money, they wouldn't believe me.

They didn't seem to understand that if I wanted to support the queen in taking back absolute power over her kingdom, my wearing her uniform would have nothing to do with it.

"What does Her Majesty have to say about this?"

"That they are a bunch of silly buggers. If you wanted her to take power, you could do it no matter what clothes you wore. She does feel that if you could resign, it would ease matters."

"Well, then I give my resignation."

"Sporting of you."

I didn't bother to tell him this was like having my cake and eating it too. I got out of the guard and built up brownie points in doing so.

"Your Grace, it is a shame that it had to end like this. You made the uniform look good. The senior officers tend to let themselves go."

"I don't know if Harold will be thrilled about not having to care for all the uniforms or upset at their loss."

"No doubt he will want to keep them as you can be recalled, you know."

Chapter 20

Escorting a young lady at a royal presentation isn't a big deal for the guy. For the girl, it is the world. Woe unto the guy that messes up.

Keeping that in mind, I gave some serious thought as to what I would wear. Normally I would have gone as a colonel in the Coldstream Guards. A military uniform always worked in those situations.

I could still wear the Coldstream uniform even though I had resigned from the regiment. I could have worn it as it was considered okay to wear a former uniform to special events. I thought it would be too close in time to do so. I wanted to get some separation.

I suppose I would wear a morning suit like most other guys. While not a peacock, I wasn't used to being in the background.

That might be for the best, as the one big no-no was to upstage the girl. At this level of society, it would be worse than upstaging the bride.

I briefly thought about going as the Crown Prince of Luna.

When I told that to Mr. Norman, he nearly choked.

I told him, "That was a joke that we made up for the Princess Party that Mary went to at her new sorority."

The sorority was having a contest, and Mum and Sally, who lived Mary's social adventures vicariously, decided she had to be the best princess there."

I continued, "They went more than overboard. Mary wore her real tiara with diamonds. She has her Princess dress collection, so she was the height of fashion.

"Dad got into the spirit of things and borrowed a brand-new glass coach from the Disney people. It was called a Cinderella coach and hadn't been seen in public yet.

"There were two coachmen, two footmen, and six white horses. I don't think the coachmen started as mice, but with Disney, you never know.

"Since I was to be Princess Mary's escort, I had to have the proper outfit. Since she was a Princess of Luna, I had to be the Crown Prince. They designed a uniform for me."

Mr. Norman asked about the uniform. "What does a Lunar prince wear?"

I replied, "A high collar red tunic, black trousers with a red stripe down the side, a belt accompanied by a dress sword, and all my clutter. That is my medals, those worn on my left breast, around my neck, and on a white sash."

"We even designed a new medal for me as the Knight Commander of the Knights of Luna. I must say it was spiffy.

"As you well know now, there was only one problem. The newspapers and TV people who covered the event seemed to think that I had declared the colony I was building on the moon as a kingdom with myself as the ruler.

"Questions were even being asked at the UN. I was surprised that it wasn't universal condemnation. It seemed if played right, some countries would even recognize my kingdom. That gave me some food for thought."

Mr. Norman asked if I had decided anything.

"I would have to be crazy to set myself up as a king. I was trying to unload responsibilities by selling many of my companies. Why would I inflict this upon myself?

"Another reason not to dress as the Crown Prince of Luna is that the young lady I am to escort would probably put out a contract on me for upstaging her."

He agreed that was the best reason for not wearing that uniform.

The young lady in question is Catalina Cardozo, the daughter of an English countess and Argentine general. She is the niece of Colonel Frade through his wife.

I called the number given to me by the countess and asked for it to be arranged for me to meet her daughter. Shortly after lunch, a meeting at their London abode was set for the next day.

I seriously thought about the moon colony on my way to meet the contessa and her daughter. Its governance had never been brought up.

I assumed it would be set up like a small city with a mayor and a town council. What never occurred to me was what flag would fly?

Right now. The Americans, the British, and the Chinese could make claims. I supposed it could be divided like Berlin had been, but that hadn't worked very well.

Historically, almost all long-distance colonies ended up with self-rule. Maybe we should start that way. I would have to think about this a lot before even opening my mouth to my parents.

The Cardozo family received me well. Catalina was a cute girl with dark hair and an exceptionally endowed figure.

I explained that I would be in a morning suit as the escort, as I had just resigned from the Coldstream Guards. The countess caught on quickly.

You resigned, so it would only be an American walking Catalina in?

"Yes, ma'am."

"'That says a lot about how the queen doesn't want a war.'

"Yes, it does."

That left a brief silence as there wasn't much else to say.

I did ask Catalina if she wanted me to wear my full medals or miniatures. She looked lost for an answer.

Her mother said, "Miniatures will be fine."

"Why, Mother?"

"If he wore the full-sized ones, no one would notice you."

"Miniatures will be fine then."

Catalina and I were attended the whole time. Before I left, the father asked for a minute of my time. We adjourned to his study.

"Richard, may I call you Richard?"

"Yes, sir."

"This is an awkward time for all of us. We are about to come to blows with Britain over the Malvinas once more. They don't recognize our rightful ownership, and it's a matter of honor. I'm not for this, but the current rulers want the war. I think they are foolish if they think they can beat the British Navy."

"Honor can be a tricky thing."

"That is why I want to personally thank you for escorting Catalina. It helps both countries save face at this time."

I will never know where my next thought came from. I will never know, it just came to me, and I spoke without thinking.

"Would Argentina like to be a part of my colony on the moon?"

"What part could we play? We are an agricultural country."

"That is what we need, particularly your cattle."

"Cows on the moon?"

"Why not?"

"How would they do?"

"No one knows. I want the colony to be self-sufficient in the long run. I would like to see if it is feasible to have cattle on the moon. I know that I need my hamburgers and steak no matter where I am."

"How would this work?"

"I haven't given this a lot of thought, but we could start with a small herd, say ten sets of cattle, two from each of the five best ranches in Argentina."

"Are you trying to start a civil war in Argentina?"

"No, if that isn't the best way to do it, your government can select those participating."

"What about feed?"

"You probably do not realize what our launch capability can currently achieve."

"There would have to be people to take care of the cattle."

"I well know that from my *estancia* and stations."

"I forgot you are a cattleman in your own right. Why don't you ship your cattle?"

"When you spoke of honor, it occurred to me that countries engaged in such a project as ours would be honor-bound not to be at war with each other."

He looked at me for a long time.

"I heard that you were the luckiest person in the world. I think there is much more to it than that.

"I try."

"There will be technical details to work out, like how to transport the cattle, not only to China but to send them into space."

I had to smile as I had another thought.

"The spacesuits will be interesting."

This picture made both of us burst out into laughter. Both of the ladies came running to see what was going on. They thought I was being given a lecture on behavior towards his daughter.

When we told them we were shipping cows to the moon, they thought we were mad.

The actual event the next afternoon was uneventful for me. I walked Catalina to the queen. She gave her curtsey and was introduced. I escorted her out. Job done.

For this, I had flown back from the moon. What a waste of my time. On second thought, maybe it wasn't a waste. What British and Argentine lives and treasures may have been saved?

The event may have been almost boring, but my call to the space center to inform them we would be sending cattle to the moon wasn't.

The screams in China were probably heard on the moon.

It only took two days for me to receive a telegram from General Cardozo that they were selecting what cattle would be sent to the moon. The new government in power since this weekend was enthusiastic.

It seems the general had contacted the five largest landowners in the country. When they realized what was at stake, they changed the government overnight.

It seems the military didn't have the power they thought they had. Colonel Frade sent me a separate telegram asking whether the cows should be pregnant when sent up or artificially inseminated later.

I sent back: it was up to them as they had control. I found out that the largest landowner was Colonel Frade and that he was in charge of the Argentine part of the operation. I had dodged a bullet those years ago.

I also knew the newspapers would have headlines saying "The Cow Jumped over te Moon."

Chapter 21

After the presentation, I flew to the US to see my family. It had been a few months, and I missed them.

They were all fine and growing in their separate ways. Dad was becoming a media tycoon. He owned pieces of the major media outlets in every major country. The only newspaper he didn't own part of was the Russian *Pravda*.

I had no idea how many television stations and networks he was involved in. He did his best to keep them all fair and honest in their reporting.

Reporters and editors are human and will let their biases influence them. Dad did his best to keep it down to a dull roar no matter the political persuasion involved.

Mum was involved in the charity world. She truly wanted to help people. It was a shame that those she had to entertain and solicit funds from were such fakes.

She, like Dad, worked hard to keep things honest. You would think charities would be doing their best to help people. Many of them were doing their best to help their upper management. Mum avoided those like the plague. If asked why she wouldn't work with a certain charity in an interview, she would advise the interviewer.

"Look at the public filings of the charity in question. See how much they pay out internally vs. what they use to help people."

That attitude didn't help her with a certain group in Hollywood, but then she didn't care about them. If they got too bothersome, they would probably disappear. I was used to Mum's foibles.

Denny was doing well with his photography studio chain. He had started filming on the teenage beach movie, which I was financing for him. He was having a ball. The tabloids hadn't reported any scandal yet, but it was early days.

Eddie had joined the junior stock car racing circuit in California. He was pretty good and had won two races. He might end up driving in NASCAR.

Mary was the star of the show. She was now attending classes at Stanford University and looked to be in line for a Nobel Prize for her work on fusion.

Her bodyguards, Jim and Sally, with Mum overseeing things, kept her in line. She was walking a fine line between being a nine-year-old and a forty-year-old.

She knew the world with her wide reading but had only a child's understanding.

The day she stayed home to have lunch with her friends at her grade school, I asked her questions. "Mary, have you ever looked at gravity as a force that could be adjusted?"

"Not really. Do you want me to?"

"It would be good if you could figure out how to create gravity that could be adjusted."

"Why would you want to do that?"

"So we could have normal Earth gravity on the moon."

"I would rather bounce around."

"Mary, playing in low gravity is fun, but it is hard to go to the bathroom there. Things might float back up."

"Oh, yuck, I will look at the equations and see if Professor Einstein missed anything. You know he still hasn't answered any of my letters."

"I bet he will after you get a Nobel Prize. Anyway, if you would take a look, I would appreciate it."

We spent a couple of days doing family stuff like going to the beach and playing board games in the evening. Like all good things, it had to come to an end. We all had busy schedules.

Before I left, I stopped by my office to talk to Jim Williamson. All the company sales had gone through. They were still slogging through all the paperwork for public offerings of the various companies.

At this point, I was paying very little attention to any of them as I had mentally written them off.

From the US, I flew to Australia. My new 707 was now in service. As my chief pilot said, "She flies like a dream."

I replied, "She can dream all she wants as long as you stay awake."

"Boss, you are no fun. Besides, that is why they invented autopilots."

"Well, I'm giving you the controls."

"It's early. Why are you giving up command?"

"I'm going to take a nap."

I think I heard him say something nasty as I left the cockpit.

In the backend, all my original stewardesses were gone. They had retired, got married, or in one case, gotten her commercial license and was flying for Qantas.

The new girls weren't as much fun. They wouldn't even play gin! Work, work, work!

Instead of taking a nap, I went to my office and read reports from the space program. Things were moving along nicely in one respect, and in another, it was an eternal logistics battle.

The transportation portion seemed to be firmly in place. Launches to orbit were routine. Work on enlarging the current space station was underway.

The Lagrange points were under development. The UN hated this. They still thought I was going to try to take over the world.

Why would I want to do that? I had enough going on in my life. I had broken down and let them have station observers on the space station in Earth orbit. All cargos were routed through the station to inspect each shipment for arms.

I hoped none of them had given any thought to the idea that I could have rocks dropped on them from space. Who needed weapons?

We had to do it in space because the Chinese were even hard-pressed to allow the UN Observers to be launched from China.

When we arrived at my next stop, Australia, I thought every politician in the country was waiting for me to lobby for something.

It was either for the oil pipeline, spaceport, or water rights. In a quick meeting, as we walked to my waiting car, I told the Australian president I didn't care where the pipeline went but to get a move on.

I stated, "Every time you have a by-election here, the route changes. If you don't have a route in two months, I will select one and make it stick.

"Place the spaceport where it makes sense. If it doesn't make sense, I will take that project over also.

"As far as water rights, the station will keep control of issuing them. Of course, anything not on land that we don't own is fair game."

"But, Your Grace, you own the entire length of the underground river."

"Then deal with the station."

Since the car was parked at the foot of the ramp, it was a very short and terse conversation. It was only after the car had delivered me to the DC3 on the other side of the airport did I realize how short of shrift I had just given a head of state.

Upon arrival at the station, I was given tours of the different areas. All seemed to be progressing per plan. At the goldfield, they had kept for my viewing a gold nugget that had been found embedded in the quartz.

The nugget was bigger than me and weighed almost a thousand pounds. I told them to keep it locked up and that it would probably end up in a museum somewhere. If a bigger one was found, melt it down and replace it with the new one.

I could tell I was anxious to get back into space with how quickly I was going through things. I did make a point of slowing down and spending an afternoon with the Aboriginal chiefs to make certain things were going as promised.

They were. I was glad to see all the children from their traditional village picked up by one of the school buses.

The one chief who had given me the hardest time was very mellow in his outlook now. It seems that since he didn't need a lot of wives to show his importance now, he had divorced all but two. They were his first wife and her sister, so they got along.

From Australia, I went on to Hong Kong. I stayed at Jackson House for two days while I checked up on events in the colony.

I had many questions for the governor-general about how he ran the colony. For the most part, I found that he was a figurehead, and the place was running on the same scale as a state in the US.

Beyond the state government, they didn't have any counties, just towns, villages, and cities with their governments.

That gave me some insights but still wasn't the answer for the moon.

I loved Jackson House and the service there. They spoiled me to no end. Life was good between Jeeves and Boris, but I had to keep moving.

My next stop was the Forbidden Palace, where I made my duty to the empress.

Chapter 22

The empress was in good spirits when I had my audience with her. She wanted to know about the newspaper headlines, which started with, "Hey Diddle, Diddle." I had to explain the nursery rhyme to her.

She liked it and wanted to get a fiddle-playing cat to take to the moon. I told her if she found one, I would take it.

I inquired about May-ling and how she was doing in school. I was told that she was doing fine. She was wrapped up in her studies and wasn't dating anyone. That was either a message of hope or loss in that statement, maybe both.

I was still mixed in my emotions about the girl. I wanted to know her better. There was chemistry between us. Did we want to spend our lives together? Unless she let me closer, we would never know.

I didn't stay long at the palace. The next morning, I continued to the launch center. I wanted to get back to the moon and get to work.

My capsule was loaded and ready to launch the next day.

I had to have my preflight physical, which was done before every flight. After answering a hundred questions like, no, I have not been exposed to the three-day measles, I was good to go.

I had textbooks to study on my journey. This time was precious to me. Nothing to do, nothing to distract me. You can only stare out a porthole at the Black for so long.

Before, my studies were all about business. Now I was reading everything known about our solar system.

I had the privilege of only having one other person on board. A roughneck named Jim was being rotated back up after his mandatory leave. No one was allowed to work there for more than a month due to the loss of muscle mass.

I have never seen anyone sleep as much as he did. He was a match for Bob, the cowboy who first took care of our horses. Three words a day were his limit. His being laconic worked for me as I was into my studies.

There was another capsule on its way to the moon. It had been launched for moon orbit just before us.

We both launched from the Earth the same day, and our equipment went through an examination at the Earth orbit station simultaneously. They were about one hundred miles ahead of us.

We had radio communications, but none of us were the chatty types.

That was why I came fully awake from my sleep when the radio blared, "Mayday, Mayday."

A small meteoroid had hit the space vehicle ahead of us. The main engine and rear side thrusters had been wiped out.

They were thrown off course. There was life support, so they weren't in immediate danger, but their craft was heading for parts unknown. We were their only hope.

Two capsules demonstrated why we always launch two at a time.

The now-famous message went out in the clear air, "Jiuquan, we have a problem." All international Maydays are sent clear to all stations. This was expected.

The news traveled around the Earth at the speed of all bad news.

Every news agency in the world was trying to transmit to the spacecraft to ask their silly questions, like are you afraid you are about to die a long and slow agonizing death?

The other craft, Jiuquan, and I opened a private channel. It didn't take long to come up with a plan. I would catch up with them and bring the three passengers on board, bring aboard as many supplies as I could from the other craft, and proceed to our Lunar orbiting station.

Like all plans, easier said than done.

First, I had to take us out of our flight path and adjust to the other craft. We were now using the call sign Adrift One. I was Lifeboat One. Or Adrift and Lifeboat.

Since we had the new computers onboard and ground support, we calculated the new course and the burn needed to parallel them. It would take two burns to catch them and to match their speed.

Also, I had to bring the craft as close as possible to make transfers. Catching them and matching their speed proved easy. Using side thrusters, I could get within fifty feet of them.

If I tried to get closer, there was a good chance of overcorrecting and having a fender bender. A fender bender in the Black wasn't to be considered. AAA towing wasn't available out there.

Provisions had been made for this sort of problem. A one-hundred-foot cable was in a locker accessible from the outside of the capsule. All I had to do was get it to them, and then the passengers could work their way over.

It turned out that none of the passengers were EVA-rated, not even the pilot. This state of affairs would have to be changed in the future, but we had a problem to solve now.

I would have to take the cable to them. This trip would require depressurizing our cabin after donning our space suits. I had to wake Jim up to tell him to get into his suit.

His was a soft suit like the passengers. Mine was a hard suit for outside work.

Once we had pumped the air out of the cabin, I was able to open the door to the outside. Using carabiner buckles, I worked my way around to the locker with cable.

The locker was hard to open as the metal was cold, but I managed. I then worked my way with the cable back to the cabin door. There I was able to attach the end of the cable to the door.

All I had to do was take the cable across to the other craft. It was only fifty feet, but it looked like five hundred miles. I attached the long cable to my suit. At least I could reel myself back in if I missed.

A miss would be dangerous because I would have no way to stop myself if the cable played completely out. The sudden stop could end up badly. Another problem for the future is the not-so-far future.

I could see a face at the porthole on the other craft. The crew had donned suits and pumped their cabin pressure down so the oxygen wasn't wasted or expelled when the door opened.

I had been keeping Jiuquan ground control appraised each step of the way. We had decided to go back to the open channel so the world would know what was going on.

If things went south, we wanted everyone to know the truth immediately. The last thing we wanted was to be accused of a cover-up.

Orienting myself, I took a deep breath and gently launched myself towards Adrift One. I had to lead it slightly as we weren't perfectly matched in speed.

I didn't want to slam into the side of the other craft, which is why I went slowly. It is a good thing I did because it was still a hard landing as those things go.

It was hard to judge as I was the only one who had ever pulled this dumb stunt. It was with relief I heard that I had landed successfully. I was clinging to a stanchion on the spacecraft. I didn't know if I could ever let go.

It took a minute for my heart rate to settle, and my breathing to get back to normal, but I was able to work my way around to the door of the craft, along with the cable.

After that, it was anti-climactic. The other crew opened the door, attached carabiners to the cable, and went hand over hand to my craft.

I went back to my craft and unreeled the refueling hose, which had been designed with this sort of problem in mind and refilled my tank with their fuel. We hadn't used much and probably could have made it without doing this, but why take the chance?

The same with the food and oxygen from Adrift. Better to have and not need. The oxygen was in all the spare canisters. The main tank couldn't be pulled across.

I did take the time to drain the spare canisters into our main tank and then refill them from the other craft. As I said, better safe than sorry.

After that, it was a matter of recalculating the burn to get us back on course to the Lunar Station.

To say I was a hero to the passengers that I had rescued was putting it mildly. I tried to explain that all our training was for these possibilities, but they wouldn't hear of it.

Many Earth agencies interviewed them the next week as we finished our trip. I refused all interviews except for one, one of my dad's. I tried to explain how it wasn't that big of a deal. It was a waste of breath.

If I heard how great I was one more time, I would throw up. Jim was the smart one. He slept most of the time.

Chapter 23

The problem had occurred a week out from the moon. The capsule was fully occupied, but we had enough food, water, fuel, and oxygen that the trip was like a standard trip, long and boring.

There weren't enough portholes for all of us to use separately. Besides, there isn't much to see out there.

Since my capsule was specially built for my height, it had extra room. The teasing about riding in my limo got old pretty quickly.

Someone was always reading the books I had brought along. One roughneck had a deck of cards. I will never know why they started with poker like normal spacers. I threatened to space them all if they continued to play slapjack in weightlessness.

Even the most boring trip ended as I had found out on my many Pacific crossings. Docking with the Lunar satellite was uneventful, and we all were glad to get out of our cramped quarters.

Jerri Cobb was waiting for us. She had come up from the moon's surface for this occasion. The occasion was our safety debrief.

Each of us was interviewed separately about what had happened and how we reacted. What problems we had to overcome? What potential hazards did we note during the event?

My contribution was that we needed a maneuvering pack on board like they used for working on the space station. Slamming into the broadside of a metal capsule wasn't my idea of fun.

An outcome of all the debriefs was that we were lucky, very lucky. What if the oxygen or fuel supplies were completely gone? The supplies on board my capsule alone wouldn't have safely got us to the moon.

An outcome of these sessions was the addition of maneuvering packs to all crafts. The addition of the packs also required training of all crew members in their use. There was no way of knowing who would have to perform the EVA.

The major change was the implementation of a project which had been under consideration. We have established a habitat at LaGrange point L1. It would have a space "tug" and crew stationed there.

It would be manned by a trained rescue crew, including medical personnel. Every possible failure was gamed. The goal was to establish the most a spacecraft could be thrown off course and the distance it could travel before the rescue crew would arrive.

The tug would be built with the ability to rescue a craft that went fifty percent further than projections in the time estimated before a response could arrive.

We were in space to stay safe for keeps, not a publicity stunt.

There went another billion dollars or so, but so what? I had it.

The plan was to establish stations at all the LaGrange points. Even the one on the other side of the Earth from the moon. The publicly stated reason was for rescue and research purposes. It did occur to me that it would be handy to control all the high ground.

I had no war plans with anyone, but as they say, Man plans, God laughs.

Once the debriefings were over, Jerri told me that I would be given safety awards for my actions on the drilling incident and the capsule rescue.

Unbeknownst to me, there had been created three levels of awards. The Safety Award was for minor safety actions, such as coming up with a good idea. The second level, Safety Star, would be for physically preventing an accident or intervening to save someone from death or injury.

The Safety Medal of Valor was the highest for risking one's life to rescue others from death or injury.

I received the Safety Star for the drilling incident and the Safety Medal of Valor for the spacecraft rescue.

I protested receiving the highest award but was overridden by the safety committee, which controlled all safety aspects and was the sole authority. Even I couldn't stop them. That is not exactly what I had in mind when approving their charter.

These awards were to be worn like all military awards. There were the medals themselves and ribbons for daily wear. Not that they would be worn on a working space uniform.

Leave it to Harold to have all my awards in ribbon form printed on a "dress" uniform. This printing included all of my awards, such as parachutist and pilot wings. This was getting silly.

After many objections, I wore the damned uniform when presented with my Safety Star and Safety Medal of Valor.

I was told that a series of awards were being created for those classified as our military ranks. The Safety awards would be for all personnel, but the separate ones for the military were for military actions.

Why this undercurrent of preparing for a war? Me being paranoid was one thing, the whole team another.

I asked my guiding committee of the empress, the queen, and the president of the United States to consider who and why military action would be taken against the lunar colony. We had no intention of instituting any actions to be a Lunar Defense Force like Japan.

To say that request put the cat amongst the pigeons was putting it mildly. Their countries all had experience with break-away groups between the heads of states. China with Taiwan, The UK, and the US still remembered the American Revolution or the American War for Independence, depending on which side you were on.

The question was raised as to how to rule the Lunar Colony. All parties recognized that a long-term tripartite commission on Earth wouldn't work locally on the moon.

I don't think they realized I owned this operation lock, stock, and barrel until this issue was raised. Who was the UN to tell me what I could do with my private property?

All parties, including me, decided this wasn't a question that could be settled in a day and would best be put aside and looked at periodically. As far as someone attacking the moon, it would take a special idiot to think it was practical.

You know that moment in a horror movie when the pretty girl says, "I'll check out the basement while you guys go upstairs."

That's how I felt when I read those words, "special kind of idiot." I just knew he or she would be showing up soon.

Now that I was back on the moon, I decided to tour the project to see how it had progressed.

The Germans had turned themselves inside out to replace our busted drilling machine. We had to pay a premium to jump our place in their production queue like people had paid Mum and Dad for their place in line for a 707.

The machine was due to be launched this week. It would take four rockets to carry everything into orbit. If I had a real budget for this project, it would be bleeding red in the books.

The machine had reached a depth of two miles. We planned to level out at five miles. That would give us insulation from anything but a major moonquake. We didn't know how strong they would be, but we did know that the moon had quakes.

The scientists told us that they would be more intense than those on Earth because water slightly erodes rocks and dirt, thus creating spaces that act as insulators from the vibration.

The moon doesn't have that, so they theorized that it would ring like a bell during a quake and last up to ten times longer than those on Earth.

The wide-open areas we had planned couldn't be as wide as we wanted, and we had to leave larger columns in place to support the ceiling. These changes still weren't enough to change the colony layout.

A series of radio relay towers linked the Earth's side to the moon's far side. That way, we could have continuous communication.

I received one of the first calls on this network. Mr. Hilton of the hotel chain asked if I would be interested in one of his hotels being on the moon.

I loved the idea and said yes. The details would have to be worked out later, and it would take a few years, but it was a wonderful idea.

It started me thinking, who else would be interested in having one of their stores or restaurants on the moon?

I was so excited about these prospects that I had a development team assigned to the project. A colony needed stores just like any other city. Shipping costs would be a little higher. Well, a lot higher, but we were getting them down.

Once the story of my space rescue hit the newspapers on Earth, we got a lot more publicity, mostly good. The story I liked the most was in my favorite scandal magazine. "The Man in the Moon Identified," the headline screamed. They had imposed my picture for the face of the moon.

Chapter 24

Later the same day, I received an encoded message from an Earth orbit satellite. They had successfully tested what was called an EmDrive.

EmDrive is a radio frequency resonant cavity claimed to be a spacecraft thruster. It was theorized to generate thrust by reflecting microwaves internally in the device.

The only problem was that this would violate the law of conservation of momentum and other laws of physics. When British scientist Roger Shawyer first introduced the drive, it was derided in the media and called The Impossible Drive.

Attempts by NASA to duplicate his results were inconclusive. The first trial had a net increase in thrust with an equal and opposite reaction.

The net increase was put down to being within the measurement error, and no one else could duplicate the net increase result.

The project was shelved until the British team came up with a thought. Why not try the experiment out in space where the purported causes of the false positives weren't present?

If this drive could work, a trip to Mars would only take ten weeks and the Asteroid Belt 135 days.

The testbed gave a large enough positive result that couldn't be attributed to measurement error or other external factors.

They started another experiment run with duplicated equipment operated by another team using the same settings and controls. If they could duplicate these results, we would have a real game-changer in our exploration of the solar system.

I was so excited by this news I gave the original team permission to start designing an actual prototype drive. This team would use Dr. Shawyer as a consultant.

He refused to come into orbit to supervise the tests. I found this to be slightly humorous.

If only Mary could come through with a device to adjust gravity, we would be all set. Since Dr. Einstein's general theory said it wasn't possible, I doubted very much if it could be done. If Mary did achieve that, I bet the professor would answer her letters.

The EmDrive would be available soon if the results were validated. A gravity adjustment device was in the long term, if ever.

A new four-wheel drive for our moon vehicles was a more useful, or at least immediately useable, technology. One of the problems we faced was wheel spin caused by bumps and different textures on the moon's surface.

A slight bump would cause one of the wheels to rise and spin, causing higher torque, which in turn caused problems when the wheel came back down.

Each of the wheels on the vehicles had a separate drive. With the direction of our new computers, the RPM of each wheel would be adjusted to a constant. This way, the wheels would be turning at the same rate when the bouncer hit the ground.

These changes would lower the accident rate of our dump trucks. I now could blame my trucking accident on wheel spin, and it had nothing to do with the high rate of speed and lack of attention. It was now my story, and I was sticking to it.

Another advance we made was the fairing covers on the capsules. The capsule had a cover over the nose during the launch to make it more aerodynamic in the launch process and to act as a heat shield.

Once in orbit, the fairing would be ejected so the capsule could separate from the launch vehicle.

We had let the first few fairings go, and they would eventually have their orbits degrade and burn up on reentry. The reentry heats were much higher.

These might take months to fall back to Earth and burn up. We now had so many launches the fairings were becoming a navigation hazard.

The design team had come up with a new design. The team called it the Hungry Hippo. The fairing would now be attached permanently to the launch vehicle. Once in orbit, the fairing would now open in a clamshell fashion. This opening would look like the huge open mouth of a hippo, thus the name.

We had been retrieving the launch vehicles all along to reuse the metal sheets as a building material for the space station expansions.

The space station was expanding continuously. I wondered if we could put one of Mr. Hilton's hotels there. It would specialize in honeymoons. Enough said.

After our leadership committee decided it would take a special type of crazy to try to attack a space station or lunar colony and decided it wouldn't happen, they recommended that I establish a lunar guard.

The guard would be trained in the skill sets of firing weapons, first aid, and disaster recovery. We would recruit volunteers on the moon and from space stations.

Weapons would fire as modern bullets contained accelerants and didn't need an external spark to set off the propellant.

The guards would be armed with shotguns using plastic shot on the space stations. These were the stations circling the Earth and moon, plus the proposed LaGrange points.

We didn't want to shoot holes in our station. That would be embarrassing. On the moon, we could use high-powered weapons. We set up pillboxes with heavy machine guns protecting the entrance to the colony tunnel.

This setup also took an interesting legal twist. I, the owner of my private company, now had my private army. The US, UK, and China had all sent trainers and helped set up the defenses, but they were mine.

The countries didn't want to take the grief that would come with the first war in space, even if they had been attacked.

I thought it was really funny when my first volunteer was Jerri Cobb. She now could claim combat training for space warfare.

As the titular head of the new moon Guard to keep the ranks in line, I had to put up a general's star. Remember that Custer didn't get his star until he was twenty-three to recognize how stupid this was.

I had to return to Earth, another downside of all this good scientific news and not-so-good promotions.

Dad had called me, and I guess he had been elected as the sacrificial lamb for this exercise.

The time lag between the Earth to the moon is a little over a second each way. That doesn't sound like much until you try to have a conversation.

"Rick, I have been asked to call you about reevaluating your priorities."

"What's wrong with them?"

"Being on Earth to run your many projects would be a better use of your time than driving a dump truck on the moon."

I didn't want to hear this.

"Dad, I'm overseeing the entire colony project here."

"How much time a day does that involve?"

I don't lie to Dad.

"Right now, only a few minutes."

"You need to be back here ground side to calm fears at the UN. Your new Lunar Guard has them in another uproar.

"Also, the EmDrive team needs a media front. Claims are being made that the rocket would be so powerful that it could destroy the Earth."

"Who is making such wild claims?"

"Your old friends, the Russians."

"Why are they doing this?"

"My guess is as a distractor from what they are doing in the Kuril Islands."

"I haven't followed that; what are they doing?"

"They have put their Bastion rockets on Matua Island, which is the center island in the chain. It had been held by the Soviet Union but reverted to Japan when the Union collapsed. Now they have these rockets, which will control a circle of five hundred miles around the chain. They have moved support personnel and built permanent structures for them."

"What do the Japanese have to say?"

"They don't like it, but their self-defense force isn't allowed to do anything except defense by their constitution."

"That seems silly."

"I remember Pearl Harbor."

"Oh."

I hoped that this turn in the conversation would make him forget the reason for his call.

"When can we expect you back?"

Well, that was a forlorn hope.

"I will check the flight schedule and see where they can fit me in."

"Good. Harold will be waiting for you. He has designs for your various Lunar Guard uniforms."

Way to go, Dad; put the boot in when you have a guy down.

I think people had been talking behind my back. I thought I could put off returning to Earth for another week, but there just happened to be an opening for my capsule to be launched back to Earth if I would leave the moon's surface today.

By the way, there is a launch to the lunar station with an opening in an hour if you leave right now.

Somehow, someway, someday, I would get even with these people.

They even thoughtfully had my reading material packed and ready to go.

The way Jerri Cobb was trying to keep a straight face told me who number one on the moon would be in my plan for revenge. Shaving cream in a flight suit gets icky.

Chapter 25

The trip back to Earth was long and boring. I caught up on my reading and my naps, and even spent time working on a speech to the United Nations.

The landing in China was normal. The capsule slightly bounced when it hit the ground but wasn't damaged.

I made my usual stop at the Forbidden City. The empress was more enthusiastic in her welcome than normal, so I knew something was up.

It didn't take long for it to come up.

"Rick, as you are aware, the Russians have established a military base on Matua Island in the Kuril Island chain. Matua itself is worthless. Its position in the center of the chain puts it within striking distance of northern Japan."

"The Russians have not done this lightly, as they can't support it from Siberia anymore. They have started at the Black Sea and come through the Suez Canal, then around India, and then north past Japan."

She continued, "This is an enormous undertaking for any Navy. They have something in mind, and it will not be to our benefit."

"Do you have any idea what it is?"

"They are talking to Japan about taking the territory back as the Soviet Union once held it. My strategist thinks it is a cover for a build-up in forces to cut the connections between China and Siberia as a prelude to invading Siberia."

"What is Japan saying about this? The Russians have taken Japanese territory, so it is an act of war. Is their defense force mobilizing?"

"The party in power in the Japanese Diet has decreed that only a direct attack on the Japanese mainland is justification for the use of force. We know better. They have downgraded their military so much they are incapable of taking the island back."

"They could ask the UN to intervene, as it falls under their purview as a country going to war with another."

"We have quietly checked, and there isn't enough support in the UN to undertake military action. It would raise their dues. We have even volunteered to provide the troops and weapons at our expense, and they have declined."

"I don't like to see any wars being started. May I think on this and see if there is an action that I may take?"

"Our people have thought on this, and there is one thing that you can do from space."

"You mean to drop a rock on them."

"Almost. Drop a rock on another uninhabited island close to them. That would send a strong message."

"Let me think on this."

I had to do some serious thinking because I don't think the Chinese staff understood the ramifications of what they were asking.

First, it was creating my army. Now it was taking hostile action against a sovereign nation. I thought only nations took such actions, not private individuals. I would have to investigate historical precedence.

Before I left the empress's presence, I shared a series of thoughts.

"There are several concerns with what is being asked. First, dropping a rock is easier said than done. Space is big, and the correct rock may not be available. Too small, and it would burn upon entry.

"Too large could be a disaster, especially in the volcanic Kuril Islands. I can see a large meteor breaking through a volcano's mantle and launching enough ash in the air to prolong winters worldwide.

"This has happened before in 1816.

"My next concern is that I have looked up the international law on this subject. If I attacked a country as a private citizen, I would be labeled a terrorist."

The empress broke in, "There are no treaties with Russia on this. We would not have to honor any extradition request.

"But there are treaties with the United Nations that state that I could be deported. China, the United States, and the United Kingdom would have to honor a request through the UN unless I was acting as an agent. If I were acting as an agent, then it would be an act of war between that country and Russia.

"My true concern is that efforts I have taken in the past have been my efforts. This action would take a concerted team effort. While I may be willing to drop a rock on Russia, the rest of my team probably isn't in the same frame of mind.

"Until these concerns are put to rest, I must decline."

I wasn't going to be the fall guy in this scenario. The empress had no response to my concerns, so I left and prepared to fly to New York City to speak to the United Nations. I had to put the fears generated by Russia to rest.

I gave my speech to the UN. I wish I could report that it was a rousing success and the whole world agreed that I had no plans to conquer the Earth or any variation thereof.

Unfortunately, it was received in a ho-hum manner. Any tinpot dictator who appeared in front of them received this same underwhelming response. Of course, I would say I was a good guy.

The Russians requested that I be extradited to Russia to be questioned as a suspected terrorist. They cited my previous actions in the old Soviet Union and the Chinese campaign in Siberia as reasons to arrest me.

Since I was under no travel restrictions, I didn't wait around in the US to see how that would play out in court. I went to Hong Kong. Let them try to extradite the Duke of Hong Kong to Russia.

I stayed at Jackson House for several days. I was able to see that Boris and Natasha had started a family. She was about to pop.

I quickly decided that she was as reasonable as all other women in the last days of her pregnancy and decided to return to orbit.

We were launching on average two rockets a day. The Gold Reef in Australia was the only thing keeping the project going. The space project was the most expensive ever undertaken.

Many projects like the Pyramids or the Great Wall had taken longer and required more manpower, but none approached the millions now being burned through every day.

Those millions added up to billions. As that senator from Illinois said, "A billion here, a billion there, and pretty soon you are talking real money."

I usually checked up on the command crew at the Earth-orbiting station. They comprised a rotating staff who were in charge of Earth orbit construction.

I was surprised as to where the conversation went.

"Rick, we have been thinking about the Russians and them accusing you of getting ready to drop rocks on them."

"I'm not, but there is no way to prove a negative. The UN practically laughed in my face. The current chairman, the gentleman from Togo, went so far as to require me to be escorted everywhere I went.

"I asked if I was in danger, needing bodyguards. He told me that I was considered the danger and that these guards were to prevent me from attacking anyone."

"That's harsh!"

"After that, I wanted to attack him."

"We have been thinking. Finding the right size rock would be next to impossible. We did some calculations and came up with tungsten rods that will do the trick."

"Maybe we should bring some up to orbit."

"I didn't make myself clear. We have the rods here. With the new computers, targeting is a breeze. We could drop one through the Kremlin front door if needed."

"Who authorized this?

They looked nervously at each other. Finally, the team leader spoke up.

"Your mother and the empress gave the orders."

I could override the empress if I wanted to, but Mum never. Well, I could say the words, and they would be obeyed, but the price I would pay wouldn't be worth it.

No one crosses Mum lightly, not even her kids. Dad could get away with it, but that was it.

Besides, after thinking about it, it seemed like a good idea. Russia may need a sharp reminder of the game they were playing.

They could try all the legal shenanigans they wanted, but if they turned physical with me or mine, all bets were off.

"How many rods are up here?"

"Ten of them."

"What size are they?"

"Eight feet long and two feet in diameter."

I did some quick calculations.

"That is over thirty thousand pounds. How did you get that much into orbit?"

A little bit at a time. Every launch has a variation in weight. We filled in the shortfall with tungsten. Once up here, we melted the metal in a solar furnace to form each rod."

"How long has this been going on?"

"Almost since day one. We thought you were aware and approved of this."

"I wasn't, but I do approve. I will be having a conversation with those two ladies."

I wondered why the empress suggested that I dropped rocks when she knew these rods existed.

Chapter 26

I had been informed before leaving Earth that the work schedule was now so complex that I couldn't come up and do whatever I wanted when I wanted. I was welcome to visit and observe all I wanted. Just don't expect to work.

I found that a little offensive since I owned the operation but decided to go along with their request. The construction crew made this request. I chose to see it as a request, but the leaders had made it in the form of an order.

As long as things were correct and on schedule, I would let them go. If things went wrong, then it would be a different story.

Going to the moon without a mission seemed senseless, so I created my mission. I would play golf on the moon. I brought my clubs with me.

Before leaving Earth, I thought about the conditions I would be playing under. Low gravity, rock for a surface, no atmosphere to create drag on the ball, no wind.

It would be interesting.

One issue that couldn't be overcome normally was teeing the ball up. You would have to tee up for every shot or risk breaking your clubs. There were no divots on the moon!

There was no way to drive a tee into the rocky ground short of a metal tee driven in with a hammer. I first thought of one of the fake grass mats with a rubber tube sticking straight up to tee the ball. I then realized that rubber wouldn't do too well in the cold, becoming brittle.

I ended up cutting an eighth-inch piece of plywood into three-inch squares, drilled a hole in the center that a standard tee would fit in, then glued the tees in.

I had a couple of hundred of these with me. I didn't know what would happen to the tee when I hit the ball. My drives would send the tees ten or more yards away and usually broke them on Earth. Who knew what would happen on the moon?

My first job on the moon was to build a driving range. Building a range seemed like an easy thing to do. The math said otherwise.

My longest drive, in theory, could go over five miles. Five miles wouldn't happen because the stiffness of the spacesuits would restrict the range of motion.

There was also the pesky fact that hitting the ball would bring Mr. Newton into play. We wore spikes in our shoes on Earth to remain solidly placed. On the moon, spikes wouldn't help. I could see taking a mighty swing and launching myself into orbit.

Of course, that wouldn't and couldn't happen, but you could end up going ass over teakettle, as Mum would say.

My solution wasn't very elegant. A little experimentation proved that I wouldn't be thrust backward if I only used my arms to power the club through the ball. A full swing would do as I feared.

That cut down on the distance a ball could be hit. This shortening of distance wasn't necessarily a bad thing. Another problem was that it would be very easy to lose a ball that you hit three miles down the fairway.

What a pity. Now my drives would only be a mile long. This distance worked out as a standard par four being 2640 yards long. A par five would be about 3100 yards.

I couldn't wait to see other golfers make the swing discovery that I had made. I would have to make certain that we had TV cameras present to record their historic moment. Snicker.

I confiscated a bulldozer and a powered asphalt roller to make my driving range. First, I made a huge flat area three miles long by a mile wide. Markers were placed every one hundred yards.

An important first step was to put a safety hut in place. This hut was a small building with an airlock and an oxygen tank. There were also suit-sized tanks along with a few K rations. Food, water, oxygen, a radio, and a few blankets made survival possible.

The driving range took me a week to put together, but it was an interesting task.

I also found out that my definition of being flat wasn't very good. Golf on the moon would be like golf cart path golf. Extra-long and strange bounces are to be expected on every shot.

I had to remake the driving range in the shape of a fan. The farther out, the wider the fan. Now the problem was keeping track of the ball.

A golf ball is relatively small and impossible to see with the naked eye at over a mile. A TV camera with a telescopic lens would be needed to track each shot. Even then, a shanked shot would be too far off course to track.

It would take a lunar rover to carry two golfers, plus a rover with a camera and operator to track the ball.

The next problem to be faced was the dust. The moon's surface is covered with dust from the many meteorites hitting it over millions of years.

There would be little distance gained from a roll as the dust slowed the ball down. It also buried the ball!

At least there would be a trail left in the dust. I even considered a metallic coating on the golf ball and bringing a metal detector along.

This game sounded less and less like golf all the time unless you chose to play golf in a supermarket parking lot.

When the range was usable, I tried to calibrate the distance for each club. My efforts were approximate at best.

I ended up using exactly 1/60 yards for a driver which would be equal to 200 yards on Earth. From there, it worked down 100 hundred yards for each club.

I could hit a two-iron 1250 yards or so. From there, each club was 100 yards shorter. A sand wedge would hit 350 yards. Anything shorter would require a fine touch with a lob wedge.

Ha! A fine touch with a lob wedge on the moon was an oxymoron if there ever was one.

My next chore was to lay out the actual golf course. As the course was relatively flat, I used devices like doglegs, sand traps, and water hazards to make it interesting.

Doglegs were easy. Sand traps were unfilled meteorite holes full of moon dust. As there is no water on the moon's surface, I plowed extra rocks on the rough to form my water hazards.

The extra rocks made the area unplayable. This area served the same purpose as a water hazard. Being diabolical, I even had creeks crossing the fairway at convenient distances.

It took me two weeks of work to have a golf course in place. One of the hardest parts was coming up with a name for the course. I finally wimped out and named it the Lunar Country Club.

The par 72 course was 59,200 yards long.

After all this work, I was ready for the first full eighteen holes of golf on the moon. I had hired a roustabout to be my cameraman for the day.

We had worked together on the driving range, so he had practice tracking the ball.

The course layout was such that it kept bringing you back to the safety hut every three holes. I never wanted to be too far from extra oxygen.

My building a golf course on the moon wasn't done in a vacuum. Well, it actually was. It wasn't built in an information vacuum. I had all sorts of inquiries about using the course.

There was even a news story on Earth about the course. Thanks, Dad.

The upshot was that many people on the moon wanted to try their hand at it. Many of them had never played golf before.

I could see that the Lunar Country Club would have to hire a pro as an instructor, open a pro shop, and even have a ranger moving around the course to keep things safe and in order.

I wonder what I could charge for club memberships. Not wanting to get into all of that, I made membership a perk for all workers.

While at first I was kidding about the professional setup of the course with shops and staffing to be safe and fun, it ended up that way.

I want to say that my first round of golf on the moon set a course record. It was a course record as it was the only round played so far.

My score wasn't one to make me proud. A 141 for eighteen holes was not a number that I was used to. Some smarty pants made a plaque up for the safety hut recording the first round of golf played on the moon.

I will get Jerri Cobb for that!

Chapter 27

Getting Jerri Cobb wasn't as easy as I thought it would be. My plan was simple—invite Jerri to play golf. Have cameras present to catch the show.

I would let her find out the hard way about the flipping effect, as I called it, for a couple of reasons.

She took a full swing on the driving range with her upper and lower body. The ball went flying off into the distance. We never found it but later estimated that it went five miles as predicted.

As she swung, action and reaction took effect. She started to flip over. I watched to catch her if there was any danger of hitting her head. She was never in danger.

She had worked in weightlessness for so long that she was able to correct her trajectory and do a complete flip, landing on her feet.

They got the camera shot.

I confessed that I knew that she would flip over and had hoped she would land on her butt. I wasn't trying to endanger her as I was ready to catch her if needed. Since everything happened slower in weightlessness, I could have caught her.

We both agreed that it was a dumb stunt, and I apologized. The next concern was that Jerri had hit the ball five miles as good as we could tell.

If word of this got out, other people would be trying to do the same thing. One of them would land on their head and crack their helmet open.

We destroyed the tape in the camera and swore the cameraman to secrecy. She was so fervent in her agreement that I believed she would keep the secret.

We later went one step further and included the information in our safety training on working on the moon. Upper or lower body actions separately. Too much motion, and you could be in trouble.

The term golf green on this course was a bit of a stretch. The greens were compacted dust that had to be filled in every time they were putted on. Sometimes even during play. The ball would leave a trail in the dust, which had to be smoothed out.

Courses on Earth had rakes for sand traps. We had hand-driven rollers for our greens.

As all these differences added up, I realized that this was a relative of golf, not golf, but it was as good as we could do, at least until we had artificial gravity. Then we would hollow out a huge space under the moon's surface. After hauling dirt in and planting grass, we would have a real course. Until then, this would have to do.

I think the golf ball manufacturers would love my course. I was losing at least one ball on every hole I played. Maybe I should buy a company. That wasn't a serious thought, but I sent a message to my headquarters to look into a golf ball manufacturer who would provide us with labeled balls for use on the moon.

The balls would be free, and they would have bragging rights. Titleist jumped all over it. Part of the deal was that they could ship extra balls to us. The extras would be returned to Earth. Titleist would then donate the balls to charity auctions.

Doing this was a win all the way around. I even went further and autographed any balls leftover from my round that I had hit and had a certificate included that this had been used in play by me on the moon. One of these fetched ten thousand dollars for Feed the Puppies. Mary told me I was her favorite big brother...today.

There was plenty of footage to send to Earth since a cameraman followed every round being played. After my first few attempts, I opened up the course to any who wanted to try it out. We even had a ranger teach course safety before letting them loose. Anyone trying to hit long using the upper and lower body would be banned. It only took one foursome being kicked off the course for the message to get out.

They were banned for a month. I posted that the next transgressions would result in a lifetime banning.

The networks on Earth couldn't get enough footage. Playing golf on the moon was the new Mecca for golfers.

I kept getting requests to play. After talking it over with the colony staff, we decided to have a trial group.

I called President Eisenhower to see if he wanted to play, gratis. He had to turn it down. His doctor told him that the stress of a launch would be too much for his heart. Besides, Ike wasn't allowed to travel alone; there would be four secret service men with him at all times. Most of all, Mamie wouldn't let him go galivanting off to the moon!

I ended up inviting Jack Nicklaus, Arnold Palmer, and Lee Trevino. They all accepted. Their cost would have been a quarter of a million dollars each for the ride up and quarters while there. We had never established a greens fee.

It was great fun playing with them. We all agreed that it would never take the place of Earth golf. Actually, we agreed that anyone who liked playing this course was a little crazy.

Lee loved it because he could finally hit a one-iron. We let him hit it all out with the cameras turned off. Jack and I caught him in mid-air. He would have landed on his head.

There was no way of knowing how far the ball traveled, but Lee claimed five miles plus.

The networks took our camera footage. They wanted it, but not badly enough to pay for a full camera crew to be sent up.

After that footage hit the air, the demand for playing on the moon skyrocketed. No pun intended, well, maybe a little.

The caverns we had been hollowing out on the moon were now large enough that we could put structures up in them. Employee housing and support facilities were in place, so the first Lunar Hilton was implemented. It looked suspiciously like a World War II Quonset hut.

No surprise there because it was four of them joined together. There were plans for a new hotel in the future, but this was a start. You got a private room for a mere one thousand dollars a night with an army surplus cot included.

We started selling all-inclusive golf packages for three hundred thousand dollars in conjunction with Hilton. Half the profits would go to charities sponsored by the PGA and LPGA. The rest would go to defraying the cost of the colony.

In time, the profits were in the millions but weren't a drop in the bucket for the program's cost. To put it in perspective, the US budget for 1964 was around ten billion dollars. My space program cost two billion. That is serious money by any definition.

If I didn't keep the money turning over, it would be sitting in banks to be loaned out. Money being pumped into the economy with nothing being created would cause inflation. The space program increased the worldwide GDP by one percent last year.

When I played the pros, I had been around my course ten times, so I had a distinct advantage. My 118 was the lowest score, but I'm not going to share the others. Well, one guy had over two hundred.

None of the scores were shared back to Earthside, that is unless the golfers themselves shared them. I never heard that they did. In this case, the score didn't matter. Playing the course was everything.

It didn't take long before the fun of playing on the moon palled on me. There was no physical work that I was allowed to do, so I decided to head back to Earth.

The PGA had come up with a modified version of the rules of golf for the moon. It didn't take long for a request for a tournament to be submitted to the colony administration.

I told the admins to go for it as long as I didn't have to be involved.

The administrators were the department heads of each group on the moon. They were running the construction operation and weren't to be confused with a government body.

One of my reasons for returning to Earth was to find out why the empress had told me to drop rocks on the Russians when she had been involved with making tungsten rods in orbit.

I even took my clubs back with me. I had requests from museums such as the Smithsonian Institution and the British Museum of Natural History to put them on display. I decided to have them kept at our Chinese launch center. They were so dinged up from the rocky moon that I wouldn't dream of using them on Earth.

The trip back to Earth was uneventful. I was able to catch up on my sleep and reading. I had read every available book about the moon and near-Earth orbit. I realized that I now knew more about the subject than any of the authors of the books.

Chapter 28

I had to find something else to do on these trips from the Earth to the moon and back. It took ten days each way, not counting launch time and downtime in orbit waiting for the launch window.

At least I didn't have to spend time on my business so much anymore. However, the trip would have been perfect to sign greeting cards and other correspondence.

The best thing was to cut down on the number of trips. Since I wasn't going to be doing any of the labor in building the colony, there weren't many good reasons for me to go up until it was ready for occupation.

My main concern at this time was why Empress Ping had told me to drop rocks on the Russians when she knew we had Rods from God in orbit. I loved that phrase. I hoped we never had to use them.

Upon landing, I spent a day recuperating and taking a well-overdue shower; in fact, I took two of them.

I had made an appointment with the empress for the next day, so I was flown in my 707 to Beijing for our meeting.

On the way there, I quizzed the chief pilot about using a fusion engine so that the 707 could go supersonic. To my dismay, I was told that the airframe wasn't made to handle the stress.

I tried a different series of questions. It started with could we take the 707 into orbit? Again, it was a negative answer. The airframe wasn't built to hold the pressure of a true vacuum. The internal air pressure would blow the aircraft apart.

I told him he was a spoilsport and went back to my office. I drafted a memo asking the design team to combine a fusion power plant with an EmDrive on a craft capable of taking off from the ground, flying to the moon, and returning.

This combination of power and drive would make it a true spacecraft. Our first test results of the EmDrive indicated it could make the trip to the moon in two days.

It would only take ten weeks to go to Mars.

I was given time to change to a suit before meeting the empress. She welcomed me warmly with a smile.

"Rick, it is so good to see you again. How is your golf game?"

"Pretty good on Earth, terrible on the moon."

"I never tried the game, so I wouldn't know how big the differences are."

"Trust me; they are like night and day. I don't think it is fair to call what we do on the moon golf. The reality of physics makes it a different game."

"I'm sure things will work out. It is giving your project a lot of favorable publicity and even some income."

"I think the ROI would be about a million years if we only depended on golf income."

"What do you depend on to turn a profit? You have already spent a large fortune."

"I'm not worried about turning a profit in the short term. The money I have is found money, and if not spent on major projects as a money sink, it could upset the world economy."

"My people have told me that if you tried to keep the money invested in the general economy, it would cause a depression that would last twenty years or more. There should be a return in the long run. Maybe not even in our lifetimes."

"Agreed. I think man has to go to space before we use up all the resources on Earth. I have read papers that state our burning of fossil fuels will cause climate change. No one can say if that will be good or bad or how far in the future it will be, but I suspect it won't turn the whole world into southern California."

"That is a nice thought, but highly unlikely. Now you asked for this meeting. I suspect it isn't to talk about the weather."

"Are the Russians still building up forces in the Kuril Islands?"

"Yes, they are. My staff is more convinced that the Russians will try to cut us off from Siberia. They have started a troop build-up in the west."

"So, do you still want me to drop rocks on them?"

"I think the tungsten rods in orbit would do a better job."

"Why didn't you ask that before? Why rocks?"

"It wasn't my place to tell you that we had snuck the tungsten into orbit without your knowledge. We, meaning the Space Alliance, decided it would be better if you found them on your own when you were in orbit."

"You guys were afraid of my reaction and wanted me far away when I found out?"

"Yes."

"That doesn't seem very smart letting me find them in orbit, where I could drop them on those that made me mad."

"What odd wording."

"I didn't think it would be polite to say drop Rods from God on those who pissed me off."

"You are probably right."

"Besides, there remains the terrorist objection. I don't want to do your dirty work, have you guys arrest me, and turn me over to the Russians. I've been there and done that. It wasn't fun."

"You are correct in your thinking. The only way you could do this is if you were the head of state of an independent nation."

"That wasn't exactly in my plans for today."

"Not today, but very soon."

"Whose idea is this?"

"I have talked with the president of the United States, the prime minister of England, the presidents of Argentina, Germany, and

Australia. They have all agreed to recognize an independent government on the moon headed by yourself."

"Why?"

"Because you can act more effectively than any of us. The tungsten rods will convince the Russians to back down. The colony becoming an independent nation is only a matter of time. We want to speed the process up to avoid a war."

She continued, "A war that would turn nuclear and destroy human life on Earth."

I thought she was exaggerating, but not by much. Mankind would be set back a thousand years or more. It might lead to the extinction of the human race, but I think we are like cockroaches. Some will always come back.

"Why me as the leader? I have no qualifications to be the head of a state."

"You have more than you think, but we want you to be a constitutional monarch. A figurehead if you will. The Russians know you and fear you. They know that you will not hesitate to do as you say."

She smirked as she said, "A demonstration of a Rod from God on an uninhabited island in the Kuril chain will bring the message home. The Japanese have already agreed to this, and it will return the islands to them at no cost to themselves."

More seriously, she continued, "This path will save the wealth and treasure of our nations. Young men on both sides will now live."

I couldn't disagree with this chain of logic. I wondered how the workers in orbit would receive this. I would hate to be King for a Day and then be overthrown. That sounded like that TV show, *Queen for a Day*. I wonder if it is still on the air.

"Who will crown me?"

"You will have to do a Napolean and crown yourself."

"I will have to order a crown made."

"I have already taken the liberty, Your Majesty."

"Oh lord, this is going to drive me nuts. Have you talked to my parents about any of this?"

"They are all for it. Their only concern is if you refuse to give your little sister the title of princess."

"That will be one of my first acts before a formal government is in place. She would make my life a living hell if I didn't. I have to do it before a government exists because any of them that know her will not want her to have any more power than she now has."

"Rick! Mary is a delightful little girl. How can you say such things?"

"Try waking up with honey poured all over you and a jar of ants waiting to be tipped over. Mary can be mean.

"Setting Mary aside, how is this going to happen? Do I write a memo to my employees?"

"Silly boy, I will submit a bill to the United Nations voting on recognizing the Lunar Colony as an independent nation. The reasoning will be that we want to avoid issues in the future by having a colony governed by several nations. They always succeed in the long run, so we want to make it a smooth transition. The bill will ask you as the head of the company that owns the colony to form a government, and we won't specify the form of government."

"So, I'm to be the fall guy if all goes wrong."

"Yes."

"What is the timing?"

"The bill is being submitted today. It will pass since Russia lost its place on the Security Council. You might want to return to the moon to set up your government."

And so, I became King Richard I of the Lunar Kingdom and Royal Fall Guy.

Chapter 29

The most obvious problem with being the King of the moon (ugh, have to come up with a better title) is that right now, I would be the only citizen.

I brought this up with the empress.

"That is no problem, Rick. All your employees on the moon can be offered dual citizenship. Even the ones from the US. US citizens lose their US citizenship if they swear an oath to another country. The answer is simple. You won't require an oath. Just hand them a passport, and it is done."

"A lot of thought has gone into this, hasn't it?"

"The various departments of state have been negotiating this for months."

"They knew Russia was going to be a problem?"

"No, they knew a colony that far away would be a problem."

'I would think people would be reluctant to accept citizenship in a country where the king has absolute power."

"They would be crazy to do so. That is why a constitution has been developed."

"What if I don't agree with this constitution?"

"Read it first before you jump to any conclusions."

"I will before I accept that I'm king of anything."

"That is wise. I think you will be okay with it. It is a combination of British law and the US Constitution. The laws are similar to Britain while there is a Bill of Rights similar to the US Bill of Rights."

She continued, "There will be no Senate or House of Lords at this time, though there is a provision that a second body may be formed at a later date if deemed necessary."

"Who does this deeming?"

"The Commons, but it requires a seventy-five percent majority, so it is doubtful if it ever will happen."

I reserved my thoughts on that. I had seen how people reacted to having a noble title. All you would have to do is offer titles to those politicians, and it would be a done deal.

"So, to be king, I have to recruit citizens from my workers on the moon and have them vote on a constitution that I agree with. If it passes, then hold elections."

"You understand it clearly. Once elections have been held, the major countries of the world will recognize your kingdom."

"And how will this mythical kingdom be financed?"

"It is thought that you will continue to fund the organization as you are currently doing."

"Is there anything in the constitution about taxes?"

"A statement that the Commons determines tax rates."

"Does this mean that they may tax me to death and give themselves a zero rate?"

"They would never do that."

What rock has this empress been living under? She has total power in China, so she has no clue how much mischief politicians can get up to.

"Rick, right now, you think I'm naïve—far from it. Remember your funds aren't based on the moon. They can't tax what isn't there, while you can refuse to fund operations. Unlike England, you truly control the purse."

"This all sounds like it is doable, but until it's tried, we won't know. Saying we are a country is one thing. Having an organization in place is another."

"That is why we are sending a person with you to attend to the details. They will have copies of the proposed Constitution after you read and approve it. We have made up five hundred passports for the Lunar Kingdom and a host of supporting documents."

"There are so many documents needed for a country that we were concerned about the weight limits on your capsule. That is why there will be three capsules in your flight."

"Why three?"

"There will be other people like your security guards along."

"Why security?"

"It wouldn't be good for there to be a revolution on the first day of the new kingdom."

"That would be awkward.

"Now for my big question. The leading countries of the world are handing me a kingdom. What do they expect in return? I'm not going to be a puppet."

"No one thought you would. All that will be asked is that you be part of the UN and sign the treaties where you will support other signatories from being invaded."

"I see. That is where the Rods from God come into play."

"Any country would be foolish to try to invade another with the threat of an attack from orbit."

So simple it sounded.

"Who determines if a country is being invaded?"

"The UN, but it will be self-evident."

"Will it? The US sent troops to Central America to subdue the banana countries for US business. By any definition, that would be an invasion."

"Surely the US wouldn't do that again in this day and age. The UN must retain the right to determine if an invasion occurs."

"And I refuse to bow to a legalist definition of what constitutes an invasion or not. I won't be put in the position of being a puppet of the world powers so they can do what they want with no repercussions."

'You can always refuse to bombard a country."

"By the same token, I can decide to bombard a country."

"Not legally if the UN has not approved the police action. Besides, while you have the physical power, your kingdom can be starved into submission. That plus the fact your citizens will still have loyalty to their home nation, and you will not be able to stop those countries from doing as they will."

"I see. This gives me a lot to think about."

I did have a lot to think about. It was apparent, at least to me, that if I didn't go along with this insane plan, they would manage to take my colony away from me and put it under their control, probably through the UN.

That part is a done deal at this point. What they are forgetting is that we are building a self-supporting colony. We had been lucky and hit an ice comet, so we had water to drink and convert to oxygen.

We were busy creating caverns to grow food. We even were importing cattle. If they worked out, we would have to look at sheep, pigs, and chickens. It would be interesting to have fish on the moon. How would that work?

Those projects were all underway in one form or another. Granted, the animals were a new idea, at least to me. I bet some committee I had in place was working on it.

The next thing that had to be addressed was control of these Rods from God. Right now, who held the "trigger," and how could I gain and keep control?

That was for later. In the meantime, I had to go back to the moon to set up my kingdom. I wondered who the old, dried stick of a person they sent to help with the administrative functions was.

I found out the day of the launch. It was good that I hadn't shared my vision of my new assistant. The shriveled-up old stick was a beautiful young lady named May-ling. You talk about being set up!

As we were being loaded into the capsule, I asked her why she was doing this.

"I have wanted to go to the moon ever since the first landing. This gives me a chance, and I can do something useful while there."

That made sense, so I relaxed and went with the flow. I had wanted to get to know her better, and now I had ten days to do so. I had brought marked-up copies of the constitution to continue my review, but it looked like this trip would be more interesting than most.

She and I would be alone in our capsule. The rest of our contingent, four guards and four clerical types were in the other two.

I did get to know May-ling on that flight. We both were attracted to each other but had never acted on it. Being attracted to someone and being attracted to someone who you liked and could care for were another.

I knew she was afraid to get close to me because she couldn't have children. This would cause problems, including a civil war in China when the secession was open.

She went on to tell me this was because of a condition called endometriosis. Her fallopian tubes were blocked by tissue that should only grow in her uterus. She was fortunate that she had low pain levels, but the pain was bad enough that the doctors performed exploratory surgery to find the cause.

We talked for many hours about our lives, hopes, and dreams. As we got to know each other better, our attraction grew.

By the time we got to the moon, we were a couple in every sense of the word.

Chapter 30

May-ling and I had a lot of time to talk before we became lovers, even after we started to make plans for the future.

We would be getting married. Events now overcame her earlier objections. Being king of the Lunar Kingdom would make me the hardest target in the world if a Chinese civil war broke out upon her demise.

We hoped that would be many years later, but one never knew.

Until she ascended to the Celestial Throne, we could live together, where we hadn't decided upon. Much time would have to be spent on the moon, but we didn't want the negative effects on our bodies with the low gravity.

Hong Kong and Australia were the strongest contenders for our residence. Hong Kong because of its closeness to China and the mere fact I was still the Duke of Hong Kong. I did wonder how that would work when I became king.

Australia had to be considered because it was the bedrock of my fortune. I made a lot of money from the businesses I still owned and my various properties, but the big moneymaker was the gold find.

There was no question as to where we would be married. It had to be in China as she was the crown princess. I had seen how fancy and convoluted one of their funerals could get. A wedding must be over the top.

We first made radio contact with our parents when landing on the moon. Anyone in the world could intercept radio signals, so we didn't use voice, even the code developed by Mary's computer.

We both had our private codes to communicate with our respective families. They were both based on the same method. This was because of its simplicity.

We each carried a novel with us. My parents had an identical copy down to the same printing and edition. May-ling's mother and grandmother had the same.

We would write our messages out, keeping them as concise as possible. We would then hunt for that word in the book. When we found it, we would write down the page number, count down to the sentence it was used in, and record that sentence number. Then list the place of the word in the sentence by counting its numbers. The numbers would be written in blocks. Since numbers could be one, two, or rarely three digits long, the numbers were separated by a comma. A dash was used to show the start of a new word in the message.

This format announced to the world what type of code was being used, but unless they had that same book, they were out of luck.

Common words would not be used from the same page twice. Too many usages with the same numbers would give a cryptologist a leg up.

I sent my messages using a book from one of my favorite authors. *Mary, Mary* was fun, but more importantly, it had many common simple words.

My test message read: 7,13,4-5,3,16-26,26,3-2,1,1.

The message we sent was simple.

"Getting married."

As almost no coded messages were sent from the moon, worldwide speculation about its contents was rampant. Many organizations and individuals listened to every message sent to pick up ours.

My favorite guess was "Aliens Found on the Moon!"

Technically there were aliens on the moon, us.

May-ling and I laughed a lot when we composed our short message. Our families knew we had been together alone for ten days, and it stood to reason that we were marrying each other. The funny part was that they wouldn't know for certain.

Our respective parents weren't greatly amused because we received a coded message telling us not to say anything. A military-grade encrypted radio transmitter would be on the moon within two weeks. Until then, say nothing.

It was terse, no congratulations or anything else.

While waiting for the encrypted radio, I carried out my original mission. The mission was to let my managers on the moon know that we were becoming a sovereign nation, with me as head of state.

In one way they were very surprised but in another not at all. The timing was the surprise. Being made independent wasn't. These were all smart people who knew their history, so they expected this or a revolution to gain independence. This way was much better.

I explained that the leading nations wanted us to be a constitutional monarchy for the simple reason that I already owned everything, and it would be awkward for anyone trying to tell me how to run my business. I said nothing about being the Royal Fall Guy to avoid early controversy. This change was going to be difficult enough without that in the equation.

I presented the marked-up copy of the constitution the UN had provided. It was mostly based on the United States Constitution, so I hadn't many problems.

The biggest change I wanted was to have the Bill of Rights included in the body of the Constitution, not added as an afterthought. I also wanted simplified wording, such as the flat statement that all citizens have the right to own and bear arms. If any citizen bearing arms causes damage to the integrity of the infrastructure of the kingdom, they would be charged under the law.

We quickly ran through the document and agreed that it would need finer wording. Changing the wording would call for a constitutional convention!

A convention was fine with me. I didn't want to be regarded as a despot.

The department heads asked how my power would be limited.

"How about if I can only exercise high justice in cases sent to me by our highest court as treason? Anything lesser would come under the court system."

The director of logistics asked, "How will we control the spending?"

"You will recommend projects as you do now, and I will provide the funding."

"What if we disagree with you?"

"My gold, my rules. I'm not giving you my money to do as you see fit. You can introduce a tax system and spend that money as you see fit."

I continued, "I will be responsible for all the expenses of the Crown."

"One other thing you should be aware of, and this is not for general dissemination, May-ling Crown Princess of China and I are getting married. She cannot have children, so a parliamentary system like Great Britain's will replace the monarchy when I die."

We talked for hours about what would be needed to become independent. The biggest concern was citizens. I told them that the major powers that supported a kingdom were willing to allow dual citizenship as long as the people didn't have to swear an oath to the Lunar Kingdom.

I explained that this had proceeded to the point that I had five hundred blank passports to the Lunar Kingdom that we could hand out as needed.

One smart butt suggested we put them in Cracker Jack boxes. I think I freaked him out when I pretended to give his idea serious thought.

I contemplated the suggestion for a while and finally said that the passports were too large to fit in the boxes. The guy who made the suggestion looked relieved when I burst out laughing.

As we were winding up with plans for another session the next day, Jerri Cobb asked if she could have a minute.

As the others were leaving the conference room, I told her, "Certainly, Jerri, what's up?"

"I suspect this has something to do with those Rods from God that we have in Earth orbit."

If anyone had known about them, it was Jerri.

"It has everything to do with them. Since I own everything in orbit, I could be charged with terrorism, no matter who launched the rods. If the King of Luna launched them, the UN would call it state-sponsored terrorism. If I only launch them when officially requested by the UN in a public announcement, I would be clear."

"You truly think that?"

"No. I think I'm being set up as the Royal Fall Guy. Any orders presented to me will be worded so that I'm held accountable, like the wooden sailing ship captains, if anything goes wrong."

"Rick, the wording of higher-level military orders hasn't changed that much."

"I didn't know that."

"Now you do. You better have tight control over those tungsten rods. I know for a fact that as things are, there is almost no security on them."

"How do you know that?"

"I have my Space Ladies sitting on them to keep them safe from misuse. You need to have a formal system like the United States Air Force's new missile command. So, they can only be launched by official orders, not by a wacko.

"Jerri, NASA would be horrified to know that you have control of weapons as strong as nuclear bombs. Why, you haven't even had combat training.

"That's a hoot. I hadn't thought of that."

"The United States is in on this, so I'm going to contact the president to ask him for help from the Air Force in setting up a dual launch key system as I have read about. I want you and your people to be the ones forming the launch team if it is ever needed."

"If they can pass the psychological exams given."

"I would hope your people aren't crazy."

"Let me see. We sit on a device that is filled with explosives and let them light the candle. Why would you think we were crazy?"

"Point."

Chapter 31

Not all the problems I was asked to address on the moon were serious. A question came up from many sources and directions. What about other sports on the moon? Golf was all well and good, but what about other sports like track and field events, basketball, baseball, or even football?

After talking it over with the safety committee, we decided we wouldn't sponsor or allow any contact sports. They would be too dangerous.

It seemed simple to do, but it was a lot of work to implement. We had to build facilities for the participants and fans to stay at. We had been planning for many visitors, so it wasn't bad, just sooner than we had planned.

We went along with all this because we would need all the favorable publicity we could get if we had to drop rods on the Russians to stop them from invading Siberia.

Then we had to arrange transportation for the sports tourists. We had the equipment, and we didn't have a price list or a method for reviewing passengers. It wasn't like getting on a plane at the local airport. Each person would have to pass a physical to make certain they could stand the stress of liftoff.

Pricing was contentious until we settled on a high price with reduced pricing for athletes with a reasonable chance of winning and demonstrating financial need. We didn't want a pay-to-win scenario.

There would be an indoor setup for the broad and high jumps. Hammer throw, discus, and javelin outside.

We wouldn't have the triathlon, but a shooting range was built. It would be more like the army shooting competitions at Camp Perry. We even invited the US Army to run the competition and invite shooters from all over the Earth. This content wasn't limited to the military only.

The army jumped on the chance. They would get to test their weapons on the moon and gain a ton of publicity.

The new Hilton was booked in hours. The additional rooms we set up weren't nearly as nice. They reminded me of Tin Pan Alley at Bowling Green State University.

The big difference was that they were set up inside the caverns we had dug into the moon, so there wouldn't be any rain on the roof. I laughed at myself when I realized that there wouldn't be any outside either. Maybe meteorites but no rain.

We were planning this for six months from now, the October timeframe. For an Olympic event, this was an incredibly short schedule for the work we had been doing; it was forever.

I fought it and lost, but we invited the Guinness Book of Records people. I fought it because my committee insisted that there be practices of every sport and that I would be the first person through. Doing it this way meant I would be the Lunar record holder in all sports. My records wouldn't last the first challenge, but I would be in the Guinness Book.

The Olympics people didn't like what we were doing. They said it made a mockery of their games. Rather than argue with them, we just ignored them.

While all this was going on, I received a thick package of documents from my parents. They wanted my opinion on the content. The request was based on my experience with Oxford University.

It seems many different professors at Stanford were claiming partial credit for Mary's development of the formula that enabled cold fusion to occur.

They were basing their claims that she couldn't have done her work without their instruction.

My favorite was a professor who had evidence that she had used the university's library. A copy of the textbook from his class was on the shelves. Even though there was no evidence that she had ever touched the book, he claimed it was the foundation for her work.

His was a basic book of Calculus 101, and Mary had been given credit for that class based on her entry exam results.

Part of the package sent to me was a copy of the book. Mary had gone through it and underlined about fifteen errors she had found in one read-through. These weren't typos in the explanation but errors in the formulas presented.

No one else's claims were that bad, but I recommended that they make an example of him. My parents were to make a public statement that they were investigating the claims one by one and making the results public.

I predicted that many would withdraw their claims when the professor was outed for fraud. Did I mention that Dad owned one of the largest news organizations in the world?

The university itself had tried to make a claim but had backed down quickly. They first claimed she was using university resources. These resources included equipment, office space, and personnel.

We had the documents to prove that I owned the lab Mary had been using, provided all the equipment, and paid for her assistant.

As far as them having a document signed by Mary giving them the rights to anything she developed while enrolled, that was a joke. She is a minor and couldn't sign anything. Our parents hadn't signed. When she wanted to do her thesis on the cold fusion formula, it was rejected out of hand as being impossible. That was in writing and signed by the department head.

Stanford gave up on that tactic and switched to bribing the family by promising to make her an honorary doctor when her Nobel prize was announced. Unfortunately for them, they offered it to Mary in a face-to-face meeting. It must have been grinding to them for a ten-year-old girl to laugh in their faces.

They immediately upped the ante to a full Ph.D. if she gave them some credit. I didn't know Mary knew the term Piled Higher and Deeper.

The next ploy by Stanford was to try to claim the rights to her physical invention. They thought that Mary had built it in her little office. They didn't know that Jackson Laboratories had built the device under a license issued by our parents as Mary's trustee.

They couldn't find the patents for the fusion devices. No applications for patents were filed. After the lab figured it out, the fusion generator wasn't that hard to build.

The judge was asked to halt production until the court case was settled. When asked to counter the request for a work stoppage, my parent's lawyers replied that it would be halted on Earth immediately.

I was told the judge grinned when he heard that but didn't make any comments other than to make a statement.

"The claimant's request is allowed, and the defendant has agreed."

You should have heard the screams when they found out the work was being transferred to the moon.

The bottom line was that my parents had things pretty well under control. I thought my suggestion about making a public example of the professor's claim and the errors in his books would scare most of the others making claims enough to drop them.

If there were still some making claims, I recommended that they play hardball and sue the first professor. Along the way, Dad was to explain to all involved what the term deep pockets meant.

It was a shame that these academics were so greedy that they wanted to steal a young girl's work, but they would pay the price.

Our drive to develop the lunar colony had gotten ahead of us. Between sports and the production of the fusion power generators, we significantly improved the launch requirements. We had the launch vehicles covered. It was the fuel and the manpower that was now our bottleneck.

May-ling and I discussed all the problems. She thought the professors' claims were silly and that they would have been sent for reeducation on a farm working in rice paddies in China.

China is China.

We laughed ourselves silly when we got the next request for sports. Someone wanted to jump horses on the moon.

That reminded me that we were having cattle shipped to the moon. When I checked up on the project, I found the cows were already here and doing well. The cows liked the lower gravity. I was told how they had to put in ventilation to remove all the methane generated by the cows. Since we had enough energy, we were just venting it to space.

It was reported by the gauchos watching them that they had been cavorting like calves. This I had to see. When May-ling and I went to the "Ranch," they were chewing their cuds like every cow I had ever seen.

It seems they had gotten used to getting around easier and went back to their old ways. The head gaucho told me that he was concerned about them losing bone mass as time went on.

I agreed this was a point of concern and for them to let me know directly if there would be a long-term problem. The use of cows on the moon was a concern, but their presence had possibly headed off a war.

The next report I reviewed addressed my concerns about fuel and personnel.

Chapter 32

Upon landing on the moon, I received a lengthy report from the development team that I had asked to scale up the EmDrive along with the fusion generation plant. After an in-depth review, they wanted me to know that they didn't think the EmDrive was the sole way to go. It would be the best solution once out of Earth's gravity well but not within it.

The EmDrive is a low-thrust drive that gets its effectiveness in shortening trip times by its capacity for constant thrusts – like the ion drives that had been hypothesized in the '50s. It can't be used to lift heavy weights out of a gravity well or against air friction, and the acceleration at any given moment would be leisurely in the extreme.

This weakness was especially true if trying to move a substantial mass. If I wanted to keep the EmDrive, it would take a hybrid system to get into space and, once in space, to accelerate to escape velocity. The EmDrive would work for the long legs between planets, during which the small amount of constant thrust would pay off in terms of providing about a quarter G of apparent gravity and in ramping up transit speed and deceleration.

At the midway point, you need to turn the drive around and start decelerating or save enough reaction mass to let the fusion flux drive decelerate you quickly.

These hard facts ended my dream of having a true space plane that could take off from Earth and land on the moon. While they killed that idea, they did have an alternate proposal. We would have to have a vehicle to reach Earth's orbit and then transfer to another type of ship. The team proposed using a ramjet to reach orbit.

The fusion-powered ramjet would be a pipe wrapped in electromagnetic coils most of its length. There would be probes in the intake for the most efficient ionizing of some of the intake air.

The more, the better. The coils and the geometry of the pipe will compress and accelerate the ionized intake air.

A wrap-around ducted fan would create greater low-speed efficiency and quietness. A different set of coils would be in place to turn the fan, making the whole thing like an electric motor instead of adding the weight of a separate motor to drive the fan.

The reaction mass used didn't have to be water. It could even be dust if you could pump the mass and prevent it from eroding the pipes and thrust channel. Their solution was finely powdered moon rock which you would keep away from the walls of the pipes by ionizing it and using magnetic flux to keep it from touching.

In some turbine engines, the combustion chambers would melt away in a heartbeat if the flame ever touched them, but the combustion air was introduced under pressure through hundreds of tiny holes in the chamber walls, creating an insulating space that prevents that catastrophe.

Their solution was similar but used magnetic flux instead of air. Liquids or gases would be the easiest, of course, and you have to remember that even if you powder it very finely, a given volume of rock is still going to have the same mass and weigh as much as a rock. And don't forget that moon rocks are igneous rocks, like basalt, not sedimentary rocks like limestone, marble, etc.

The RJ space scientist who wrote about which mass to use stated: "We'll throw rocks!" This statement confused me, but then came the explanation about the technical details—you're still throwing rocks, albeit very tiny ones. Is that cool, or what?

One thing about the proposed drive is that it eliminates volatile and explosive chemicals and produces no pollutants. The drive would use no onboard reaction mass to get to a very high speed and altitude and use 100% of the weight of reaction mass to generate thrust instead of most of it getting burned up to generate mostly waste heat.

This drive would be used to get to near-space altitudes and hypersonic speeds before transitioning to the EmDrive because while it works in space, it would be useless in lifting heavy weights out of Earth's gravity.

We would use a lifter with ducted fans to get a space vehicle to, say, 40,000 feet and then launch the space vehicle from there. The only reason this would work is we now had an affordable and relatively lightweight source of large amounts of electrical power.

Some waste heat captured for the operation won't hurt. The high compression end of the ramjet will have to be resistant to high temperatures but transparent to magnetic energy, a tough goal.

There were advantages in this sort of system as it would head off the critics claiming climate change leading to a "nuclear winter", causing global cooling and a host of other adverse ecological ills.

It would prevent the rise in power of the Islamic nations by eliminating the West's dependence on oil fuels. There was rising international concern about exported Islamic extremism as they now had money.

It didn't take long for me to realize that this was the way to do it. I explained it all to May-ling, and she agreed that it sounded best. It was nice to have someone to talk things over with.

As we were discussing the new fusion device and how it would help the world, plus the problems that it would cause, I had a thought.

May-ling and I built on this thought. As a fusion plant was put into an area, we would hire displaced workers to put in underground utilities. This was being done in some high-end communities now. The profits from the power generation would pay for this effort.

Displaced workers who were too old or couldn't learn a new trade could operate backhoes and other equipment. The underground utilities wouldn't have as many power outages as above-ground stations and would relieve a landscape cluttered with poles and wires.

The wires would be buried in the ground but put in a trough that would be underground. This would prevent damage to the wires and allow the easy pulling of new wires, rather than digging everything up. If new technologies like the fiber optic cable worked, that could be run parallel.

We could even pay higher wages so that the entire community would get a boost. Since we own the power companies or partner with existing companies, we could spend money outside the local area.

Even after the current distribution system was put underground, there would be new construction. This, along with workforce retirements, would keep all employed. There would always be those classified as unskilled labor we needed to provide work.

Suppose we did get ahead of the curve on underground utilities. In that case, we could partner with construction companies to put in new roads and bridges while updating the current infrastructure. Unless the politicians chose to interfere, we should have an age of full employment and prosperity.

This addressed my concerns about India and other countries. I wondered how Africa would change and grow once it was hooked up.

We talked about having fusion engines in cars and trucks, but that wasn't feasible. The power generator was too large to fit currently and would generate more power than ever needed. Of course, if you wanted your eighteen-wheeler to be able to fly, it might be worth looking at. We laughed about that for a while and decided it wouldn't be the safest thing to have.

I could see it, the truck heading down the highway with the motorcycle cop behind and the truck lifting into the air and flying away, right into the side of a mountain. No, not a good idea.

Now the big fanjets on jumbo jets would be a different story. Those fanjets burn a lot of jet fuel to produce direct thrust and turn the big multibladed fans that produce most of the engines' thrust.

The waste heat of the fusion power plant could be used to superheat air and expel that as thrust the way conventional jet engines do and capture some of that thrust, the way conventional fanjets do, to turn big, ducted fans for the thruster.

Instead, use the magnetic fields generated by your fusion generator to a) turn the fans directly or b) take the place of a jet engine compressor by using the magnetic fields to compress intake air and move it down the pipe to be heated further and expelled as thrust. And none of these methods produce any carbon dioxide or burn any oil at all.

As an alternative, ramjets do the same thing as turbojets but have to have external rocket bottles to get the aircraft moving fast enough to dynamically compress the air and burn the fuel for a faster engine.

With fusion-powered magnetic fields, we could create a magnetically driven ramjet capable of accelerating an engine to hypersonic speeds, as much as ten times the speed of sound in the atmosphere without burning any fossil fuels.

Suppose you use this to gain altitude till the air is too thin to work as a reaction mass. In that case, you can seal the intake and start dumping reaction mass, such as water, from onboard tanks into the engine, and it instantly becomes a rocket motor, but with no combustion byproducts, just water vapor.

On reentry, reverse the process once the air is thick enough to act as reaction mass. This will give you a fusion-powered space plane with no smoke and no fuss. Carry enough water on board, and it will take you to the moon.

May-ling and I went over this information several times, as it was all new to us. The message was you can generate heat or magnetic fields or both with the fusion power plant. We could use magnetic fields to compress and "push" air or water down a pipe, and by injecting heat, you can expand that reaction mass exponentially so that thrust is increased.

Some thrusts could be recaptured to mechanically turn fan blades for low-speed (up to about 600 mph) flight, or you can use the magnetic fields to turn the fans.

If the pipe and reaction mass carried on board are kept clear of obstructions, the vehicle rises above the atmosphere for flight and continues to accelerate as long as the reaction mass is held up.

Getting out to Jupiter, we could capture its atmospheric gases and convert them to reaction mass or harvest ice from its moons to turn that into the water for reaction mass.

That meant it might be possible to have my envisioned space plane after all. I sent a message back to the design team that I wanted both options looked at. One of the questions was, which option would be best for a heavy lifter, both for taking a load out of the atmosphere and for providing a reasonable-sized long-term habitat for going to the outer reaches.

Chapter 33

You would think that I had enough on my plate with the spaceship project and the Lunar Games, as we were now calling them.

I still had to figure out how to create a kingdom on the moon, and there was the little item of a wedding.

The wedding would be an enormous worldwide event. I expressed my concern to May-ling about having the time to help with the wedding plans.

When she was done laughing, she told me all I had to do was show up dressed properly on the wedding day. Undoubtedly, I had to attend some other events but would have nothing to do with the wedding planning. This was her territory.

She confessed that since it would be an extremely large wedding of public interest, there might be some help from various palace officials.

Since there hadn't been a royal wedding in China for over a hundred years, they were checking on traditions and looking at modern equivalents. The only equivalents I could think of were British royal weddings.

Since I knew nothing about weddings, much less royal weddings, I was happy to be set aside. I was to show up at the appointed time and place dressed as I had been told.

There was the matter of the rings. I was responsible for obtaining them. We considered ourselves engaged, and I hadn't even given May-ling an engagement ring. What sort of fiancé was I?

The moon doesn't have too many jewelry stores, none to be exact, so I sent a message to Mum explaining I needed help deciding what size ring I should be buying. I was thinking the bigger, the better.

Since it was in the new codes being used, I could explain completely what I was facing. It took several days, but she came back with a reply that a five-carat perfect diamond would be best. My thought that bigger was better would end up with something too large to wear comfortably.

It had a high price tag, but not so high that someone would try to cut May-ling's finger off to steal it. She was always accompanied by bodyguards, except for our trip to the moon.

We both agreed that the females had set it up in our group, namely Mum, the empress, her mother, and the queen.

I left the design and stone up to Mum. I told her that cost wasn't an issue. It had to be perfect. While she was at it, she would obtain a matching set of earrings, a necklace, and a bracelet. Might as well go all the way since we had gone all the way.

May-ling and I agreed that I wouldn't take any steps towards independence for the moon colony until we were self-sustaining in the basics: water, food, atmosphere, and energy.

With the fusion device, energy was solved. The embedded ice comet took care of water and the atmosphere for the foreseeable future. Food was the only question left.

We met with our Farm Committee, not an imaginative name, but it addressed the issue. The committee was pleased with how things were progressing.

We needed land, soil, light, and water like any farm. Huge caverns had been cut out for farming, and more were being formed every day. The cutting machines could cut out a one-hundred-square-yard field in a day. This was as large an unoccupied area that could be formed without support columns.

Occupied areas were kept down to fifty square yards. This exceeded our estimated safety requirements by a factor of five. It wasn't like we couldn't just cut more of them out as needed.

That gave me a terrible thought. If we cut out enough caverns, the moon would be made of Swiss cheese, not green cheese. I decided not to share that with anyone. It would get me thrown out of an airlock.

Soil was the difficult part. Before, we had been hauling water to the moon, and now it was dirt. Granted, it was the most fertile soil that could be found, but we were shipping dirt at the end of the day.

For light, we would use what were called grow lights. These were used in greenhouses. I learned that growers of marijuana used them. Now that was an interesting thought. What would be legal to grow on the moon?

Not that I wanted any part of drugs and their downsides. The question was rather how it would be decided what would be allowed. Once decided, how would the laws be enforced? What form of punishment would be used if broken?

May-ling and I agreed that the conditions we had previously set for declaring independence had been met. We had enough food supplies on hand to last three years, so we should grow crops by then.

With seed and soil in hand and light fixtures in place, we couldn't wait to start planting and harvesting our first crops.

As far as meat went, the cows were doing fine, other than a tendency of trying to jump around as calves do. We lost some due to broken legs. We solved that problem by raising them in pastures with lower roofs. Even the exuberant calf would learn not to jump if it gave them a headache.

Pigs, sheep, and chickens were on the way to being the most common meat sources. The Chinese wanted to include dogs. That was the only real disagreement that May-ling and I had. She thought a dog roast was wonderful.

We settled on me not asking for vegetables being served raw on the moon, and she wouldn't eat dog while here. What we did on Earth was our own business.

Declaring independence sounded simple. The Americans and many other groups of people have done it in the past. The only problem was that we didn't have any permanent residents, much less an independence movement.

Everyone on the moon was a direct or indirect employee who I was paying.

We discussed this for hours on end and finally concluded that one person, me, would declare the moon to be an independent nation.

Now all I needed were citizens. We decided that citizenship would be offered to everyone on the moon or who had been there in the past.

Like lawyers in the courtroom, I didn't want to ask a question I didn't know the answer to. Dad agreed to run a discreet poll on people who worked on the moon or had been there to see how they would react.

The questions asked were a bit loaded. It was made clear it would be a dual citizenship situation and that the Lunar Kingdom would have no income tax on money earned.

There would have to be reciprocal tax agreements worked out with each nation that had people working on the moon, but the individual's taxes would be lower than if taxed solely on Earth.

With free food and housing provided to employees, they would make out like bandits. Even those stationed at the launch center had free housing.

Dad also surveyed the nations involved to see how their citizens would react. The answer was that they couldn't care less. Now the politicians were a different story. If one party thought it was okay, the other would oppose it on general principles.

The only thing we could do was to ignore the politicians. What were they going to do? Declare an embargo? Our launch center is in China, and the new one in Australia will keep launching.

The UN could declare all the sanctions they wanted against those countries, but a war wouldn't result. Between the two countries' resources, nothing could be cut off completely.

Push came to shove, I had the Rods from God.

It wouldn't come to that because I had been assured by the major countries involved that they would recognize the Lunar Kingdom.

Actually, they had committed to recognizing a government of the moon. They hadn't specified a type. I didn't see how I could declare myself president or prime minister, or even a great leader of a country of one. King it would have to be.

May-ling wanted to know if I would be Lionheart or Crookback.

Only time would answer that one, other than I didn't have a hump. Hero or villain was the real question. History would have the final say on that. I wouldn't be around, so I wasn't going to worry.

I spent days writing the Lunar Declaration of Independence. I couldn't claim that anyone was picking on me. What was my reasoning?

The long commute and different living conditions were the only logical answers I could come up with. The answer also reminded me that my citizens had to return to Earth every three months and spend a month there, or they would lose bone mass and not be physically able to return.

After many reviews by May-ling and me, I sent it Earthside for review by the nations involved. That proved to be a mistake. As each state department nitpicked it to death, it became a worthless document.

They wanted a declaration of independence with me surrendering all rights to their respective governments. I decided sod that; it was a game of silly soldiers.

I issued my original proclamation to the UN. As I thought, the screams were loud, until they weren't. As long as Australia didn't decide to seize my goldfields, I was the economic engine for the world. The Rods from God made me the supreme military power. I had a hard time wrapping my head around these facts, but facts they were.

Once the UN recognized the Lunar Kingdom and me as its rightful ruler, things started to fall into place.

Chapter 34

While setting up the Lunar Kingdom, the rest of my projects kept moving along. The science team working on the spacecraft had developed a new plan.

The more they tested the EmDrive, the less they liked it. On paper, it would create a significant amount of force. The reality was about one percent of the theoretical output. As they put it, the energy being produced appeared to be going somewhere else, like another dimension.

Like a good team, they brought not only the problem to my attention but a possible solution along with it. The team advocated building a reaction drive that would be mass-efficient by taking advantage of the large power output of the fusion plant.

The plant would have huge power production from a very small mass, which would create a lot of acceleration out of a very small amount of reaction mass. It would accelerate the reaction mass to extremely high speeds.

In the case of the interplanetary space thruster, it would first take the reaction mass and heat it with the waste heat from the fusion plant. It would use water or other vaporizable liquid to be effective, the easiest to handle, store, and move.

They explained to me that water vaporizing expands by a factor of 1000+. That is, if you flash water to steam, one cubic centimeter of water wants to occupy 1000+ cubic centimeters of space. You can accomplish this by heating water above the boiling point under pressure, 'superheating" it.

You can use the electrical output of your power plant to confine the water while you heat it and direct its "explosion" once you release the pressure.

It will ionize by putting enough heat and electrical energy into it, an important next step.

The next step is the same kind of electromagnetic drive they had already discussed, but by lengthening the "pipe" and adding coils, you can keep accelerating the mass–and you can still do this with charged rock dust–to very high speeds, theoretically to a large fraction of the speed of light. This drive takes a hell of a lot of power, but that we have.

As an illustration of what they were talking about, in terms of the force of impact, they used the example of six .50 caliber machine-gun bullets simultaneously hitting a structure such as a Nazi airplane with the same force of impact as a six-ton truck at 30 mph.

Run a truck into a parked WW II airplane and its curtains for the airplane. That's with a two-ounce bullet at about 3000 feet per second. Accelerating a smaller mass to a hugely higher speed still gives you a similar impact, using a lot less mass than a bullet.

Assemble a thrust pipe, say, a mile-long in space, obviously impractical in the atmosphere, and accelerate small masses with very powerful magnets to very high speeds, and we would get decent accelerations using very little reaction mass because the energy input makes up for the smallness of the mass.

By reducing the mass that must be packed, we could move large payloads long distances at high speeds.

They called this a hyper-speed reaction drive.

I think I understood what they had written and gave them the go-ahead to build a testbed in orbit.

Anything to make the solar system more accessible.

I wondered where the energy generated by the EmDrive was going. If we could figure that out, it might be viable after all. I asked the team to put it on the back burner for now but not completely shelve it. Maybe assign a couple of interns to keep looking at it.

Another project brought to my attention was the need for a bank in the Lunar Kingdom. Any respectable kingdom would have its coinage. I only laid down the law on one thing. I was not to appear on any of the coins. Enough is enough.

There would be paper money by necessity, but every Lunar dollar would be backed by gold and exchanged on demand at one of the branches. At this time, they would only be on the moon.

Each bank would have on hand enough gold coinage to cover a significant number of redemptions. It would also be kept in our Australian vaults and at the main branch on the moon enough to cover all the paper issued.

The twenty-dollar gold piece was the most frequently used in circulation. The coin had the classic picture of the moon on one side. They became known as loonies.

Most of our expenditures on Earth were through my companies, so they were in American, Australian, or Chinese currency. The Lunar currency at this time was only used on the moon, I think mostly for the crew's eternal poker games.

No one could use our currency as a reserve currency because there was so little of it. We did have the problem that the loonies fetched about double the price as collector's items.

I tried to cool that market down by announcing in one of my press conferences that we would mint as many coins as the market would bear. I thought that would discourage the outflow of coins. It didn't.

We had included the date and an Australian mint mark on each coin without thinking. Next year every collector will be buying the new dates. If we opened another mint, it would be Katy bar the door.

I don't know how she did it, but my sister Mary talked me into selling proof sets of each coin at a premium for Feed the Puppies. At the rate she was generating money for her charity, the dogs would be getting fat.

Then there was the Jerri Cobb life story. My old studio would be making the picture, and I was asked to do at least a cameo. I couldn't say no, and it sounded like fun.

Jerri herself was hired as a technical advisor for the movie. I heard that she was having a good time in Hollywood. She had been seen with Frank Sinatra, John Wayne, and James Garner at various restaurants. She was alone with each of the gentlemen when spotted.

I didn't read too much into it as I had been in those same tabloids many times. Still, one must wonder.

Anna Romanov was playing the part of Jerri as expected. She told Mum that she enjoyed this movie more than any she had done in a long time.

It was more action and adventure than any she had performed previously, and it was exciting.

Jerri even wrangled a trip to the moon for Anna to feel the real thing. We destroyed all the cabin footage where Anna didn't do well in weightlessness.

The studio was also making the movie I had promised Denny. The good news was that he hadn't been involved in any scandals. He appeared to be growing up or at least learning to be discreet.

On top of all this, I was informed that the golf course I had built on Lassetter Station was now complete and waiting for me to be the first to tee off.

I requested the Australian president to stand in for me as there was no way I could work it into my schedule. That was when I found out that he didn't play golf. I put plan B into action. I told them to have a soft opening. Allow people to play on the course, and we will have an official opening later.

Then there was the wedding. From being told that I would have nothing to do with the plans, it changed to putting my blessing on everything. I learned very quickly this was a proforma request. I think I was being trained to say, "Yes, dear."

It was probably in the bride's chapter of the woman's handbook.

One decision was placed squarely in my lap. The honeymoon. Where would we go? The answer was obvious, but that thought was shot down immediately.

I was at a loss. It would probably be some island in the Pacific. We were too well known to spend it somewhere like Paris. The Papa-Rats-Eyes would be all over us.

I asked all my acquaintances for suggestions. Queen Elizabeth offered Balmoral Castle, but I thought the weather would still be too cold and damp. No matter what I thought, I knew we wouldn't spend all our time in bed.

Maybe a grand tour of the world. We could use the 707 and change our flight plans to keep the press away once in the air.

Then the question became what cities and how would security be handled. May-ling and I had a series of conversations on this. She understood the problems we faced and wasn't demanding in her requests.

We finally agreed to rent a small island in Tahiti and stock it for a week. Security would be the Chinese Navy circling the island. I wondered if I should have a navy, but that seemed silly.

All joking aside, it made me wonder if I should have some armed spacecraft. That would freak the UN out, but it was like owning a gun. When you needed it, you needed it right then, right now.

Chapter 35

I dislike most politicians, and now I have found bankers fall in the same class. I know that is extreme in both cases. They aren't nearly as bad as people who have tried to kill me. They are more like ducks trying to nibble me to death.

The UN wanted to know what kind of king I would be. An absolute monarch, a constitutional monarch, or would I rule by the grace of God? I found the last to be highly insulting.

The other two were reasonable questions. How could I be a constitutional monarch when there was no constitution? I would have to start as an absolute monarch no matter the endpoint of the process.

Besides not having a constitution, I had the money. In Great Britain, the House of Commons controlled the purse and, through it, the entire government. The monarch could dissolve the parliament but would have no money to run the country.

If I dissolved my house or parliament, I could still run my country, as I had the money. This state of circumstances left me as an absolute monarch. I wasn't about to turn over control of my purse to others.

There were many questions I had to settle. The biggest was the succession to the throne. May-ling and I would have no children. Denny would be the next logical person. Don't get me wrong, I loved my brother, but he was not the one to run a country,

He was just as liable to bring *droit du seigneur* back. He would have a very short reign. Eddie and Mary were too young to tell, though Mary showed signs of being another empress.

After thinking hard and long, I discussed my conclusion with May-ling. When I died, the Lunar Kingdom would become a republic. She wouldn't lack for anything as she would probably be the empress of China by that time.

That was another concern. I would be ruling from the moon, she from China. That would be a long commute.

Since these events would be far in the future, we hoped, we decided not to worry about them. However, I would have to include my succession in the constitution. It would be something like, if there were no heir to my body, then the title of king would dissolve.

We would clarify that any titles granted before that event would be maintained, but they would be courtesy titles. They would only continue as long as the holder's lifetime and not be inherited.

I had one of my many teams working on writing a constitution. I had so many teams working on the various projects I joked about starting interleague play.

While May-ling and I fretted about governing, the bankers of the world were becoming a nuisance. They were going on about routing numbers, clearinghouses, and a bunch of other stuff that I had heard of but knew nothing about setting up.

It seems writing checks was more complicated than I thought. The result was another team. Jim Williamson hired a retired banker from Wells Fargo to consult on what we needed.

I wasn't at the first meeting. I avoided meetings like the plague. I was told the consultant almost went into shock when he learned that all our deposits were backed one hundred percent in gold.

When he recovered enough to comment, he explained that everyone in the world would move their money to my bank as it was one hundred percent insured. Depending on the rate of interest we paid on deposits, money would flow in and out at unprecedented rates.

People would take advantage of high-interest rates elsewhere until things looked unstable, then flee to the safety of the Bank of Luna. These transfers would drain cash from weak systems, making them weaker.

The solution proved to be simple. We limited savings accounts to Lunar citizens and made it a felony for anyone to act as a front for others. I'm certain people would find loopholes, and we would have to plug them, but it was a start.

The constitution team came back with a document that May-ling and I could live with. It allowed an elected house to give the monarch advice, but only advice. In turn, I, the monarch, would owe them an explanation of why I wouldn't follow their advice. "Because I said so" was not an acceptable answer. The lawyers had fancier words, but that was the gist of the matter.

We sent a copy to the major countries globally, the UN, and all incoming Lunar citizens for comment.

We got many comments back, and I decided on which had merit, almost none. Then following the spirit of explaining, I wrote a plain English answer and turned those over to the lawyers to convert the country and UN level comments to legal gobble-de-gook.

My future citizens received the plain English version.

Suggestions that I liked were having a contest to pick the country's flag design and our national anthem.

I had announced that comments would be open for two weeks. The international community almost unanimously replied that their input would take a year or more.

My reply was, "Two weeks."

I hadn't given it any thought, but of course, it all came out in the press. The press wasn't kind. It was reported as a power play by me to take the moon. They played up the monarch aspects with no limitations other than those I imposed upon myself.

No taxes and free food and shelter were ignored.

Although I had assurances from the US president and the queen of England that my kingdom would be recognized, both countries' governing bodies passed resolutions condemning my proposed actions.

The specter of using objects in space to impose my will on Earth and make myself emperor was raised.

The politicians were aware that I was trying to develop a bank based on a gold-backed currency, which also scared them. Even the controls about noncitizens having saving accounts were discounted. I could change that at a whim and beggar nations.

The Russians at the UN tried to introduce a resolution condemning me as an international terrorist and have me taken into custody. How this was to be accomplished while I was on the moon wasn't addressed.

China used its power to block this resolution.

The first person I called was the president of Australia. They could occupy my goldfield and shut everything down.

"Mr. President, how are you today?"

"I'm fine, Your Grace, and you?"

"As you can guess, I'm a little flustered by the world's reaction to my plan to create a kingdom on the moon. As you well know, it wasn't my idea, but at the suggestion of those who are now yelling the loudest."

"That's the way it always goes. How can I help you?"

"Australia hasn't come in on either side of this issue. Where do you stand?"

"Our position is that since it doesn't affect us, we have no position."

"So, there is no internal pressure to seize the goldfield?"

"There is always pressure to seize Lasseter's Reef. No more than usual. It is to our advantage to have you own it."

"How is it to Australia's advantage for me to own it?"

'Can you imagine what would happen if our politicians had unlimited funds available? The country would all be on the dole and nothing produced. Everything would be imported. Other countries would soon be eyeing our wealth. No thanks."

"Is there anything I can do that will help you maintain your position?"

"More jobs are always good."

'I will contact my space-vehicle design team. The team has several things in the works. I will have them contact you to carry out the work in Australia where practicable. I'm certain you will help them choose a location for the work and the new jobs."

"That will help immensely in keeping my party in power and our position unchanged."

We said our goodbyes. That call relieved one pressure. Before I could relax a little, the pressure was notched up to an unprecedented level by May-ling.

She came into my office in tears. I jumped up and hugged her.

"What's wrong, dear?"

"I think I'm pregnant!"

"Why do you think that? We only started having relations two weeks ago."

"My period is almost two weeks late. I have never been a day late since it first started."

"Could it be that being on the moon has changed things, lighter gravity and all that?"

"I suppose so, but if I'm pregnant, it is a disaster."

"Why is that? I think it is the greatest thing in the world."

"Our child would be considered illegitimate and could never occupy the throne. Maybe I should look into having it removed if I'm pregnant."

"I won't stand for that. Our child has a right to life. If the child cannot inherit a throne, so what?"

"Our son would become a symbol and excuse for any group that wanted to take over the government. They would claim he was the rightful ruler. Not only that, look up the historical record of children that have been in that position. It never ends well for them."

"Then we had better get married real soon."

"If we get married quickly now, the world will figure out why."

"Not if it doesn't come out till later that we got married on our journey to the moon. We can go through the formal ceremony later and let our earlier marriage come out. No one could question us then."

"How can you do that?"

"I have the solution at hand. The lunar orbital station has sent down the logbook from our capsule. It seems I forgot to fill it out because of other events on the flight. They want me to update them right away."

The log read that Pilot in Command Duke of Hong Kong Richard Jackson performed a wedding between Ping May-ling and Richard Jackson on the third day of the voyage to the moon.

Chapter 36

May-ling and I both signed the log as witnesses to our wedding. She giggled as she saw that I had married myself, and then her. Did that make me a bigamist?

We talked about the legality of what we had done. It wasn't in the jurisdiction of any country. It was the same as a ship in international waters. We were in international space or maybe extraterrestrial space at the logged time.

I didn't see how any precedent would outreach the PIC or captain doing what he saw as his duty. I could see that this would have to be addressed somehow in the future as I didn't want a captain to toss a person out of an airlock because they were spreading cookie crumbs.

Mind you, they were a tremendous nuisance, and maybe a few lashes would be in order.

We also sent a coded message to my parents, May-ling's mother, and the empress, informing them that she would be returning to Earth as soon as possible.

We further sent that it was the best news possible and that we had jumped the broom on the trip to the moon. My parents would probably have to explain the last, but I doubted anyone else would understand, even if decoded.

We had no idea how radiation and lower gravity would affect the fetus if she truly were pregnant. We weren't going to take a chance.

When I asked for my capsule to be readied to return to Earth, I was told that the launch lineup was full for the next two weeks and that she would have to wait her turn.

I didn't realize how protective I was of my new bride until I stripped the paint off the walls with my cursing. I informed them that all space operations were to cease until May-ling was off the moon with a nurse escort and on her way to Earth.

That got everyone's attention.

Jerri Cobb was on the moon and got elected to talk to me. She asked me if I could tell her what was so urgent.

"May-ling might be pregnant, and she can't be here."

"Other than the fact you aren't married, why the secrecy?"

"We are married."

"How? I would have to officiate here on the moon."

"We got married on the way here."

That stopped her cold.

"You performed your own ceremony?"

"Yes."

"How can that be legal?"

"How can it not be legal in extraterrestrial space where there are no laws? I was the PIC at the time. There is no controlling authority."

"That is a loophole that has to be addressed!"

"I know and will have our constitutional people draw up wording limiting the captain's authority in space. At the same time, we can't tie their hands as who knows what emergencies might arise?"

"Why aren't you going back with her?"

"Until we get this kingdom business straightened out, it wouldn't be wise for me to be on Earth."

"I thought it was being considered a joke by most people."

"Not hardly, since I will be forced to be an absolute monarch and will have the economic power to bring down any nation; the people in the know are scared."

"Why will you be an absolute monarch?"

"Day one, I will be the only citizen; so, ipso facto, my power is absolute over my kingdom of one."

"What about day two?"

"What powers would you have me surrender and to whom?"

"I guess you would have to have elections."

"And then?"

"Along came Jones?"

I had to chuckle at that.

"In England, Parliament makes the laws, but the queen can dissolve Parliament and call for new elections. What she cannot do is control the purse."

"Well?"

"I own all this, and you want me to give it away and be a figurehead for a bunch of politicians?"

"Sorry, Your Majesty, it won't happen again. You will be better than any of those."

"As king, I will have control over the Rods. Those we don't want to lose control of under any circumstances."

"Oh, God no."

"You might want to start thinking of a design for our military uniforms and how it is to be structured. I would think more like the US Marines and Navy than the Army or Air Force."

"I agree our craft will operate more like blue water ships than land-based flight crews. Even on an aircraft carrier, it is a Navy function."

"Can I count on you to keep this all under your hat for a while?"

"Most certainly. The rest of the Space Ladies and I know we would have never achieved our dream without your efforts."

"The comment period will be up in three days. I intend to finalize the constitution and put it to a vote of all on the moon and those who have been here. We have logs, so we know who all eligible voters are.

"It will be almost impossible for there to be any voter fraud. There are only a couple of hundred voters. They will be required to present themselves at a polling place. That will be here on the moon, at the orbital stations, or on Earth.

"Before casting a ballot, they will have to declare themselves a citizen of the Lunar Kingdom. Passports have been made with their pictures inserted. When they are given those, they can vote on the constitution."

"How do you think it will go?"

"No income tax on income earned in space for the first five years, free food and housing along with a clothing allowance. I think it will pass overwhelmingly.

"Especially, there will be no constraints about surrendering the Lunar citizenship at any time. Of course, they will then owe back taxes to their home country."

"As I said, Your Majesty, this is a wonderful place to live and work."

"China has agreed to set up a residential zone on Earth that will be considered embassy territory so taxes will not be charged while they are on Earth. If anyone leaves the compound for anywhere but their home country, it will be like going off on a foreign vacation.

"If they go to their country of origin, then that country's laws will be in effect."

"Okay, I will smooth things over with the scheduling people. They have to understand that the owner can make and change the rules. You have been going along with them, so they thought they had full authority."

"I appreciate it, Jerri. As you can expect, May-ling is all over the place in her thinking right now. She needs to be on Earth under the care of her doctors and be with her family."

"She will be on the first vessel up in the morning. Transfer to your capsule to return to Earth will be a priority."

"Again, thanks, Jerri."

"My pleasure. They will all understand one of these days why you got on your high horse."

"That would be nice but not necessary."

"My, but we are becoming the king."

"Go on, get out of here!"

"Yes, Sire!"

"Be gone before I call the headman!"

We were both laughing as she left.

The coded message to Earth about May-ling's condition had only been sent hours ago. My parents demanded clarification of my message.

I wrote a reply but was smart enough to share it with May-ling before transmitting it. She suggested that I drop some of the words I was using. She thought my reminding them I was about to become king of the moon wasn't needed, and their demands weren't appropriate. I didn't want to start a family feud, so I backed down a lot. I told May-ling to explain the situation to everyone when she arrived on Earth.

In the meantime, I replied to my parents that May-ling would explain all. What a cop-out. I loved it.

I heaved a sigh and thought at least this was the worst to my mind I would have to face as a husband. It would be smooth sailing from here on out.

Hey, one can dream, can't one?

After May-ling had departed back to Earth, I thought long and hard about my reaction to my parents' request. It was a request, though I had interpreted it as a demand, which would have been uncharacteristic of them.

There was a problem, and it was me. Why was I so touchy? Maybe this sudden wedding and impending fatherhood and being a king had stressed me more than I thought it had.

I have been through some tough events in the last few years. Escaping from Siberia, chasing down May-ling's murderous uncle. They hadn't affected me like this.

I couldn't change things as they were and had no desire to do so. I would have to be more measured in my reactions as things weren't about to calm down soon. If I wasn't careful, this all could blow up in my face. I could end up with one of the shortest reigns as king of all time. Tossed out of an airlock on my first day was not a goal I strived for.

Chapter 37

Our first order of business was to get May-ling back to Earth. I had burned up any goodwill I had with the scheduling people, so we made certain to make the launch window.

When it came time to part, we hugged each other. We both hoped my love was pregnant. It would both simplify our lives and make them more complicated than ever. The complications of having a child seemed wonderful to me.

It was hard to wrap my head around the idea that I might be going to be a father, and at the same time, it was a wonderful feeling.

I thought that I should be stocking up on cigars to hand out.

May-ling promised me she would send me a message as soon as she knew for certain. It would be the words smile or frown, depending on the result. Smile, of course, meant she was pregnant.

The last thing I gave her before she left was the gold wedding ring. She would wear it discreetly. She would return it to me for the formal presentation at the formal show wedding.

She told everyone "Hi" from me and let Mary know if we won the election and I crowned myself king, I would declare her the Lunar Princess. This declaration was to short-circuit the campaign I knew she would mount. Besides, my little sister is a princess in her own right. She deserved the title.

At ten years old, a princess, a self-made millionaire, and in line for a Nobel prize. She is an overachiever. I wonder where she got that?

Our hugs and kisses all done, May ling got into my, now our, capsule and left for the Earth. A fully trained nurse accompanied her. The nurse was at Jerri Cobbs's insistence. Jerri didn't know it, but May-ling and I had decided to ask her to be a godmother to our child.

Once May-ling was safely off the moon and had transferred safely for the trip to Earth, I turned to the upcoming referendum on the proposed constitution.

Even though I knew the logic was sound and there were many reasons people would vote for it, I was still nervous. I went over the plans for each polling station and then made inquiries if all had been set up as requested.

My second radio message to the station at L1 received a curt reply. I was getting to be a nuisance in my worry, so I tried to find something else to do.

I pored over the plans in place and found something we had forgotten. I sent an emergency message to Earth that we needed "I voted" stickers for every polling place.

Yeah, I was too deep into the weeds on this. I had to back off.

It finally became time to vote. I was first in line on the moon and cast my ballot to great fanfare and publicity. I was surprised. I don't know why so much attention was paid to this Earthside.

Every major news outlet was covering the event. I asked a news reporter from Dad's TV stations why this referendum was of so much interest.

He wanted to turn it into an interview, but I wouldn't do that. He looked at me like I was crazy when I asked my question.

"Rick, there hasn't been a new kingdom founded in over a hundred years or more. Of course, people are interested. Your rise to public fame has been meteoric, and this seems like a natural culmination of events.

"From nowhere, you have shown yourself to be a humble hero, natural athlete, and actor while having the business acumen to become the richest person in the world.

"Now you demonstrate that you are the most powerful person on or off the Earth."

"I have a hard time thinking of it like that. I have just let events flow."

"If you don't get it, I will never be able to explain it to you."

All I ever wanted to be was in the in-crowd at Don's Hamburger Shop in Bellefontaine.

We had scheduled the election day to be ten hours long. This schedule gave Earth workers time to do their jobs and still make the polls.

Halfway through the election day, the Earth polling center received a phone call from the United Nations demanding that we halt the referendum.

They reasoned that they didn't have any observers in place to ensure that it was a fair election. A few quick phone calls revealed that the Russians were behind this. They wanted to stick a spoke in my wheels any way they could.

Since I held the election, I had to make a quick decision. I declared that the election, which was centered on the moon, only concerned the moon. It was beyond the scope of the United Nations.

If I chose to apply for membership after the election, they could have observers present. Until then, buzz off. Not that I said that, but that was the way I felt. What I truly felt was, "Get the hell out of my business!" I didn't think that would play too well in the press.

The urgent news releases on my denial of halting the elections were about fifty-fifty. Half the headlines read, "Jackson refuses an honest election." The others were, "The UN overreaches again."

Since this was the press's normal reaction, I decided not to make any statement on the issue.

Soon after this news pronouncement, trouble started at the Earth polling station. The rest of the polling stations were proceeding quietly. This orderliness was expected as only eligible voters were on board each station. There were no opponents to the referendum or the constitution itself present, so they were quietly voting.

On Earth, it was different. Some people got through. They made it no matter how the Chinese authorities vetted people to come to the launch center. Like most elections worldwide, protests or lobbying was set up outside the polling place limits.

They had signs that they waved at entering voters and even tried to engage them in conversation. The signs read such intelligent slogans as, "Say No to the Despot." My favorite was, "Don't lose your head over King Richard."

The launch center security people left them alone as long as they waved signs or spoke to willing people. There were only half a dozen of them, so trouble wasn't expected.

An hour before the polls closed, they made their move. They charged into the polling place with homemade Molotov cocktails. The time it took them to pull them from undercover and light them gave the security people time to act.

Unlike the US, where the police would demand they halt and arrest them, the Chinese killed all six. This reaction must have been expected because the UN was once more demanding that voting be halted and the election invalidated within minutes.

This time the Chinese didn't defer the decision to me. They told the UN the election wouldn't be halted, and the election was considered valid.

When I heard about this, I wondered what sort of people would have committed to what had to be a suicide run.

Once the polls closed, it only took half an hour to count the four hundred and eighty-six ballots cast.

The referendum passed in a landslide. There were four hundred and fifty-seven votes for and twenty-eight against. Once the results were announced, it was noticeable that none of those against the constitution renounced their Lunar citizenship.

World reaction was scattered all over the place. The general population was for it or indifferent. Few thought it concerned them. Governments were a different story. As expected, Russia declared us a rogue state. The UN waffled, wanting to know what their member states wanted.

It was the large powers that were of the most concern.

China and Australia sent me congratulatory messages and recognized the new Lunar Kingdom. The Senate of the United States and the House of Commons in Great Britain were split along party lines.

Since both governments had liberal majorities, the conservatives took the opposite view. In both cases, an emergency vote in the Senate and the Commons was against recognizing my Kingdom.

Two days after the election, I was asked what I thought about their governments not recognizing me. I replied that each government had to do what its elected officials decided was best.

Since they didn't recognize my government, I wouldn't recognize theirs. The reporter to whom I made this statement thought I was joking.

I explained that if I didn't recognize a government, then citizens of that government would be allowed to open savings accounts in my bank. We would reciprocate if they didn't care about the Lunar Kingdom and refused to do business with us. This reciprocation included doing nothing that would harm their economies. Allowing their citizens to bank with us would cause an outflow of their cash, resulting in problems for the government.

This statement opened the gates of hell, at least in the halls of the two governments. The US wanted to declare war on us; the UK caved immediately and asked to exchange ambassadors.

Fortunately for the US, a vote in the House and Senate to declare war failed. I think the people in the Pentagon knew about the Rods from God and woke a few people up to the real world.

They also caved and revoted to recognize my government when the vote to declare war failed.

When that last bit of news came in, I was a mess. The stress had been mounting for a long time. Now it was over without me having to bomb my home country.

I wouldn't have done it under any circumstances, but they thought I was like them. I had made no threats other than the indirect one to wreck their economy. They read the rest into it.

Chapter 38

Once the referendum was over, several things had to happen quickly. The most important was to establish an elected government. One of my ubiquitous teams reviewed possible candidates for the various positions.

Our parliament would have twenty-five members to start with. This number seemed too few, but there weren't even five hundred citizens.

Those identified had been approached to see if they were interested in being in the first elected body of the Lunar Kingdom. All but two expressed an interest.

The position was a part-time one as they would only meet four times a year until events made it necessary to meet more often. They could call emergency meetings as needed.

They would be paid a thousand Lunar dollars a session. Sessions weren't expected to last more than several days at the most.

When my team reported this to me, I snorted. The team hadn't seen politicians in action. The people selected weren't politicians by trade but would quickly become one.

Once a politician, they would try to get more power. This power was defined in personal money, power over money, and other politicians.

Since they were limited to serving a maximum of six one-year terms, I hoped that the corruption would be kept under control.

We asked these people if they were interested. We didn't offer to support them. Anyone else was encouraged to step forward to run for office.

We did this because it would be embarrassing if no one wanted to be in my parliament.

Unfortunately, most citizens thought the fix was in, and no one else stepped up to run for office.

There was one parliamentary position reserved for each major base. This distribution included the Earth station, each of the LaGrange points, two for the launch center because of its size, and three for the Lunar base.

As other bases were added on, they would have an elected representative. All other members were at large.

A civil service had to be set up; think small county government in the US.

It seemed to never end. There was a school board election, a post office set up, a police department, a fire department, a public health department, and a library system.

Everything I had taken for granted on Earth needed to be recreated on the moon and to a lesser degree on each station. I'm sure there were others that I had forgotten about, such as power and sanitation. All these things were to be free as they had been in the past, but that would change as the kingdom grew.

My long-term plan was not to have personal ownership of the kingdom but to turn it over to its citizens. Once it was self-sustaining, I wouldn't have to be an absolute monarch but would become a constitutional one with limited power.

As the elected officials took office, I informed them they had to set up working committees to sort these issues out.

They liked the goal of becoming a constitutional monarchy rather than me having all the power. As the sole proprietor, the members didn't catch me moving space transportation from the Lunar Kingdom into a privately held company. I would still have the power, just not so public.

They could make all the rules they wanted, but they wouldn't be allowed to run wild.

A real thorn in my side was the bank issue. Every time I thought things were settled, new issues cropped up. The latest was from my team.

The team wanted to set up a retail bank to serve our general citizens, a commercial bank to serve businesses, an investment bank to manage investments for large customers, and a central bank to set Lunar fiscal policy. Like they had in the US, there would be a Fed to independently monitor the banks and an FDIC to insure bank deposits.

I had studied enough banking to know this was a recipe for disaster.

Our first bank branches would handle both retail and commercial customers. Under no circumstances would there be an investment bank. I had read about the problems they could create. There would be no "too big to fail" on my watch.

There would be no failures on my watch since I was backing everything with gold. As far as a central bank to set kingdom financial policy, they could have one, but it wouldn't have the power to change the amount of money in the system and destroy the common man's savings. Thank you, Adam Smith.

Wanting an independent watchdog over the banking system was a fair request. I did have to ask why the team recommended an FDIC. Their reply was astonishing. Everyone else has one. Not everyone else was one hundred percent gold-backed.

All the newly elected members of parliament assembled on the moon in our brand-new capitol building. Think larger than normal Quonset hut. It was done up nicely inside. The cost of transporting all the wood must have been astronomical. I didn't look at the pricing.

I had told the construction team and designers I wanted it done right as it would be a historical site one of these days. I didn't want people to think the king was cheap.

I couldn't get the banking system out of my mind. The system had to be done right, or there would be major problems down the road. I didn't want the moon to be looked at as a third-world country.

Hmm, moon, third-world country, there had to be a joke in there, not that I would spend any time on it.

Everyone, including me, had glossed over one type of bank: a private bank. They were for the rich, but when I thought about it, the only thing they did differently was provide financial advice to their members.

Unlike an investment bank, a private bank provides advice to its clients. The private bank would only invest funds directed by its members if they agreed with the advice.

The trick was to be able to give good advice. Most clients wouldn't be able to buy a large selection of stocks in a sector to minimize their risk with any one company as I could.

That did give me an idea. What if we set up a fund that would buy a large selection of stocks in a market sector like transportation? Our clients then could buy a share of the fund, thus spreading their risks over a large area.

The more clients who participated, the larger the fund, and the lower the overall risks.

I didn't want to set up the fund myself. Also, there was no reason to limit the funds to our bank's clients. After all, the more investors, the lower the individual risk and a better chance of higher returns.

I had Jim Williamson set up a team, well I called Jim, and he informed me that I now had a team manager to handle all the teams I had in place. There were too many for him to handle anymore.

I still think we should set up league play between the teams. I had no idea how that would work, but it seemed like it would be interesting. How would we judge the teams? They all had different projects.

Setting that aside, the new team worked themselves out of a job quickly. The team found a firm in Boston investigating the possibilities of such a fund. They called it a mutual fund, as its members mutually supported each other.

Their board was reluctant to start the fund because of the initial investment. My team set up a meeting with their president. Since I was still on the moon, it had to be on an encrypted radio channel, but it worked out fine.

You could tell the president of Fidelity was in a little awe talking to the king of Luna. That didn't prevent him from some tough bargaining. In the end, I was in a fifty-fifty partnership with Fidelity Investments and the first-of-its-kind mutual fund.

It would take a while to set the fund up as there were many government hurdles to jump through, but by the time it was in place, my bank clients would have one of the best investment choices in the world. At least for a person without a fortune.

My team of advisors told me this would become the investment vehicle of choice for the small investor. They predicted that many companies would adopt it as part of their retirement plans.

As king, it was my job to take care of the citizens of my country. This mutual fund was a solid first step for making it financially sound for everyone.

Next, I had to look at the kingdom's defenses and alliances for our external security.

While all this was going on, I received word from May-ling that she had arrived safely on Earth and sent our pregnancy code. I was going to be a Daddy!

While I glowed on the outside, inside, I was scared to death. What did I know about being a dad?

Chapter 39

It was time that I checked up on how the colony was progressing. I had received continuous written reports, and they were encouraging, but I wanted to see where we were at with my own eyes.

I believed the reports and knew that the truth could be told in many different ways to create a false picture. I didn't think that was happening here but didn't want to relearn my lessons the hard way.

Rather than make people feel that I didn't trust them, I asked Jerri to take me on a tour of the colony with her department heads present to describe each of their successes.

When I had this conversation with Jerri, she smiled and said, "That's a good way to see the real project progress without people thinking you are spying on them or trying to catch them out."

"Why, Jerri, how could you think such as thing as that?"

"That's easy. You can be read like an open book. Never try to play poker."

That was one piece of advice I had already taken to heart. My face revealed my emotions constantly. No wonder I almost always lost playing gin on the airplane. I had finally started winning a few hands, and the flight crew all moved on. The new ones didn't play at all.

The overall colony condition was great with my poker face or lack thereof aside. The main living and working areas were five miles deep. It was now a shirt-sleeve environment. Wherever possible, there was a brown carpet made up of what NASA called Velcro.

All of us wore slippers that had Velcro on the bottom. It took a while to learn to walk with the slippers wanting to cling to the floor, but things were much easier once one got the hang of it. Instead of wanting to bounce upwards on every step, we now had a graceful-looking glide to our step.

Velcro was one of the best results of the NASA program of inventing new materials for life in space. I didn't mind giving credit where it was due, so I had good things to say about NASA's efforts in this area. Though tempted, I didn't make any snide remarks.

The grow lights were on every ceiling. They were on timers to start dimming at our designated twilight until "sundown," and then they would slowly ramp back up. They weren't a perfect solution, but they helped with peoples' circadian body rhythm.

The area that contained the housing was coming along well. There were single-family dwellings and an apartment complex.

They were divided into small neighborhoods that had their own park. The parks had soil that was growing grass. There were small trees and other plants, but they didn't have any size yet, so it looked like a large playing field.

These housing units were built because many of our Lunar citizens who spent a lot of time on the moon wanted their families with them. I could hardly say no, as I had had May-ling up with me. It didn't take long for a community to develop.

While I and the department heads were walking through the area, children were running around.

They had taken off their Velcro shoes and were playing tag moon style, with a lot of bouncing around. These kids were becoming proficient in low-gravity maneuvers.

It was a Saturday, so I understood why they were out playing and not in school. Thinking of the school had me ask to see how it looked.

Each house in the area was a version of your basic Quonset hut, but the owners of single dwellings had individualized them. Mostly paint and small plants, but they looked good and would age well.

Someday we will replace these houses with better ones. I owned all of these and let the families live there rent-free. I could upgrade them at will.

I mention this because the children had decorated the school, or a mad graffiti artist was at work. It was a unique look.

We went inside the schoolroom. There was a teacher there doing some work. I asked her what she was up to. She told me that it was hard for her to keep ahead of the children. They were letting them do their lessons at their own pace, and it wasn't easy to keep ahead of them.

I asked her about boring subjects. She informed me there were no boring subjects, just boring teaching. If each child was allowed to absorb at their own pace and interest, they weren't bored. Since this matched my own experience, I was pleased.

After the housing area, we went to the industrial zone. There was no heavy industry with noise, air, or water pollution. It was all light assembly work. Heavy assembly was performed in the upper caverns, which weren't connected to our air or water supplies.

I had to stop and watch a fusion reactor being assembled. It was fascinating both in function and how simple a device it was. If RJ Research ever filed a patent on these, the reactors would be duplicated within hours.

There was a super clean room where computer chips were being made. No one could go in when the automated machines were running. You could enter wearing clean room garb and even a portable oxygen bottle when they shut down. This room was seriously clean. They were achieving success rates unheard of on Earth.

I asked what class the clean room was. I was told that it was less than one particle of .5 microns per cubic meter. I had asked what the class was because I had heard the term. The answer was meaningless to me. I nodded my head wisely and moved on.

There were small specialty shops making furniture and other housing fixtures. They were an ingenious adaptation of raw materials found on the moon. Who would have thought moon dust would be soft to sit on? It was embedded in an aerogel which had a texture like foam.

These small businesses had been set up by spouses of those with full-time jobs working for the colony. I thought this was wonderful.

Next on my tour was the shopping mall. The stores in business were along two sides of a town square. These were the name-brand stores from the Earth. There were even a couple of chain restaurants. I was happy to see the Golden Arches. I needed a burger and fries.

While the stores carried the more expensive items, small stands were set up in the town square. This area looked more like a flea market.

One enterprising young lady named April Lewis had set up a stand advertising guided tours of the facilities. She also had a message and delivery service and a line of moon shoes, those with Velcro attached.

April would go a long way, in my estimation.

There was an area set up for tourist facilities. So far, there was only one hotel, the Hilton, but others were being erected. There was one small building in the center.

I asked about it. The building was for the on-moon safety orientation every visitor had to go through. They had to pass two exams, one written and the other practical.

They had to demonstrate they could put on a spacesuit in less than one minute. If the tourists couldn't, their movement around the moon would be severely restricted.

The Sports Arena was set up next to the tourist area. At this time, it was a large open field planted with grass. Bleachers were being set up around the field. This setup wasn't going to be fancy like the Olympics. It was like going to a high school football game. There was even a concession stand that would have been right at home at BHS.

I didn't know what they were doing about outside events and didn't ask. I would have to do each event once soon enough.

Our farm was impressive. The grow lights made the area bright. There was grass everywhere, and nimble cows eating like crazy. The gauchos who had accompanied them from Argentina told me this was a wonder to behold. They sent videos home of the cows leaping around the field, where they were played on Argentine TV. There was now a regular program where Argentines could tune in and see how "their" cows were doing.

There were pigs, sheep, chickens, and ducks, but none were as interesting as the cows. Then there were several hundred acres of corn, wheat, and other plants. I wasn't interested in these, so I spent little time there. I did learn that the plants were growing taller than on Earth. With the lower gravity, this was no surprise.

The utility area was interesting. This was where we made our air by electrolysis, melted ice for water, and made our energy with the fusion reactor that had replaced the solar panels.

Since they were all closed units, there wasn't much to see. The message I took away was that the ice comet we had found had enough water to take care of a population of a million people for a hundred years or more.

I don't think we will be reaching a million people anytime soon. We should be bringing ice comets from the solar system's outer reaches by then.

Chapter 40

Now that the constitution referendum had passed, it was time to crown me king of Luna. I had agonized over this for weeks. Who was I to crown myself king?

I went around in circles, trying to come up with an answer. It finally dawned on me the real question was, if I didn't do it, who would?

By letting someone else crown me, I would recognize their authority to make me king. The reverse of that was that they could unmake me king.

If I allowed a religious body to crown me, I would, in effect, claim to be king by the grace of God. That was a no-go as far as I was concerned. Not only wasn't I claiming God's backing, but I also didn't want any religious leader to think he had a claim on me.

Listen to a priest on what is right or wrong. Yes, I would do that. Let them dictate to me the religious beliefs of my kingdom and its people, never. History showed that it never worked out too well.

I never understood all the hoorah about religion anyway. Of course, there was a creator. Did the creator follow the flow of every atom in the universe? How was I to know?

Are the religious rules good rules to live by? Yes, otherwise, we would be beasts at best. At least the animals we called beasts had a consistent code. Mankind had shown that it was capable of any misdeed and atrocity.

To my mind, the do unto others as you would have them do unto you made common sense. That, along with the other teachings of Christianity. That was the New Testament. The Old Testament seemed a little harsh to me, though, at times, I had practiced an eye for an eye and a tooth for a tooth.

I was of the school of thought of the whole head for an eye or tooth.

I decided that Napoleon had the right thought when he crowned himself emperor.

One of the questions I had to answer some time ago was where would I be crowned. On the moon was a no-brainer. What location on the moon? By that, I meant in what building?

The main colony was the logical place. The only problem was that there was no large public building yet.

We would need several of them for the future: one to house the parliament, another the civic functions, and a palace for me, the king, to live in.

None of these existed yet, so I decided to have it on the sports field. It was a large open space where all could see, and bleachers were in place.

The bleachers could seat the entire population.

The palace, when it was built, would be one of the ubiquitous Quonset huts with a façade to make it look a little classy. I had thought about having a false front that made it look like a real castle but decided that was too much.

Instead, I went, with a lot of input from May-ling, with the English Tudor look. Behind the building would be a large walled area for gardens or whatever struck our fancy. I even thought about an inground swimming pool.

What I was calling a Quonset hut was not like the simple ones we had used for the first housing. This building was six of them joined together.

There would be a family space on the second floor. The first floor would have offices, meeting rooms, and a large open room that could be used for large events such as a ball.

I had learned enough about how things were done in England and China to know that there would have to be a certain amount of ceremony and entertainment by the Crown.

For the crown that would be used in the coronation, I had chosen a simple circlet of eighteen-carat gold. I toyed with the idea of calling it the Crown of Charlemagne as Napoleon had called his but decided that people would read too much into it.

The circlet would have as its front peak my coat of arms. All the jeweler had to do was attach an enamel pin to my coat of arms. Harold had these made up to wear on my suit coats. I told him that I could remember who I was, but he told me that some people had to be reminded.

When he said that, I nodded my head and went on my way. Later I wondered who he meant had to be reminded, my visitor or me. Never try to trade wits with your valet. It is a no-win situation.

Later on, more formal crowns for May-ling and me would have to be designed, but I intended to dump that chore on her. Trying to tell your wife what your hats should look like would be a disaster. I would surrender up front.

As far as the clothes I would wear, I let Harold come up with those. He had much more experience with this sort of thing and understood what it took from studying at his father's feet.

I knew that I couldn't get away with my rodeo riding outfit of boots, jeans, and cowboy hat. Nor my casual golfing clothes. The closest I could imagine was what I wore for formal Knights of the Garter events.

He came up with a red tunic, along with black trousers, a sash around my waist rather than a belt. This sash would be black. Another sash, white satin, would go from my right shoulder to my left waist. I would wear my honors on this sash that wasn't on the right breast of my tunic.

All my honors would be the full medals, no ribbons, or miniatures for this day.

I would wear a sword at my left hip. Though the sword had a fancy gold-encrusted hilt, it was a working blade. This sword had been given to me at one of my medal ceremonies. It was sad that there had been so many I couldn't remember which one.

The attendees would be everyone in the colony who didn't have a critical duty and guests from the Earth. These included Queen Elizabeth and Prince Philip, Empress Ping of China, and President Kennedy.

Lesser country heads such as Germany, Australia, and Argentina would also be present. It was a big deal for these people to come to the moon. It would make my reign recognized as legitimate and demonstrate that travel to the moon was now normal instead of a grand adventure.

I also invited people who had helped me on my journey to this point in my life. Dick Wyman and his wife; Chief Redfoot; the entire upper management staff of Jackson Enterprises; Mr. Monroe; John Wayne; The Beach Boys; Frank Sinatra; the Downings; and Anna Romanov, to name a few.

And, of course, my immediate family.

For the ceremony, a platform had been set up in the center of the sports field. It had two levels. The highest level was for the TV cameras. My coronation was to be a worldwide event. This publicity was once more to show that we were legitimate and create more interest in the moon.

Did I report that a team had been put in place to design the ceremony and its fittings? I loved my teams. They made my life so much easier.

When it came time for me to enter, they played the same music as Mary had at her entrance as a princess at her sorority. It made for a triumphant entry, I must say.

There were seats on stage for my immediate family. I noticed that Mary was wearing her tiara. My little princess. The only person missing was my wife. She and her mother had remained on Earth.

We agreed that we didn't want to take any risks, as her pregnancy was already high-risk.

This situation had put us in the position of telling the world why she wasn't present and that we had already performed a wedding ceremony.

The talking heads had a field day on that one. Was it legal for me to perform my wedding and do so in extraterrestrial space? What they thought was meaningless to me, but I did like the use of extraterrestrial space. It took space further away from Earth's authority.

One idiot even questioned if a baby not conceived on Earth was human. He was yanked off the air shortly after that. Not even the tabloids went that far, though they did wonder if it was an alien that had impregnated her and that I was marrying her to protect her honor.

I mounted the platform and picked up the crown, setting all the nonsense aside.

I swore a simple oath.

"I, Richard Edward Jackson, crown myself king of Luna and swear to protect and honor all my subjects to the best of my abilities, so help me God."

Chapter 41

I returned to Earth for my formal wedding to May-ling. I had to laugh when I found out the procedures for a wedding in China.

The wedding ceremony had three parts. The first was the true wedding, where the couples exchanged vows in a government office and signed the paperwork.

Next was the celebratory wedding dinner with the bride and groom's families, then the public reception which the guests attended.

Since we had exchanged our wedding vows and recorded our wedding in the capsule's logbook, we had married traditionally. There was no point in sharing that the vows and logbook signing occurred several weeks later.

The wedding invitations were presented in a long red envelope, similar to the traditional *hongbao* in which money is gifted to people at weddings, during Chinese New Year, etc.

The "double happiness" character Zhuangzi appeared on the envelope, hand-delivered to the guests a few weeks before the wedding. Those in other countries were sent in an embassy pouch and hand-delivered from there.

The invitation itself included the dates for the wedding banquet, order of birth, and names of the bride, groom, and respective parents.

Details for the dinner venue and the timing for the cocktail reception and dinner were included.

For weddings where guests may not be familiar with Chinese customs, a red packet was included with the invitation.

I dithered for several weeks, figuring out who to ask to be my best man. I had no one whom I could call my best friend. I could ask many solid acquaintances, but I had to think of the ramifications of having one of them at my wedding party.

The tabloids would have a field day. The sad part is that they probably wouldn't have to make anything up.

I finally asked Dick Wyman if he would stand with me. He had helped me in my early days in Hollywood, and he would be considered a nonentity by the press. Besides that, his wife Jane would keep him on the straight and narrow.

My brothers Denny and Eddie would be escorts. My only hope was that May-ling's maids of honor were all schoolmates of hers and older than the boys. Still...

A *Feng Shui* master chose the wedding date to choose an auspicious date to ensure the success of our marriage. I didn't know the details, but the Chinese zodiac sign and May-ling's birthday details played a big role in choosing a date. This method of choosing was more to placate the traditionalists rather than a family belief.

What was different was how the wedding photographs were taken. They were done before the wedding breakfast so they could be displayed there. They were to be taken in romantic spots. The ones on the moon were my favorites. We had those taken before May-ling returned to Earth. That bit of planning was the same military precision as the rest of the wedding.

The Earth photos were at what were considered romantic spots around Beijing. My bride had a different outfit for each of the fourteen spots. Some were formal, others fun, some traditional, some Western, and most segments of Chinese society were represented between the groups.

There was no wild bachelor party, no party at all. The Chinese aren't big on alcohol, and the women ruled the roost during party time.

On the day of the wedding breakfast, I had to retrieve May-ling from her bodyguard, who consisted of the maids of honor. They wanted me to do silly stunts like using a hula-hoop. I chose instead to go old school and bribe them with money envelopes.

They were even going to resist until they saw the lunar thousand dollar bills redeemable in gold. Go big or go home worked well in this case.

At this point, May-ling and I bowed to her mother and the empress before I took her home. Home today was the Royal Suite at the Double Happiness Hotel.

From there, we went to the wedding breakfast, which was being held in one of the large halls in the Forbidden City. Any other venue would have had the press all over it.

Tables at Chinese weddings are decorated with flowers similar to Western weddings. Lilies are the type of flower most commonly used for weddings as the Chinese name for lilies sounds similar to a common idiom that means "happy union for a hundred years," *bainian haohe*.

This flower also has another connotation. It is known as the flower that brings sons to the happy couple. Orchids were also used to represent a happy couple, love, wealth, and fortune.

Even the family gave gifts in the traditional red envelopes. May-ling and I were gifted a home, really a castle, by the empress.

The wedding bed preparation, or *An Chuang*, took place on an auspicious day and time, two to three days before the wedding. A female relative of good fortune carries out this tradition. The female of good fortune has parents, a husband, children, and grandchildren. An aunt filled this role, where the bed was dressed in new red color bedding and pillows with a mix of dried fruits and nuts such as longans, persimmons, and red dates.

The combination symbolizes a sweet and long-lasting marriage blessed with fertility and well wishes. No one can sit or sleep in the bed until our return together at the end of the night of the wedding.

We had to go through the hair-combing ceremony. It is a ritual performed the night before the wedding to symbolize us entering a new stage of adulthood in our respective homes.

We showered with pomelo leaves to cleanse off bad spirits and changed into new red clothes and slippers. I was glad to see one of my showerheads in use.

May-ling sat in front of a mirror while I sat facing the inside of the house. Our respective parents prepared a pair of red tapered candles and scissors, one stick of incense, a wooden ruler, a hair comb, and red yarn with cypress leaves.

A woman of good fortune, once more the aunt, lit one stick of incense and a pair of red tapered candles to start the hair-combing ceremony. While she combed the hair, she recited blessings to the bride or groom:

> "May the first comb bring you a long-lasting union.
> May the second comb bring you a harmonious union.
> May the third comb bring you an abundance of descendants.
> May the fourth comb bring you prosperity and longevity."

After our hair was combed four times, the woman of good fortune clipped the red yarn with cypress leaves and attached them to our hair, and the ceremony was officially completed.

I might note that there were TV cameras at every point of the ceremony for broadcast after the wedding day.

Her mother gave May-ling a set of dinnerware from the Ming dynasty, dated 1580. These were a national treasure and only would be brought out for show on special occasions, never for actual use.

Without opening the red envelopes decorated with the characters for happiness and wealth, I knew the sum would be an even number divisible by eight. They would not be large sums, as money was our last worry. It was the thought that counted.

A bridesmaid had the duty of receiving and recording our gifts. I had worried that Denny might try to gift us with a ridiculous amount, like a million dollars. Later, when he married, we would be expected to gift him and his wife a larger amount. Denny pleasantly surprised me with twenty-four dollars. He's not always a brat.

My parents gave us a house in Malibu high in the foothills overlooking the Pacific. While entirely different from our home in China, most Americans would call it a castle.

Mary gave us a certificate for a puppy. We would pick it out and keep it at home in the US. I was afraid it would end up on the menu if left in China.

The wedding dress that May-ling ended up choosing was in the *Qun Kwa* style made of two pieces: a decorative jacket over a long, embroidered skirt.

This traditional Chinese red wedding dress was embroidered in real gold and silver threads with both a dragon and a phoenix, giving the attire the modern Chinese name of "dragon phoenix coat" or *Long Feng Gua*.

Along with the dragon and phoenix, five bats were embroidered on the coat, symbolizing five blessings.

She wore the gold diamond-studded tiara that I had gifted her a long time ago. To say it is spectacular was an understatement.

I was told that she had tried over twenty different dresses before she said, "Yes, to the dress."

I didn't know that women talked to dresses, but I quickly learned not to get between a bride and her wedding. No matter what the logbook legally said, this was our real wedding.

For this part of the ceremony, I wore a Tang Suit. The Tang Suit is a long sheath paired with a Mandarin collar jacket with intricate frog buttons down the front. The jacket was also red and adorned with dragon and phoenix symbols. No bats for me. I guess I didn't need any blessings.

I didn't wear any of my honors to not upstage the bride. Not upstaging the bride was a tradition that crossed all cultures. I think that was because there were women in all cultures.

I mentioned earlier there were TV cameras. Later I learned that everything was being broadcast live around the world. Not all networks chose to air it, but those who aired the wedding had high ratings. In China, every TV set was tuned to watch the wedding.

Chapter 42

The wedding ceremony was a combination of East and West. Mostly East, but May-ling did have a white dress sent from America. The other Western part was the alcohol.

The meal in the afternoon of the third day was the highlight of the wedding. It was a feast for all the guests invited to the wedding. The eight-course meal plus dessert:

The first course consisted of sweet and sour pork, prawns in mayonnaise, fried fish sticks, and pork balls with sauce, completing the four seasons dish. The prawns were chilly but fresh, representing the winter solstice.

After that, Shark fin soup, with a generous helping of crab flesh. This meal was best eaten with black vinegar. The acrid taste of the black vinegar created a harmonious union with the slimy paste that made up the shark fin soup.

Then there was fried chicken meat draped with sliced mango as dressing. Separated by a border made out of pineapple, the duck was set in a stew of brown sauce that delivered a strong duck flavor.

Then came steamed fish in soya sauce and mushrooms. The flesh was slick, indicating good preparation. There was no fishy smell.

Next were simple prawns fried in curry paste. The inner flesh of the prawn had the scent of curry on it like a finely fried curry prawn would have.

My favorite was sea cucumber with white mushrooms as a topping. The sea cucumber flesh was so tender and juicy. It would take a good chef to make it into a slimy juicy piece. An inexperienced chef would end up with a turgid, hard piece. The sea cucumber, marinated perfectly in the stew of mushrooms, was the crown jewel of this eight-course meal as far as I was concerned.

Then came fried rice wrapped in lotus leaves.

The rice was soft and aromatic, with a hint of nuts and mushrooms.

The feast must end with dessert. Sweet *lai chi* syrup with sea coconut. I had to ask what the brown flesh floating inside the syrup was. It was the coconut.

The feast was not a sit-down and eat-until-you-burst meal. There was time between each course. I was required to mingle with the guests and drink wine with the men. After my first glass, my server told me he would switch me to water.

I would have been falling down drunk if he hadn't. I made certain he was given an extra tip.

May-ling was setting a new trend in Chinese weddings. Since there were many international guests, she changed her wedding dress several times during the day. I should call it a meal, but it was so long and drawn out that it was more of a long party.

After the first three courses, she changed into a Western-style wedding dress, white with all the bows, etc.

After the next two courses, she changed into a Han-style dress. It consists of the *yi*, an open cross-collar garment; *ru*, an open cross-collar shirt; a shan or open cross-collar shirt worn over the *yi*; and then the *qun*, a skirt worn by women or men.

I refused to be involved with this. I had worn a kilt, but a skirt was going too far.

I did agree to wear a Zhongshan suit which combines traditional Chinese and Western clothing styles.

Zhongshan suits have four big pockets on the front, two up and two down, equally spaced left and right. There are five central buttons on the front and three smaller buttons on each sleeve.

Zhongshan suits can be worn on formal and casual occasions because of their symmetrical shape, generous appearance, elegance, and stable impression. At least that is what they told me.

The terms *cheongsam* and *qipao* both refer to the same style of dress. The term *cheongsam* originated in the south while *qipao* is primarily used in the north.

Meanwhile, a different style of dress that is common in southern China is the *qun kwa*.

These dress styles were explained to me, but I don't know if I wasn't listening or just didn't understand because I couldn't remember anything about them the next day.

While I was a heathen on wedding dresses, the women of the world weren't. Later, women's magazines worldwide discussed the pros and cons. I knew this because Mary brought out a new clothing line. These were prom dresses based on the wedding dresses.

My opinion was asked as I had been to the wedding and seen the different styles. It only took Mary and her female designers about ten minutes to declare me useless. I was proud that I could fake it for that long.

My last uniform of the day was my king-of-Luna regalia. May-ling had her glory with all the brilliant dresses. Now I was allowed to show off a little. It turned out a good thing that it worked out that way.

As it was late in the day, I hadn't had a drink for several hours, so I was completely sober for what was about to happen.

Men were now approaching our table and that of the empress and May-ling's mother. That wasn't unexpected as people had been coming up all day to pay their respects.

Their biggest mistake was shouting, "Death to Tyrants." That gave a little warning.

They all had swords like many other guests in full military mess dress. These weren't the gilt-decorated swords that most of the men were carrying. These were killing weapons.

I had enough warning to draw my sword. Mine was patterned on a US Calvary 1865 sword. It did have a fancy hilt, but the blade was sharpened, and all business.

Two of them came directly towards May-ling. They must have thought my sword was for show.

The movies have sword fights as long, drawn-out scenes. In real life, they are short and brutal.

As they charged May-ling, I stepped in front of her. The lead man slashed at me, but I parried it easily. His mistake was getting too far ahead of his partner.

After parrying his strike, I thrust straight out, piercing his stomach. The sword wasn't made for that, but my Hollywood reflexes led me to that. It worked as the sword went in clear to his backbone.

As he fell, my sword came out. Luckily it hadn't stuck on the bone, and it came out before the body tightened upon it.

The next guy came at me with his sword raised high like he would split me in half. I stepped forward so I could be inside his downstroke and slashed his throat.

My fight was over.

I turned to help with the others when I heard gunfire. The attempted assassins learned an old lesson the hard way. Don't bring a knife to a gunfight.

After that, the screaming started, and people went under tables or headed for the doors. It was all over, but they didn't know it.

My family was standing their ground. Both Mum and Dad had pistols drawn. Mary had a pair of Fairburn-Sykes ready to gut anyone who came near.

Even Denny and Eddie had grabbed table decorations to brain anyone who attacked them.

The royal family and other dignitaries, me included, were hustled out of the room by palace security.

A TV cameraman tried to follow us down the hall to the next large room but was stopped. That was when I remembered that this had been broadcast worldwide.

I hoped there was some delay, or the scene would be brutal. There wasn't a delay, and it was brutal. I was the star of the show as the cameras had been on May-ling and me when it started.

I didn't believe it was me at first when I watched the tape. I had a calm look that turned into a killing rage within seconds when it started.

The investigation started immediately. I gave a short, written statement, then an excuse to return to our rooms where May-ling and I changed out of our blood-splattered clothes. She had a little on her. I looked like I'd had a bath in it. Pro tip— when cutting someone's throat, don't stand in front of them. The blood spray is horrendous.

A reporter intercepted us as we returned to be with the rest of our families.

"King Richard, why did you kill those men before finding out if they meant to harm you or May-ling?"

How do you answer something like that? I ignored her and walked on. May-ling waved her hand, and a security guard dragged the reporter away.

The head of palace security reported it was too early to know where these men were from or who was backing them. It was noticed that the men had steel dental work as found in Russia.

I was ready to drop the Rods from God on Moscow right then. I mentioned that to May-ling in a rather loud voice. She quieted me down and told me that I could do that right after the wedding dinner was completed.

That settled me down. I didn't want to get indigestion from taking out a major city.

Chapter 43

The aftermath of the assassination attempt was incredible. The attempt had been live on worldwide TV, and the crews had good camera angles. No one could be accused of a cover-up on this one.

At least, that is what I thought. The conspiracy nuts had plenty of reasons that something was being covered up.

I was portrayed as a mass murderer. How they got that when I only killed two guys, I don't know. Why didn't I wait for the police to arrive and take care of things?

Duh, I wanted May-ling and me to live.

One thing that they got right was my incredible reach with a sword. At six feet five inches and a three-foot sword, I could hit someone almost ten feet away from me. That second guy never got within six feet of me before I slashed his throat.

My extensive background with a sword came out. I was acknowledged to be one of the best swordsmen in the world. They even interviewed Basil Rathbone, who was considered the best.

He said he might have taken me in his younger days but not now. This endorsement brought back my Robin Hood movie and every sword and board scene I had ever done. I had not used a shield, but it was good technobabble for the audience.

There was endless speculation on who had ordered the attempt. The Russians pushed the theory that supporters of May-ling's Uncle Haoran were behind it.

We had no evidence that Russia was involved except for the dental work. The money trail was a dead end. It was like these people had never existed. They were checking into how they got an invitation, as they had been tightly controlled. At least we thought they were.

May-ling and I had intended to take off on our honeymoon immediately after the wedding reception. The trip was held up for two days for our part in the investigation.

I don't know why it took so long. My statement consisted of, "Two guys were coming at me with swords drawn and shouting threatening remarks, so I killed them."

May-ling's statement was, "Two guys were coming at my husband with swords drawn and yelling threats, so he killed them."

We added that by the time our two attackers were down, we heard gunshots, and the other bad guys were down.

Later we were told the hold-up was to get more security in place for our honeymoon.

Our honeymoon trip was to an island near Tahiti. It is a private island with only a main house and several small houses and workshops for live-in staff.

We got there by flying to the main island in my 707. There was a fighter jet escort all the way. On our take off until well out to sea, there were Chinese Shenyang J-5A fighter jets, licensed production of the radar-equipped Russian MiG-17PF, then McDonnell F-4B Phantom IIs from the aircraft carrier the USS Coral Sea CV-43.

It was strange flying with these jets on my wings. The pilots must have been under strict orders as they didn't pull any stunts. I would have loved to fly either of those but had to settle with showing off to my bride by piloting my flying hotel.

I did this for the takeoff and two more hours then grew bored. May-ling and I retired to our room and renewed our mile-high club membership.

We landed in Papeete and changed over to a twin-engine aircraft for the final leg to our island. The French got into the aeronautical circus with their new Mirage III escorts.

There was also a chase plane behind us for the whole trip, so the various militaries got to show off, and the world got to follow us on our honeymoon as there was live TV onboard.

I didn't ever check, but I just knew the bookies in London and Las Vegas were making book on our being attacked.

As we came near our island, we could see ships circling the island. They were Chinese Navy ships charged with keeping intruders away from the island.

Unwanted air visitors were kept away by the USS Coral Sea, which was over the horizon. May-ling and I were amazed at all the security until we thought about it. I was king of a sovereign nation, and she was the crown princess of the largest empire on Earth.

To each other, we were Rick and May. We didn't give much thought to how the rest of the world saw us. Archduke Franz Ferdinand and his wife Sophie's assassination set off World War I; our deaths would match that.

Most of the time out of our sight were roving patrols of the Chinese Army. They were headquartered on the next island and used small boats to circle our islands. They also ran foot patrols.

I thought this was overkill until I learned what overkill was. The Space Ladies watched the entire honeymoon trip with their trigger fingers on the Rods from God. Any large formation coming at us would be destroyed.

I asked Jerri who could send a formation that large against us. Her answer was shocking.

"What if the US had a change of policy?"

The house we were staying in was well set up. It was an island house up on stilts. Not that large with three bedrooms. The covered veranda was enormous. One end was left open for sunbathing.

We had elected to prepare our meals, so the only time the staff came near the house was to replenish the foodstuff. This service was when we were at the beach or early in the morning before we woke.

We spent our week walking on the beach and snorkeling in the clear waters. I even taught May-ling how to surf. The waves were like the infamous Teahupoo off the main island. They were more of the four-foot variety that gave a nice long ride without the dangers of the crossflow or undertow of the Teahupoo.

If May-ling hadn't been pregnant before this trip, she would have been now. We are very compatible with our tastes. We experimented a little then settled on what we liked.

We walked and talked about our childhoods, our dreams, and the cold hard practicalities of our world. May-ling wanted to bring prosperity to all Chinese. I wanted to open the solar system to all of mankind.

While different, we had a common goal: to improve living conditions for all. We realized that the Earth's resources would be used up with the current population growth. We needed to obtain more. Space was the obvious answer.

Like all good things, our honeymoon came to an end. The trip home was the reverse of our trip out with all the attendant security. I realized that this would be our new way of life.

Our quiet week had made us forget the glare of publicity we lived in. I started to look back at my days hitchhiking with nostalgia. Hours would go by with no one giving me a second look.

When we got back to China, I sent inquiries to the US, China, and the French as to the names and ranks of every person, both onsite and staff support, involved in our security on our honeymoon.

As king of the Luna Republic, I issued an award for being on the "Honeymoon Cruise." It was a ribbon to be worn on their uniforms. Then I let the press know that I had done this. That forced the hand of the three military establishments to let their troops accept this foreign award.

It also set the stage for other awards and recognition in the future. The Honeymoon Ribbon became a bragging rights award.

I checked with Jerri Cobb on the moon base construction status. All was going well. We now had enough food supplies on hand to last until the first food crop was harvested. I was still nervous. We were trusting that the first food crop would turn out well.

I asked Jerri to keep bringing food up to the moon as much as possible. I was informed not to teach a Space Lady how to use her thrusters. That had been in the plan all along.

Since I wasn't needed on the moon, I decided to head to Australia to check up on things there.

Heretofore, I would hop on my jet and fly to the country. I was now a visiting head of state, so arrangements had to be made in advance.

I had to fly into Canberra to meet the prime minister and the royal governor before proceeding to Lassetter Station. May-ling stayed in China for a series of government meetings. Better her than me.

One nice thing about being a king is that no one asks you for a passport. One was never required of Queen Elizabeth of Great Britain. Now I didn't need one either.

I didn't have a staff that traveled with me. I soon learned that I had better get one on board, if nothing else to coordinate travel plans, contact my offices, and provide security.

Chapter 44

My trip to Australia was worthwhile. I was given updates on every major project at both of my ranches. They were both ahead of the projected schedules and turned their first profits.

The goldfield had been profitable from day one, but now the rest of the ranch was coming into its own.

I even took the time to play a round of golf on my new golf course. There were TV cameras everywhere I went nowadays, so I wasn't surprised when a crew followed me around the course.

Luckily, playing on the moon hadn't ruined my Earth game. The course was designed so that a reasonable golfer could have an enjoyable round from the gold tees.

It was also set up that if you played from the black tees, you were in for a miserable day if your game wasn't right on. These tees were meant for a pro tournament. Several foursomes had played from the black tees once.

No foursome played them twice. Even my pro friends who had initiated the course reported they were nasty.

The Aborigine chiefs told me that all my promises were being kept. They felt like they had the best of all worlds. Health care, and the ability to roam as they wish.

I noticed that the one chief who had divorced his wives so that he was down to two now had two more. From the screeching coming from his house, he hadn't learned a thing.

As I had feared, the cattle had worn a track into the fields as they followed the irrigation systems around. A series of portable fences had been put up to encourage them to use a different course every few days.

I talked to May-ling every day. We were both enjoying our days. She loved learning how an empire was run, and I loved seeing the things I had set in motion be successful. I guess we enjoyed the same things from slightly different directions.

It was early days, but her pregnancy was proceeding with no problems. Her only complaint was that she had as many doctors following her as security people.

I received word that a scaled-down prototype hyperspeed rocket different from the EmDrive had been assembled in a polar near-Earth orbit. I couldn't get up to orbit quick enough to see what was going on.

Upon arrival, I saw a weird-looking contraption. It was a twenty-foot diameter sphere, with a pipe about a quarter-mile long on each side transfixing the sphere.

I wasn't that good at estimating distances in space. I had been given a written specification for the craft.

I was told that each pipe or tube was the engine. There was one on each side, so there was no need to rotate the craft to go in the desired direction.

There was no true front or back to the craft, but they labeled one side front for ease of conversation. The other end was called the back.

When you wanted to accelerate to the front, you would fire up the engine in the back, thrusting in the direction you wanted to go.

When it was time to slow down, you would turn that engine off and turn on the engine on the opposite side of the space vehicle. Small chemical-powered thrusters could rotate the craft into position for thrust or braking if we lost one engine.

Losing two engines would not be good.

The fusion engine generated the power for these engines based on Mary's formulas. The engine would first take the reaction mass and heat it with the waste heat from the fusion plant.

At this time, water was being used as the heat transfer mechanism. The fusion reactor would heat the water, and in turn, the water would be contained as ionized superheated steam.

The electrical output of the power plant confined the superheated ionized steam while heating it and directed its "explosion" once you released the pressure.

The thrust pipes, a quarter-mile-long in space, would not be practical in the atmosphere and accelerated small masses with very powerful magnets to very high speeds. We would get decent accelerations using very little reaction mass because the energy input makes up for the smallness of the mass.

By lengthening the "pipe" and adding coils, we could keep accelerating the mass, and we were using charged rock dust to very high speeds, theoretically to a large fraction of the speed of light.

By reducing the mass that must be packed, we could move large payloads long distances at high speeds.

The team designed two major pipes in each direction in case of an engine failure. There were also shorter-length pipes surrounding the major pipes. These pipes at small angles from the major pipes would be used for steering. They also were gimbal-mounted so we could go in any direction. Without them, we could only go straight out. Not good if you want to circle a planet.

When done, the whole contraption made me think of a World War II sea mine with its horns sticking out.

It was the most unlikely-looking vehicle for space flight I could imagine.

From the outside, the sphere looked like it had plenty of room for a crew. However, so much equipment was crammed inside that the two crew members would barely fit. At least there were bunks and a combined shower bathroom. Food would be eaten in your bunk or flight seat.

I was assured that if this prototype worked out, the full-sized vehicle would have enough room for a crew of five to be comfortable.

I did everything but stamp my feet, but I wouldn't be allowed on the test run to the moon and back. The plan was to go to the moon, slow to a stop, and then return. This plan would test the acceleration and braking power of the engines.

Jerri Cobb was there for the test. I thought for certain that she would be one of the two. When I mentioned that she told me that her flying days were pretty much over. She was now on the administrative end of things.

The way she eyed me when she told me this, I think she was trying to send me a message. I chose not to receive it. I did, but I wasn't going to let her know that.

The moon test went off like a dream. The test plan was for the engines to be run at one-quarter speed and be ramped up if things went smoothly. Things went well, so they ramped it up to a comfortable one-gravity acceleration.

After one and three-quarter hours, they had to go to the reverse engine to slow down. They came to almost a dead stop at the moon in three and a half hours! This speed was a real game-changer.

The two Space Lady test pilots reported all instruments were nominal during the trip. As soon as they returned from the moon, a crew started tearing the prototype apart looking for any hidden problems.

There weren't. Three days after the test flight, I authorized a full-sized hyperspeed craft to be built. None of our spacecraft had been named before. The overall space program was called that, or program for short. The various craft had numbers.

I agreed that it was time to name the hyperspeed spaceship. I canvased people on what to name it. The most common name mentioned was Ares since his symbol was a spear.

The only problem was that Ares is the God of War, not exactly the image we were going for.

I made an executive decision to name it Zeus, whose symbol is a lightning bolt. This design was painted on both sides of the vehicle. Does a sphere have sides? I guess the engine pipes defined them.

I called them engine pipes; others called them tubes. Common use had them as thrusters. Common use won out.

One thing we hadn't counted on during our test run was that our thrusters were pointed away from the moon. They were aimed at the Earth. All that reaction mass was coming out the back and igniting the atmosphere, setting off the largest light show ever seen.

There were reports that we were in the end days, or nuclear war had broken out. A news release sent out under my name settled things down, but I got a lot of abuse in the press.

I did get one interesting request. An advertising agency wanted to know if a stencil could be attached to the thrusters so that the flames could be used for advertisements.

That reminded me of a science fiction novel I had read a long time ago. The advertising executive Don Draper, whom I met several years earlier, probably read the same story. I told my staff that we wouldn't be doing it.

Another update I got was from the R&D team working with the EmDrive. The drive had been set aside for the much better drive we now had. Only a caretaker team of interns was working with it now.

That team had an accident. The wrong material had been used to line the reactor. It was only a thin coating plated on. When the reactor was energized, it collapsed its test stand.

It was like the weight of the drive had increased many times over. They estimated at least twenty times.

They wanted to investigate this phenomenon. I gave the go-ahead. This accident could prove interesting. Was it possible that gravity could be increased?

Chapter 45

We were going to Mars the same as we went to the moon. Cautiously. We would send two vehicles, establish a station in orbit around Mars, and then have two landers go down. Again, why take risks when we didn't have to?

I shuddered when I thought of what NASA had planned for a lunar mission. They were planning on taking wartime risks when they could only win bragging rights.

Why the military went along with this, I will never know. I do know that the military followed orders, but there are limits. The NASA administration was a top-level political appointment, so I understood that.

As far as the astronauts themselves, you would always find a few brave souls who would go where no man has gone before.

The prototype had done well, and I had authorized two full-sized vehicles. I was surprised when I was told they were ready a week later.

It seems the thrusters, each a mile-long tube, were already made. They were nothing more than a pipe wrapped in copper coils. When the pipes or tubes were made for the prototype, it was cheaper to keep production going and make the full-size tubing.

It was only the cost of the material. The setup costs of the line would have far exceeded the material cost, so some smart person kept the line running.

The sphere in the middle with the fusion generator was a simple matter. We had the generators in orbit and the metal plating to make the fifty-foot diameter spheres.

Assembly was done in another week. It took longer to get the furnishings for the crew's quarters in place than the assembly. They were good to go with food, water, and oxygen.

I didn't mention another hundred or so fiddly bits that took another week. Things like heating arrangements, radio installations, and water-filled compartments comprising the outer hull, protecting the craft and personnel from radiation and small meteor hits.

Just like the station orbiting the moon and our other vehicles, the water compartments were self-sealing and had automatic filling from extra containers built into the hull for that purpose.

If a meteor hit was extreme, the entire tank could be jettisoned and replaced with a spare. Too large of a hit, and it would be all over. It was impossible to eliminate all risks.

One month after I gave the go-ahead, the spaceships Zeus One and Two left for Mars.

Mars was at one of its closest conjunctions with Earth, at forty million miles. The round trip would be two and a half months. They would circle Mars, take many pictures, and return to Earth.

While all this was happening, I was back down on Earth with my wife. Our time was either spent at the launch site or in the Forbidden Palace. We both were sensitive to the assassination attempts.

After five weeks, we received a radio signal from Mars that Zeus's fleet had rounded Mars and headed home. All their mission parameters were in the green.

I took a bit of a chance and authorized the construction of a Mars station to put in orbit and another one to send to the asteroid belt. There was also going to be a fleet of six ships to accompany the stations.

If I thought there was an uproar about going to the moon, it was nothing compared to circling Mars. I had messages from heads of state from all over the Earth. The UN got into the act.

They all demanded to know what my intentions were. I hadn't thought this part through. My only thought was that it would be cool to go to Mars and take some pictures.

After that, setting up a science station and creating another colony as part of the kingdom of Luna never entered my mind. What did enter my mind was that I had never settled on a real name for the moon kingdom.

Kingdom of Luna, Lunar Kingdom, The Royal Lunar Kingdom? I had used variations of this at one time or the other.

I had a brilliant idea. I pulled out our constitution and read what it said. It called us the Kingdom of Luna and the Solar Reaches. What the heck are the Solar Reaches?

I quickly called the constitution team leader and asked him what they meant when they wrote it.

His reply wasn't very helpful, "Whatever you want it to be. We weren't sure if you would claim other bodies in the solar system, so we left it vague."

The press picked up on this before any government agencies. The headlines were about Emperor Jackson of the Solar System. This emperor bit was starting to get out of hand.

I called my parents, and they agreed to fly to China, where we had a meeting with Empress Ping. May-ling and I sat next to each other, holding hands. We were both in shock over this turn of events.

You would think a simple denial by myself would close the issue, but I knew better.

We discussed it for several hours, lunch was brought in, and we continued past dinner. The best we could come up with was an announcement that a science base would be established on Mars.

Furthermore, I had no intention of claiming the entire planet but would probably set up the base as a province of the Luna Kingdom and Solar Reaches.

The Luna Kingdom and Solar Reaches would recognize any country's claims to establishing a base on Mars for a region extending one hundred miles in all directions from the center of the established base.

Once this was released, the UN wanted to know how I had the right to dictate terms to the world governments. This situation kept getting messier and messier.

I even thought about going the whole hog and declaring everything in the Solar System but Earth as mine by right of the first occupation. That meant I would have to send expeditions to every major body in the Solar System. Pluto would take over three years round trip.

Working the math of that trip made me rethink claiming everything. Anyway, I didn't want to be seen as greedy.

May-ling came up with my answer to the world.

"You will have to judge me by my actions. I have no intention of trying to seize all the Solar System. I can say or do nothing that will convince anyone otherwise, so this is my last comment on the issue."

That didn't stop the speculation in the press or various governments passing resolutions that no one could own the entire Solar System.

The pressure was mounting to blockade the moon when that became moot. Our first crops came in. It was fast-growing red winter wheat. As a proof of concept, it was wonderful. We had imported tons of foodstuff, but now we could grow our own.

Other than the issue of bone mass deterioration by an extended stay in low gravity, we were independent.

As a precautionary step, I requested the government of Australia to raise the taxes on the gold mine by ten percent. This higher tax rate gave the politicians more money to play with and a reason not to participate in an embargo.

As far as the taxes went, they were immaterial at this point. My riches were such that we couldn't even keep track of my worth on any given day.

Between China and Australia, we were set. Of course, when Empress Ping found out about my voluntary tax increase, she wanted her share.

Instead of money, we signed a formal mutual defense treaty between our two nations. If this didn't send a message to Russia, nothing would.

Our first harvest was announced to the world. We had requests from many different universities requesting samples for testing. I thought this a reasonable request until Dad brought up the fact that we didn't know the nutrient properties of the new crop and wouldn't for a while. If they were poor, we would lose our ability to be food-independent.

Before sending any out to universities, we decided to test it on a known population. The cows loved it and gained weight. The gauchos limited the percentage fed to them at forty percent to avoid digestive problems but other than that, it was wonderful.

The wheat was milled and baked. It was found to be like any other bread. Some of the bread was frozen, shipped back to Earth, and sent to all world leaders who wanted to declare an embargo.

We even had special wrappers for each loaf telling how the wheat was raised on the moon and baked there.

Mary got ten loaves somehow to auction off to Feed the Puppies. Those dogs must be getting fatter!

My supporters like Queen Elizabeth and President Kennedy were sent extra loaves. I think the publicity surrounding the moon bread did more for my public perception than any news release I had made to date.

Chapter 46

While I was getting pilloried in the press and various politicians were grandstanding, things weren't looking that bad. No one was trying to kill me or invade the moon.

There were no more than the usual threats against my family. They had been coming in regularly for the last several years. We ignored the single threats from the nut jobs.

Any group that threatened got a discrete warning. A copy of the FBI file telling how some Soviet agents were decapitated was leaked to them. It was surprising how that cooled the ardor of everyone but the most militant and suicidal.

Mum and an old friend from the war, Pippa Doyle, would visit them. No more problem. The two women were reenacting their youth.

There weren't any repeated threats.

Trying to think of ways to sweeten my international reputation, I asked the security group on the moon what would be the ramifications of allowing some national groups to set up a science station of their own.

They came back with a proposal to build separate tunnels for each group. They would live and work there. We would allow them access to our town square with its shops, restaurants, and food courts.

The foreign contingent wouldn't have access to our working areas. When they came to town, they would have to come in a group. Our security team would watch them on closed-circuit TV. There were only two exits to the work areas, so we set up guard stations.

Their only purpose was to stop the foreign contingent from going to those areas.

The only thing that was truly secret was fusion device manufacturing. That was segregated in its tunnel network and had a strict security entrance for all visitors. If you weren't authorized, you didn't get in.

We sent invitations to the US, China, Great Britain, Germany, Australia, and Argentina. In other words, all our partners in the space program. Transportation would be at our expense.

Providing transportation would also allow us to inspect everything being sent into orbit. Not that the CIA or MI6 would try to put something over on us.

They all jumped at the opportunity to have a laboratory on the moon. I had to laugh when I saw a NASA contingent coming up to investigate how to work in a low-gravity environment. A former colonel and failed politician by the name of John Glenn was the lead on that project.

For some reason, Jerri Cobb put herself back on flight status just for his trip.

No one tried to sneak anything with them on the first trip. My security team would keep close tabs on them but felt the attempts would begin after the fourth or fifth trip when we would be getting complacent.

A betting pool was started when the first contraband would be found. I doubt if my people would become complacent. My entry was on the ninth trip by the Americans.

I had the Americans correct. They tried to bring two Minox cameras up to the moon on the fourth trip.

While others were not trying to sneak stuff up yet, it didn't mean they were walking straight and narrow. Within two days of being in the settlement, they were all trying to get a map of our entire layout.

They started by trying to bribe the bartenders. They didn't know that our security people staffed the two bars they had access to. We had gamed out what we thought they would try. This one was obvious.

Our bartenders proved to be very bribeable. The money would go to security's Christmas and New Year party funds.

The maps sold were fake. Four different editions were being sold, supposedly from different stages of construction.

Each map was correct in detail for the zones they had access to and the adjacent zones. It was after that they became confusing.

I suggested they put an X on each map, as it marks the treasure in pirate maps. A good case was made that this would be a dead giveaway that they were fake. Darn, I wanted to have some fun.

A fifth map was made and posted on a public bulletin board in the food court. It didn't have an X. It did have an area marked fusion production.

We had a camera and operator stationed there around the clock. It was fun to watch the map discovered and copied as discreetly as possible.

If you could get past security into the production zone, this map would lead you to an empty area set up to capture people by the simple expedient of closing a blast door.

There were attempts to get past the security screening to the production area. Everything from fake IDs to fake delivery boys. The offenders were given verbal warnings the first few times or made to perform silly things like posing for a picture wearing a lampshade.

When our people got tired of it, they PNGed them and sent them home. Being declared persona non grata was the end of your field career in the spy world.

The different countries were also doing some serious scientific work. That part was welcome. They weren't required to share it with us, but that didn't matter. Our camera and computer systems were capturing everything that they were doing.

The Russians wanted to send a team-up, but that was a bridge too far. There was no way I would allow those thugs inside my perimeter. They cried to the UN, but that didn't get them anywhere.

The Russians kept pleading they were only out for the good of all. They were even negotiating with the Japanese over the Kuril Islands they were occupying.

I could understand the Russians negotiating as a delaying action. The Japanese should be screaming about the invasion of their territory. I asked the empress about this. She told me the Japanese didn't want any war and that they correctly thought the Russians were using the Kurils as a staging base and had no interest in staying.

There wasn't much we could do until the Russians made a move. Or was there? I bounced my idea off the empress. She loved it.

I had my foreign minister contact the Japanese to initiate a conversation. Since she spoke Japanese fluently, May-ling was my acting foreign minister.

The negotiations on this would take a while, and we would have to give a lot of assurances, but I thought the Japanese would go for it.

The engineering team brought forward a problem that would keep our space speed down. Theoretically, we could approach light speed. Doing that and meeting a grain of dust would be a disaster.

They proposed using thrusters on one side of the spacecraft to move forward. We would use the ones in front to throw out plasma in front of us. These thrusters on the front side would destroy anything in our way or coming at us. Well, not a full-sized planet, but a school bus-sized object would be erased.

The obvious drawback was that now we had to overcome those thrusters with higher thrust from the rear. Since we had plenty of energy, it was no problem.

We rigged up the prototype for remote control and tested it. It worked like a charm. Radar would pick up anything as large as that mythical school bus, and we could turn to avoid it. Anything small we would plow through.

If we reached .5c or half the speed of light, we would travel to the asteroid belt in half an hour. The only problem with that was we would blast right by it. We needed to slow down, so halfway there, we would have to brake to come to rest. So, allow two hours to get there and stop.

Mars was now a fifteen-minute trip. This changed everything.

I also realized that my doodles on the back of a napkin were probably wishful thinking. Even if the speeds we realized were only one-tenth of my projection, we could do the asteroid belt trip in less than a day.

The team that had come up with the deflectors, as we were calling them, also realized the ramifications of what we had. There were five of them. Counting my parents, May-ling, the empress, and me, altogether ten people knew what the possibilities were.

The team was working and living in the secure area of our moon base. I gave them each a two-million-dollar bonus for allowing themselves to be sequestered for the next two months. That should give us time to go out to the asteroid belt and see what was there.

The good old prototype was converted once more. We used this machine because no one paid attention to it. The world was following our machines that were traveling to Mars. It was well known the prototype wasn't set up as a long-term living arrangement, so it only was used to test new materials.

Chapter 47

Now things were getting interesting. The nations of the world were in an uproar about Mars. If the asteroid belt was now thrown into the mix, I didn't know where it would end up, but it wouldn't be good.

Since the prototyping team was the only one who knew that we could reach the belt in two hours, I talked it over with them. One of them suggested that we load the prototype with every bit of metal detecting gear we could find and send it out to the belt to do a preliminary survey before we said anything.

What we found, or didn't find, would dictate our timing. If the belt was worthless, it didn't matter if everyone knew it was a quick trip. If we found medium or neutral results, we would delay the announcement until we could identify the cream of the crop.

If it turned out that the belt was a bonanza, we would keep our capabilities secret as long as we could. At the same time, we would be mining like crazy. We would also be keeping track of what this would do to Earth prices. Most importantly, we would be expanding our space manufacturing base.

If it was a bonanza, a cold hard fact was that we would have to be prepared to defend it not out in the asteroid belt but in low Earth orbit.

These thoughts were the basis of the plan we put together. Since the team had voluntarily sequestered themselves, granted they did it for money, I told them their names would be on any finds we claimed.

When I made that statement, I realized that we needed a method to record claims in the Lunar Kingdom and the Solar Reaches.

We also needed a shorter way to refer to our country. The United Kingdom of Great Britain was known as the UK. We needed something similar.

LK seemed weird to me. LKSR was even worse. I talked it over with May-ling on a call, and she asked me why I needed a new name for Luna. Duh, everyone was already calling it that. I can make things complicated at times.

Sidetracking myself seemed to be a favorite pastime anymore. I had so many different things coming at me from so many directions it was easy to go, "Shiny!" and chase it.

I had the government team look into a claims system to get back on track. A primary location and orbit had to be defined to record a claim. There also had to be a claim marker on site.

There was a system in place to define locations. It was based on the celestial sphere. This sphere is an imaginary sphere of infinite radius centered on Earth.

Extensions of Earth's north and south poles define the north and south celestial poles.

A projection of Earth's equator defines the celestial equator. The celestial sphere can then be divided into a grid, just like the Earth is divided into a grid of latitude and longitude.

Stars, planets, and the Sun are "attached" to this imaginary sphere. The celestial sphere (with the stars attached) rotates in the opposite direction as Earth rotates.

To explain the sky's daily motions, you can imagine the sphere rotating once in 23 hours 56 minutes (using a star as reference).

Two coordinates allow for locating an object in the sky: azimuth and altitude. Their value depends on the location of the observer's azimuth: use as reference the north direction (close to Polaris), and the range of values is from 0 to 360 degrees. 0 degrees is N, 90 degrees E, 180 is S, and 270 is W. Altitude: use as reference the horizon. The range of values is from 0 degrees (horizon) to 90 degrees (zenith).

This system gave the location of the object being claimed as it was found. It had to be tracked for a distance to establish a series of points that would then describe the object's orbit.

The rules for a claims office were developed, but the office wasn't opened yet. Even the opening of such an office would generate many questions I wasn't ready to answer.

As an added distractor, I decided we would land on Mars and start a permanent base. A permanent base was in the plans all along, but we wouldn't proceed as long as there was controversy. Now controversy would be welcome.

"Hey, Earth, see the 'shiny!'"

And how they saw the shiny. I was glad that we had started some actions to defend our Earth orbit facilities because it looked like we might need them soon.

Both Russia and the United States announced they were in the process of a series of launches to build their Earth orbit stations. I trusted the United States to a point, but the Russians not at all.

The way I looked at it, the US would not try to capture our station. Instead, they would wait for the Russians to attempt to take the first and largest one and then come in to save the day.

Once they saved us, they would be there to stay collecting all the information on our operations that they could, just to keep us safe, you know.

We had a few nasty surprises in store for the first group to attempt to take the station. There would be no need to rescue us.

Both the Russians and the United States must have been planning their missions for some time as within two days of my announcement that we were landing on Mars as a precursor of establishing a permanent base, they both launched.

The Russians from the Baikonur Cosmodrome and the United States from the Vandenburg Air Force base.

We had no right to try to stop them, so we let them come on. The Russians launched three rockets with an estimated five soldiers on board each. The Americans sent four rockets with six soldiers on them.

It was ironic that the group the Americans sent was the 7th Cavalry. The Americans had the edge in manpower, twenty-four to fifteen, but the symbolism was terrible.

At least the commander's name wasn't Custer.

We had to wait until hostile action was taken before we could react. I announced worldwide that we welcomed Russia and the United States to space but declared an exclusion zone around our station of twelve nautical miles. This distance coincided with the international ocean boundaries of a nation.

Anyone violating this boundary without our permission would be considered hostile and dealt with accordingly.

We knew full well the Russians would ignore this claim and attack us. We were prepared. No one was taking us seriously as the station was manned, or in this case, womaned by the Space Ladies.

The Russian team was presumably Spetznaz and not deterred by an inferior women's force. Several things were in our favor. The Russians had not been in space and couldn't be used to fighting in zero gravity.

That was good, but the station's exterior had fifty-caliber machine guns attached. These were remote-controlled and could be fired from the interior by using TV cameras for the optics.

I was able to get back to the Earth orbit station using the prototype before the Russians arrived. My beginning there was important because I would be responsible for the first war in space. I intended it to be a short one.

Better than the machine guns, we had shoulder-fired antitank missiles.

The Russian capsules were heading towards our station, so I radioed to them and the whole world that they weren't welcome and would be fired upon if they came within twelve nautical miles of the station.

As their capsules came closer, I announced their distance, first at one hundred miles, then fifty miles, and twenty miles. They made no response to any of my announcements.

At ten miles, I announced they had demonstrated their hostile intentions and would be fired upon if they didn't immediately fire thrusters to leave our zone.

They didn't, so I gave the order to fire at five miles. There was no gravity to affect the flight of the missiles, so they went straight and true. Each of the three capsules was hit by at least two of the ten rockets fired.

The Spetznaz troops were suited up, so there were three survivors. We took them on board and immediately sent them back down to Earth in a waiting capsule.

There the soldiers would be in Chinese custody. I then announced to the world, particularly the Americans, that things were under control, and we needed no help. Due to the recent excitement, we weren't accepting any visitors.

The Americans stayed in orbit for two more days and returned to Earth. Their public announcement was that they had demonstrated that America's ability to put men in space was a success.

The late-night comedians had a ball with that one.

In the meantime, I took the prototype back to the moon and turned it over to the asteroid belt exploration team.

Chapter 48

The team went out to explore the asteroid belt. It was a quick trip there, and once they arrived, the search began. Before the team left, we knew a few things about the belt for certain.

The asteroid belt is a torus-shaped region in the Solar System, located roughly between Jupiter and Mars. It has many solid, irregularly shaped bodies of many sizes that are much smaller than planets, called asteroids or minor planets.

This asteroid belt is also called the main asteroid belt or main belt to distinguish it from other asteroid populations in the Solar System, such as near-Earth asteroids and Trojan asteroids.

About half its mass is contained in the four largest asteroids: Ceres, Vesta, Pallas, and Hygiea. The asteroid belt's total mass is approximately 4% of the moon's.

Contrary to popular opinion, the asteroid belt is mostly empty. The asteroids are spread over such a large volume that reaching an asteroid without aiming would be improbable.

It was theorized that there are three basic groups: carbonaceous, silicate, and metal-rich.

Since the area covered is so large, hundreds of thousands of asteroids are known, and the total number ranges in the millions or more, depending on the lower size cutoff. That number makes people think it's a dense, hard-to-navigate area.

Over 200 asteroids are known to be larger than 100 km, and a survey in the infrared wavelengths has shown that the asteroid belt has between 700,000 and 1.7 million asteroids with a diameter of 1 km or more.

After their preliminary survey, taking trips every day for two weeks, the team reported the following.

Carbonaceous asteroids are carbon-rich. They dominate the asteroid belt's outer regions. Together they comprise over 75% of the visible asteroids. They are redder in hue than the other asteroids and have very low albedo. Their surface composition is similar to carbonaceous chondrite meteorites. Chemically, their spectra match the primordial composition of the early solar system, with only the lighter elements and volatiles removed.

S-type (silicate-rich) asteroids are more common toward the inner region of the belt, within 2.5 AU of the Sun. The spectra of their surfaces reveal the presence of silicates and some metals but no significant carbonaceous compounds. This lack indicates that their materials have been significantly modified from their primordial composition, probably melting and reformation.

They have a relatively high albedo and form about 17% of the total asteroid population.

M-type (metal-rich) asteroids form about 10% of the total population; their spectra resemble iron-nickel. Some are believed to have formed from the metallic cores of different original bodies disrupted through collisions.

It was this ten percent that interested us the most at this time. The team spent two trips prospecting M-type asteroids. What they found was incredible. Nine out of ten visited were iron ore.

One out of ten were heavy metals such as lead, gold, silver, and platinum. The last three were the most interesting, but we immediately needed the iron ore ones.

Another interesting find was signs of water vapor on Ceres. This find gave us further independence from Earth.

The next week, the team set up beacons and claim markers on the major finds. We opened the claims office sub rosa to register the filings.

Every day the team reports were like Christmas morning. There was no doubt that we would mine and process ore out in the belt. Plans were underway to set up permanent operations.

We could make any steel combination we wanted with iron ore, heavy metals, and carbon. No doubt there would be tungsten and cobalt deposits to be found.

The various asteroids were not solid chunks of minerals. They would have to be mined just like ores are on Earth. Mining would take specialized equipment.

Getting into full production was a matter of months if not years.

The expedition to Mars was announced with great fanfare. The projected journey time to Mars was like a slow boat to China to keep the hyperspeed rocket secret. We were taking days instead of hours.

The average person on Earth approved of our venture. Why not? It wasn't costing them anything and was entertaining. The politicians were still screaming to the high heavens, not that they cared about Mars, but that they weren't benefiting from the journey.

How dare I, Richard Jackson, sponsor a trip to Mars and not allow them to reap any rewards. That was Un-American, Un-British, Un-Peruvian. You get the idea.

Depending on the political party, I was a traitor to mankind or a hero for advancing man in space. Those who made me a hero also held out their hand for supporting me.

I did the only logical thing and ignored them all. The politicians have no way of knowing that this was a sideshow to hide the asteroid belt venture.

The more I ignored them, the more rabid the statements were. I wondered if I would be declared an outlaw and my kingdom, a group of bandits.

My Lunar population followed all this with glee. My people saw us doing things that others had always wanted to do and doing them.

Of course, the groundhog politicians were jealous.

The slow trip to Mars was completed, and the crew was setting up for landing on Mars with pictures back to Earth. We were past masters at this. This time we didn't feel the need to have a permanent station in orbit before landing on the surface.

Building a station in Earth's orbit and moving it to Mars took time. We might have been able to do it if we weren't busy constructing a station to move to the asteroid belt.

The station going to the asteroid belt had hyperspeed capability built in. It was more like the largest spaceship ever built than a space station. It was designed to get it there quickly and move it around as needed. The asteroid belt covered a large area, and we didn't want our mining operations to spend excessive time traveling.

Even the mills and smelters would have the same propulsion in them.

The expedition landed on Mars, and a Luna Kingdom flag was planted. A plaque with one hundred square miles claimed was mounted on a tall cairn we made for the occasion. It even had a sentence that stated that I was most definitely not claiming the entire planet.

The landing ceremony was all done in front of TV cameras. Jerri Cobb was the face of our space program, so she was the one to first step on Mars. She paraphrased her famous line from when she stepped on the moon.

"Another small step for a woman and another giant leap for mankind."

You would think this would settle the issue of whether I was trying to control the solar system. It didn't make a difference. The UN ambassadors kept making speeches, deploring my attempts at domination.

They demanded I turn over all my space operations to implement responsible oversight. They didn't clarify what I was doing that wasn't responsible.

I was getting bored with the uproar at the UN. It was a lot of hot air with no meaning. They couldn't enforce anything. All they could do was whine that I wouldn't share my toys.

The Russians took the opportunity to make a lot of noise about us murdering their peaceful scientists. We released their peaceful scientists' names, ranks, units, and serial numbers.

You would think they would have been embarrassed. The Russians doubled down and presented us with the list of degrees each of their scientists held.

There was no doubt that the Spetznaz team sent were elite troops. Still, I wondered what having a degree from the Russian War College in Logistics or Mobile Warfare had to do with my space station.

The Chinese refused to send the Spetznaz back to Russia, which worked well. The troops all requested asylum as they would be punished and even executed for failing their mission.

Tongue firmly in my cheek, I publicly thanked the Americans for sending troops to orbit to help us if needed. Thankfully we were able to handle matters on our own.

I think every book on warfare ever written talked about the advantages of holding the high ground. Our ground didn't get much higher.

In fact, I was over the moon with the success of my life and family so far. I really was over the moon. I was in orbit, ready to land back on the moon to check up on the asteroid belt exploration.

We had a code name for our operation. We called it "Tonka".

Chapter 49

Through May-ling, I negotiated with Japan about using an uninhabited island in the Kurils to drop a demonstration Rod from God.

The Japanese demanded one hundred million dollars and a guarantee to remediate any radiation damage. The money was highway robbery.

The drop was to tell the Russians they had no hopes in this area. They would have to leave the Japanese territory. The Japs should be paying me!

There would be no radiation damage to remediate. It would all be impact damage. There was a good chance there would be no island left to remediate. I didn't mention that to the Japanese.

I paid the money but made a few mental notes about any future dealings with the Japanese. They wouldn't defend their territory and demanded that I pay to defend it for them.

What comes around, goes around.

We made public my plan with great fanfare with announcements to mariners and airmen. The usual suspects made the usual outcry. Like the little boy who cried wolf, it was easy to ignore them. They would probably have the same fate one day.

On the given date and time, a Rod was released from orbit. Everything went as planned. The island didn't disappear completely. What had been an island was now an atoll. The crater in the center of the island filled with ocean water and left nothing behind except a ring of high ground around the new body of water.

The ground left behind was scoured of all life. There was nothing left but bare rock. If that didn't send a message, nothing would.

We had done the math on the estimated tsunami wave. We had been conservative in our wave height estimate. It was two feet short of the estimated height.

There was no loss of life due to the warnings given. I did begin to understand why the Japanese demanded so much money. I had to change my attitude quickly when I viewed the damage from the air.

I even offered another fifty million dollars to help replace the damaged homes, stores, and fishing fleet. Most of the fleet had sailed far enough away that they weathered it okay. Those who thought adding longer lines would account for the sea level rise lost their ships.

So those who planned poorly for the wave were rewarded, and those who took their ships to safety didn't get new boats. Life isn't fair at times, but what can you do?

After my demonstration, China demanded the Russians remove their troops from the Kurils. Not only did the Russians ignore this demand, but it also triggered their attempted invasion of the mainland.

The Space Ladies watched all of this from orbit as the Russians loaded the troop carriers. I instructed them to activate their TV cameras and make the feed worldwide when they reported this.

For some reason, the UN didn't carry on like they usually did. It took three days for them to complete the troop loadings, so the entire world knew what was going on. Speculations were running rife as to what actions the Chinese would take.

The empress publicly announced a treaty with the Kingdom of Luna and the Solar Reaches. She was invoking the mutual defense clause of the treaty.

Now the UN decided to start lamenting the whole situation. If I didn't know better, I would think they weren't on my side. Come to think of it, they weren't on my side. They weren't against me; they hated the power that I had.

When the self-defense clause was invoked, I announced that the Kingdom of Luna and the Solar Reaches (that name was a pain) would honor its commitments.

The Rods would be dropped on the fleet if it sailed. The Russians tried to blackout the news from their troops, but Voice of America ramped up its station in Cincinnati, Ohio. That station was so powerful that it was said that your dental fillings would pick it up.

I don't know about that, but Dad reported that a pile of metal junk lying on the floor in the garage at Jackson House picked it up.

There was a mutiny in the Russian fleet. Enough of the soldiers had seen the results of the drop made. They wanted no part of it. It wasn't much of a mutiny as the officers offered no resistance.

I was told later that the general in charge of the operation ordered his two aides to arrest him and declare the mutiny over. The fleet wouldn't sail with any troops on board.

The Russian admiral was fine with this as he didn't want Rods dropped on his ship any more than the next soldier. The troops were unloaded and went into stand down.

In Moscow, the politicians went crazy. They demanded the general's and admiral's heads for treason.

To help matters along, I announced to the citizens of Moscow that a Rod would be dropped on their city if the Russian Congress pursued their plans of invading China and Siberia.

In response, the Congress had tanks rushed to the capital to surround Red Square and protect them. The tanks arrived and surrounded the square as ordered. However, the guns were all facing inward.

A stalemate ensued.

The Russians on the Kurils asked for asylum from Japan, and Japan refused. Next, the Russians asked China; China accepted. The soldiers were disarmed and loaded on ships to be sent to Siberia.

Not as prisoners but as paid workers to improve the Siberian infrastructure such as railways, roads, harbors, and airports.

In response, Russia attempted to nuke my Australia operations. The two missiles launched were shot down from space. Again, all this was televised from orbit.

Even the UN was silent when I gave the Russian people an ultimatum: replace your leaders, or I will do it by dropping a Rod from God on the Kremlin. Since this would also destroy the entire city, the citizens broke the stalemate.

The soldiers surrounding Red Square had been neutral to this point. Now they made it clear that the Russian government had to be replaced.

The higher-ups in the Russian government who thought they could win a war had been publicly identified for some time. It was no surprise when most of them were identified hanging from telephone poles in Red Square.

The Russians take their change in government seriously, their revolutions even more so.

The Russians had three different governments in the next three weeks. They were all military juntas. The military groups were more than decimating each other. By the time the third group came to power, they were toppled by university students.

Unlike most student revolutions, they were realistic in their expectations. Their first and only act once a parliament was in place with a prime minister was to appeal to the UN to become a protectorate until they had a functioning country.

The UN acted as a functional body for once and set up a mission. The mission was entrusted to the armies of Germany and the United States.

They were picked because of the forces arrayed since World War II to protect the Fulda Gap. This gap was a low land corridor that the Soviets planned to use for their tanks to invade Germany.

Now the gap was used to send troops into Russia.

They used both the northern and southern routes through the gap.

The northern route through the Gap passes south of the Knüllgebirge and then continues around the northern flank of the Vogelsberg Mountains.

The narrower southern route passes through the Fliede and Kinzig Valleys, with the Vogelsberg to the north and the Rhön Mountains and Spessart Mountains to the south.

Leaving Germany, they still had to transverse Poland. Poland objected to a huge army blithely passing through its borders for some silly reason. The UN passed the hat, and a large sum of money made the Poles see the light.

I came up with a significant part of that bribe. You would have thought this would have raised my esteem in the eyes of the nations complaining about me. It didn't. No matter how they complained—the world's focus was on UN troops going into Russia.

They were called UN troops, and they wore UN armbands but were very much national troops of Germany and the United States under their country's command.

The UN had tried to install Swedish officers at the highest levels but were told to go pound sand.

Free elections were held once under firm UN control with units in all major cities. The poor students who stuck their necks out to bring peace to the country lost the election by a landslide.

At the same time, any candidate with the word communist in their past also lost. Most of the winning candidates were free-market types, so I took a chance and propped up the Russian economy using the UN as my vehicle once more.

The UN bureaucrats were sorely disappointed when they found out they couldn't get their hands on any of this money.

In a bit of historical irony, my reputation improved most with the Russians. They said that the tsars used the knout. King Jackson used the Rod. I was considered a strong leader.

Chapter 50

We needed a station in the asteroid belt as soon as possible. Using our previous methods would take the better part of a year.

We hoped to have one in place using our new technology within two months.

The first big improvement we made was changing from the idea that we were launching manned space capsules.

The launch payload was to be freight. Instead of a capsule under the Hungry Hippo, it was a freight container, based on my shipboard cargo containers.

Since it would be an unmanned vehicle, we could increase the thrust in order to take heavier loads into orbit.

Previously, we had shipped individual panels up to orbit and assembled them there. Now we assembled the panels as much as possible before launch. The entire assembly was fitted together on the ground to ensure everything was correct and would fit.

The assembly was then disassembled as little as possible and still fit in a container and sent upstairs.

Once in orbit, the parts were taken into a large, enclosed area. The station would be assembled in this pressurized heated warehouse. While still weightless, the workers wouldn't need the bulky suits.

Self-repairing water-filled containers protected the warehouse, like all other buildings in orbit. These containers gave protection against radiation and small objects.

I say small objects because we now had to worry about workers' lost objects. Getting hit by a rock or a wrench would have the same effect. This problem would only get worse over time. We had to come up with a barrier that would intercept these.

Every part had been labeled, so it was easy to fit them back together. Once the fit was correct (sometimes a hammer was used to force a fit) the parts were welded together.

We had quality inspectors check every step of the way. Even the hammer fits had to be just so.

The most time-consuming part of the job was running all the wiring. Wiring troughs had been designed, so it was easy to pull the wire once it was decided what needed to be pulled.

We had a large crew doing the assembly and wiring. The warehouse was large enough that each worker had a personal room. It was like a one-hundred-room hotel. We had kitchen staff, a manned medical facility, and a gym.

The crew was working seven shifts. The traditional three shifts and then four three-day, four-day off alternating groups each doing twelve-hour shifts.

It must have been hard doing the scheduling, but it worked. Something was happening twenty-four hours a day, seven days a week. I would have messed up the workload in two or three days.

While the construction was going on, all the needed items for housekeeping were being sent up. There was plenty of water at the station, but we intended to capture an ice comet or ice-coated asteroid as soon as possible.

We could produce all the water and oxygen needed using a fusion reactor. That, plus the fact we now could reach the asteroid belt in a matter of hours, gave us a huge safety net.

The workers thought they were building a station for orbiting Mars. Maybe the fact that all the drawings were labeled Mars Station influenced them.

It was good that the drawings were mislabeled because the media on Earth were giving regular reports on our progress. There would be a huge fallout when it was realized that the station wasn't going to Mars.

The station was designed to hold twenty staff in which to base the prospecting and mining operations. It would be a retreat for those working the belt.

There would be rooms for individuals. Staff would have permanent ones, and miners and prospectors would use theirs hotel style.

We had again included a medical setup. It was intended to stabilize injuries until we could get them back to the moon base, where we had a full hospital setup.

My arm was even twisted into allowing a small bar in the recreational facility. There were strict controls on how much could be served, and anyone going out to the belt was cut off eight hours before their flight.

I wondered how long it would be before a problem emerged. I just hoped no one was killed. At the same time, going out for three or four months required some R&R. This wasn't the submarine service.

To get the station into place, we had a weird-looking transport made. It was a hyperspeed-capable framework. The station or any other object we wanted to move fast would be placed inside the frame, and away they would go.

Even though the station could do the flight, we wanted to save the wear and tear on the huge object. We weren't planning to install drives on the stations built for our partners, so we would need the framework.

The station was finished in six weeks and sent out to the asteroid belt. Work immediately started on the real Mars station.

The media kept trying to find out where the first station had gone. We didn't respond to any questions, but Norad gave us away. They kept a close eye on everything we did and leaked it to the press.

It wasn't a big deal. The UN couldn't scream any louder about my actions.

What was a big deal was a phone call I got from President Kennedy.

"King Richard, we need to talk."

"How can I help you, Mr. President?"

"First of all, let's drop the titles."

"Call me, Rick."

"And I'm, John."

"Okay, John, what can I do for you?"

"Our Congress is getting antsy about your gaining power."

"I've not gone out of my way to do so. Events have been forced on me."

"I know and understand that, but the result is you have the high ground, and it makes them nervous."

"I would think it would be your military that was nervous."

"They are way beyond nervous. The chief of staff and his crew can't find a way to counter any threats you may make, and it terrifies them."

"What do you want me to do about that?"

"Is there any way you can help us set up a presence in space?"

"I could, but what about the rest of the world? The UN will be screaming about you having an advantage."

"Let them scream."

"That's all well and good, but they will be screaming at me."

"It seems to me that you are getting good at ignoring them."

"True, but I know that I will pay for it someday."

"John, you said, 'A presence in space,' does that mean it doesn't have to be a military one?"

"Correct, our people feel that if they can get a foothold in space, they can work out the rest."

"How would you like a station in orbit around Mars? I would charge you for transportation but would gift you the station, and your people would have free rein as what they do with it."

"In principle, that would work. I would have to pass it by some people and work out the details, but that sounds super."

"It ought to help in the next election."

"It won't hurt, that is for sure."

While nominally a Republican, the Republican candidate would be Richard Nixon. I disliked that man from the first time I met him. I felt he and Lyndon Johnson represented the worst of American politics.

While JFK's personal life was questionable, he was true to his country and beliefs.

"Is that all, John?"

"For now. My people will be calling your people on the details."

"Okay, tell them to call the launch center in China and ask for the Mars station team lead."

"I'll do that, have a good day, Your Majesty."

"You too, Mr. President."

I don't think I'll ever get used to this king stuff.

I had another message waiting for me after that call. One of the asteroid belt exploration teams had found an asteroid comprised of an ore heavier than anything that had ever been identified.

They were returning to the moon with several hundred pounds as samples. I made arrangements that some of the samples would go to every team on the moon and Jackson R&D on Earth for testing.

Who knew what properties it contained? We couldn't count anything out.

Since I had offered a Mars station to the United States, I felt I had to do the same for all my allies. Would it make sense for them to have a separate one, or could some of them share?

I couldn't think of a real reason for Argentina to have one, other than the prestige. At the same time, I could understand how they would feel if left out.

The assembly building in orbit could handle a station four times the size of the one sent to the asteroid belt.

The radius of the one sent to the belt was ten yards, giving over 4000 cubic yards of space. A radius four times as large would result in 268,000 cubic yards. You could cram a lot in that area.

Maybe two of them so that the nations could select who they didn't mind being on board with to avoid problems.

I will make my team and the other nations sort that out. I think I have caused enough trouble for today.

Chapter 51

Since I had committed space on the Mars station to all my major allies, I needed to reveal the latest flight capabilities. Being able to get around most of the solar system in a matter of hours was a game-changer.

The only technology not available to my allies was the fusion devices. That was going to be closely held for the foreseeable future. Even the factory on the moon where they were assembled was compartmentalized.

The finished units were sealed, and the fusion process would halt if anyone tried to open them, so it would be hard to duplicate the process even if one had a working reactor. We controlled the ones we had very closely.

This state of affairs would change in the next month as we started replacing power generation stations with them. The coal mine workers who would be the first displaced were being retrained to install underground wiring for electricity.

The word I got back from the training center was that the miners now thought they were on a gravy train with the easiest and highest-paying jobs they ever had. If this attitude continued, keeping people on the job would succeed.

The joke on nighttime TV was that the only group being hurt by all of this was Borax soap makers.

I thought there would be more controversy and interest in our new accelerated flight times. The public reaction was more ho-hum, so what else is new? They were used to the breakthroughs in the space program so much they were taking them for granted.

The ones most affected were the national militaries. They were almost in shock. All their doctrine and battle plans had been going out the window. Now their plans were long gone. How could any of them fight a war with me occupying the high ground so decisively?

Talk about entangling alliances, everyone wanted a mutual defense pact with the Lunar Kingdom and the Solar Reaches. At least the Pitcairn Islands hadn't applied. On second thought, they were a British protectorate, so they had applied.

One of the things that I knew intellectually but didn't take to heart as I was too close to it was the true power in Britain. I had been associated with the royal family for so long that I thought of the queen as the true power.

Parliament was the power as they were the ones that had the diplomatic power. The queen was a tremendous influencer but didn't make the final governmental decisions. I found them more difficult to deal with because of the political infighting.

It made me long for a central government with an absolute monarch at its head. Not really. I grew up in the Republic of the United States of America and loved how it worked.

My love continued as I learned that it had warts called political parties. George Washington had it right.

At the same time that our flight capabilities were announced, we opened the claims office on the moon. There was an outcry about not having access to our claims office because it was on the moon. How was anyone going to be able to file a claim?

They seemed to miss the point that they would have to get to the asteroid belt to make a discovery worth filing a claim on.

Silly me authorized a P.O. Box on Earth in each of our allied countries for people to make inquiries. There were some legitimate inquiries, mostly from school classrooms.

The bulk of the mail was an attempt to file a claim for larger asteroids or any other one in a celestial catalog of our solar system. They sent the catalog number of where they wanted to file.

Some of the more serious ones included the US one hundred dollar filing fee. At least they read the filing instructions. Well, almost read them. No one had planted a plaque or plotted an orbit.

We returned those fees with a note not to send money until they met all the requirements.

The claims office opening did give rise to a new situation. We needed to become members of the International Postal Union and issue our kingdom's stamps.

Tradition did catch up with me. While avoiding it on our currency, my profile appeared on the higher-value stamps. These new stamps set off a stampede in the world of philately.

There were no commemorative stamps to be issued. Only one set of common denominations. They wouldn't change until the die wore out.

I didn't want to start a market in our stamps. It didn't work. The usual suspects ran up the prices. The most expensive were low-numbered plate blocks.

Crane Currency company in Massachusetts printed our stamps and did a professional job of quality control and security of the stamps themselves.

You can only obtain stamps by buying them from our post office. The office is located on the moon.

Stamps could only be purchased by a moon worker who would ship them down to Earth. We finally limited how many stamps a week could be bought by an individual. This limit was a pain as it required record keeping.

The postmaster, a part-time position, finally issued booklets with serial numbers. The booklet had to be presented when people wanted to buy stamps and to record purchases.

Some workers claimed they had lost their booklets. They were able to buy new ones for an exorbitant price. It was amazing how often the lost booklet was found.

Unlike most postage stamps, the most valuable ones had a Lunar postmark. These postal covers became a business in their own right.

I finally gave up the battle and told the post office to sell whatever people wanted and let the chips fall where they may.

It quickly became apparent that some of my citizens wanted to explore and mine in the asteroid belt. As part of generating a real economy, there had to be a way for my people to earn money that wasn't directly from me. Eventually, I hoped for an American-style economy.

I even imagined the day would come when I could turn over the entire moon infrastructure to the Lunar government and have them maintain and expand it through taxes.

While participating in the economy, I didn't want to be the economy.

I turned the problem over to one of my teams in my think tank. The term think tank was new and had a catchy ring to it.

They came back with a plan to loan money to miners and prospectors. The Lunar Bank would give loans to qualified people to start their businesses.

The mainstay of the proposition was a small exploring/mining vessel. It would support a team of five explorers or miners in the asteroid belt.

There would be two variations of the small ships, one with many sensors and detectors for making new finds. The second ship would be set up with a large hold and mining equipment.

The new business people would lease the ship from us at a favorable rate. We would guarantee prices, both for buying and selling. There would be no company store mentality here.

Every ship would have a safety inspection performed before departing on a job. This inspection was to be performed before leaving the station on every trip. The equipment that we leased to them would be kept in tip-top shape.

All this seemed simple. Then the requests started coming in. The ships had room for five; were they required to have five people?

Some had four children that would have to go along with them. Could they get a larger vessel?

If children were to be gone for long periods, how would they receive their schooling?

Would AAA have a ship to help stranded workers? No, but we would have a rescue ship on standby.

Claim jumping was a possibility. I made that a capital crime with the death sentence. The felons would be cast out of an airlock. Since I as king constituted the court of last resort and appeals, I would have the sentence carried out immediately.

This draconian measure got all sorts of screams when it became known on Earth. My reply was, "Don't try to jump a claim, and there will be no problem."

My citizens were all for the law.

Getting tired of all the questions sent my way on the exploring and mining issue, I set up a mining and exploration commission. They operated the claims office and now the entire mess. Thus, another government bureaucracy was born.

I was on record as hating bureaucracies, but now I understood why they were needed.

The final straw for me to set up the mining and exploration rules was to allow dogs or cats on the ships.

My new bureaucracy decided that cats were okay as they would use a litter box. It would be hard to take a dog for a walk.

The no-dogs rule got a lot of complaints from Earth dog lovers. A survey of new prospectors revealed that none of them were dog owners.

This state of affairs was announced to the world that each request to be accompanied by a dog would be based on the owner's methods for handling all the issues. To my knowledge, no one tried to take a dog along.

Chapter 52

Then there was pressure from my partners to let them in on the action. The other nations wanted the right to file claims in our office since it was set up to handle them. It was also the only one to file claims in the solar system.

The UN talked about setting up a claims office, but that was all it was, talk. They couldn't even get enough agreement to bring it to a vote.

The Claims Commission released a statement that its rule would recognize any claim filed by any individual or other organization that met the claims conditions.

The news release set off the crying once more. I had a monopoly on space. One idiot in the US House of Representatives wanted my kingdom to be charged under the Sherman Anti-Trust Act.

After a long conversation with my brain trust, Mum and Dad, an announcement was made that the Lunar Kingdom and the Solar Reaches would lease exploration and mining craft to anyone who could afford it.

Only the largest companies and governments could afford the public lease price. We knew full well that this would allow spying. Whoever leased our spacecraft would be trying to reverse engineer them.

The true secret part of the spacecraft was the fusion engine. Everything else was already in public literature. At least the theory, not actual blueprints. Building a hyperspeed rocket would be simple, but it would go nowhere without a significant power source.

Opening up the asteroid belt to exploration set up what became known as the Great Space Race. It was good that we had production facilities in place to handle the demand.

The Lunar prospectors and miners were picky about what they claimed and worked on. If the asteroid was a piece of slag, they bypassed it.

The Earthlings claimed everything they could. It was claimed if the asteroid was large enough to hold a plaque and beacon.

It was a good thing that we had set up a rescue service. The statistics were interesting. Ninety-eight percent of the rescues were Earthlings. Only those sent by the US who had NASA training did well.

The explorers sent by several large companies were a mess. Safety rules were guidelines for them to follow if they felt like it.

One spacecraft disappeared for several months. The wreckage was found on one of the larger asteroids. It looked like they had tried to open the fusion reactor.

Opening the reactor would not only shut the fusion process down, it also set off the thermite charge that we put into every reactor produced. The stickers on the outside of the reactor warned of immediate death if the reactor was opened. This group learned about it the hard way.

Our safety committee released the results of their investigation. Once more, there were complaints about not warning that the reactor's opening would set off an explosion.

I attended that news conference. When asked, my response was, "What part of immediate death do you not understand?"

At that, I walked off and ended the conference. The questions would only get more stupid after that.

My government had already claimed the five largest asteroids.

In order they are:

Ceres is the heaviest asteroid ever found in the asteroid belt. It has the largest diameter and is the fourth brightest asteroid seen from Earth. Ceres is considered a possible protoplanet and is so large that it is considered a dwarf planet, like Pluto.

It is the largest minor planet in Neptune's orbit and the 33rd largest known object in the solar system. It is also the only object in the asteroid belt to be surrounded by gravity. Its core is rocky, and its mantle is icy.

It is speculated that Ceres may have an internal ocean of liquid water under its icy mantle, and water vapor emissions have been detected, which is very unusual for a large asteroid. We are going to check this out as soon as we can.

Its surface is broadly considered similar to a C-type (carbonaceous) asteroid, but it has spectral features of carbonates and clay absent in other C-types.

Vesta is the second most massive asteroid found in the asteroid belt. It also has the second-largest diameter and is the second-brightest asteroid as seen from Earth. Its orbit is moderately inclined and eccentric, and it has a relatively fast rotation for an asteroid.

Its density is lower than Mercury, Venus, Earth, and Mars but higher than most asteroids and all moons except Io. It is thought to have a metallic iron-nickel core with a rocky olivine mantle and a rocky crust. It is also considered a protoplanet by many scientists.

Pallas is the third most massive asteroid found in the asteroid belt. It also has the third-largest diameter and is the third-brightest asteroid seen from Earth.

Based on observations, its surface is likely composed of silicate materials containing little water or iron. Its orbit is unusually highly inclined, and its orbital is eccentrically great.

It is thought to have been a protoplanet because it seems to have undergone some thermal alteration and partial differentiation (forming layers).

Hygiea is the fourth most massive asteroid found in the belt and has the fourth largest diameter. It is also a C-type asteroid, like Euphrosyne, and is the largest class C-type asteroid found.

Evidence indicating that the asteroid had ice water in the past has been found on the celestial body. It has a relatively low density.

Euphrosyne is the fifth most massive asteroid found in the asteroid belt and has the twelfth largest diameter. It has a primitive surface and a C-type asteroid, the most common type.

Being a C-type means it is very dark and is depleted of hydrogen, helium, and other volatiles. Its orbit is tilted, which is unusual. Its orbit also has a high inclination and eccentricity to it.

Having claimed these five large asteroids didn't mean that we knew what we had or that they were worth having.

It just made sense that since they were the largest, it would be enough to mine if they had anything worthwhile.

The smaller asteroids had the possibility of having valuable minerals. This possibility was proven by a family that found an asteroid with five tons of almost pure gold.

I was glad that it was one of my Lunar families. The interesting part is that they didn't retire with their wealth immediately. It seems the Trump family was into chasing wealth.

As if we didn't have enough going on, I set exploration flights to all the other planets. One of the nice things about being king is that you can tell people to do this or that, and they will.

Before that, my teams would question me on the wisdom of an approach. Now they went ahead and did it. I would have to watch that carefully. I let it be known that yes-men weren't needed, but I'm not certain the message was getting through.

I started to make a point of rewarding anyone who had a real question about my requests. I even started carrying gold coins for immediate recognition of minor thoughts.

Major thoughts were given rewards both in money or titles. The titles would only be honorary, and I had yet to award one, but they were available.

You would think that all these happenings would dominate the news. The headline story for days was that May-ling is pregnant. Speculation was running rampant if it would be a boy or a girl and if they would be king of Luna or emperor of China.

To me, it was a no-brainer. The child would be king or queen, emperor, or empress of both. They would rule their problem as I would be gone by then.

My job would be to raise them right so the child wouldn't be an entitled monster but rather a caring ruler. I would have to talk to Queen Elizabeth and Empress Ping about how they achieved it with their children.

I recapped what had happened in the last six months in a free moment.

The Russian problem seemed to be put to bed; at least they weren't trying to kill me or conquer the world anymore.

Travel within our solar system has become a reality. Thinking of this, I decided to make James Burk, the leader of the hyperspeed development team, a duke. Since titles had property associated with them, I would name him Duke of Ceres.

Not that I was giving him the large asteroid, just a large portion of the surface area. It would be interesting to see if he could do anything with it.

Jim has a good sense of humor, so I hoped it would go over well.

Then there was the minor point of me becoming a king. I'm still not sure how that happened, and I certainly didn't deserve such a grandiose title, but what the heck, as the kids were saying, go with the flow.

Most amazing of all, I had married the love of my life, and we were expecting a child.

As I sat musing about life in general and where it had taken me, an urgent message was forwarded to me.

One of my teams had developed a form of antigravity!

Finished for now.

To be continued....

Back Matter

The next in the series is Book 16, First Steps[1]
Enelsonauthor.com[2]
The Solar System's Tallest Mountains - WorldAtlas[3]

For information on hiring Janet E. Rupert to edit your fiction project, email:

janeteditorrupert@gmail.com

---

1. https://www.amazon.com/Richard-Jackson-Saga-First-Steps-ebook/dp/B0BM4GRJVY

2.   https://www.enelsonauthor.com

3.   https://www.worldatlas.com/articles/the-solar-system-s-tallest-mountains.html

Other books by Ed Nelson
The Richard Jackson Saga
Book 1 The Beginning
Book 2 Schooldays
Book 3 Hollywood
Book 4 In the Movies
Book 5 Star to Deckhand
Book 6 Surfing Dude
Book 7 Third Time is a Charm
Book 8 Oxford University
Book 9 Cold War
Book 10 Taking Care of Business
Book 11 Interesting Times
Book 12 Escape from Siberia
Book 13 Regicide
Book 14 What's Under, Down Under?
Book 15 The Lunar Kingdom
Book 16 First Steps
In the Richard Jackson World
Mary, Mary
Stand-Alone Story
Ever and Always
Cast in Time Series
Book 1: Baron
Book 2: Baron of the Middle Counties
Book 3: Count
Book 4: Earl
Book 5: Earl of the Marches

Did you love *Lunar Kingdom*? Then you should read *First Steps* by Ed Nelson!

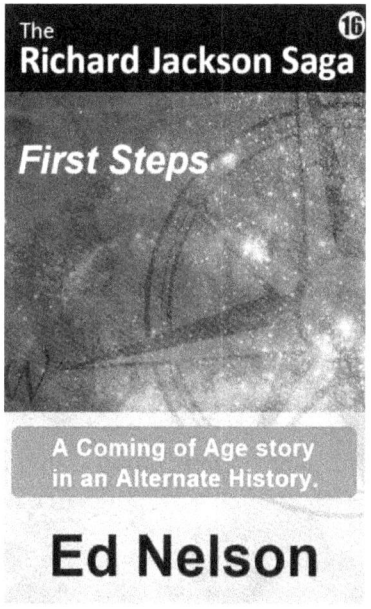

Coming-of-age stories don't have to be all teenage angst. They can be fun-filled adventures that become more serious with age. With humor, we follow a young man's coming of age in the late 1950s. Starting in the summer before his freshman year, he goes through high school and beyond. He finds wealth as an inventor and fame in Hollywood as he searches for a girlfriend. Wealth and fame prove far easier than girls. The 16th book, First Steps, has Rick continuing to explore the moon and outer space. Danger, fame and fortune, and adventure seem to be his lot in life. He and his wife are expecting their first child. He continues to affect the world around him in economic, military, and even religious matters. Gravity control opens the moon and the rest of the solar system. It is found that Man has had visitors in the past. This tongue-in-cheek saga is all true, give or take a lie or two.